MY CHAMPION

BEWITCHED AND BEWILDERED

ALANEA ALDER

MY CHAMPION

www.sacredforestpublishing.com
P.O.Box 280
Moyock, NC, 27958
Digital ISBN- 978-1-941315-16-3
Print ISBN- 978-1-941315-17-0
Sacred Forest Publishing

Printed in the USA

Cover Design and Interior Format

DEDICATION

~Omnia Vincit Amor- Love Conquers All~

To those who feel broken, may you find the ones that show you why your pieces are different and that by being different you are all the more precious, for there is only one of you in the entire universe and you have a special place that is all your own in this world, you just have to fight for it.

PROLOGUE

DECLAN SAT UP IN BED and immediately swung his feet over the side to stand. He couldn't catch his breath. Clutching at his chest, he staggered to the bathroom. He splashed water on his face and took deep breaths.

Eva didn't die. Eva didn't die. He repeated this to himself over and over again like a mantra. Adriel hadn't lost his mate, neither would he. Closing his eyes he saw his mate's mouth open and screaming, yet he couldn't hear her from the other side of the locked door.

Fate, I would accept an eternity alone to save her any suffering.

And even though his heart and soul protested the thought, he knew he would rather never meet her than for her to suffer the terror of dying in a fire.

Keep her far, far away from here, he pleaded to any god that would listen.

CHAPTER ONE

KARI DELANEY LOOKED UP WHEN she heard raised voices from the other side of her door. Seconds later, Marcus Recher stormed into her office, an expression of fury on his face. Her personal assistant, Avery, was trying in vain to keep him from entering the office. He had a hold of Marcus' arm in an attempt to stop him, but Marcus dragged him along.

Kari raised an eyebrow "So, to what do I owe this honor?"

"Why wasn't I given the Jepson account?"

"That is because Jepson himself told me he did not want you. He said you were an ill fit for his organization." Kari fought the urge to roll her eyes. Jepson actually called Marcus an ingratiating asshole and flat out refused the man as a personal assistant. Unfortunately, Kari couldn't help but agree. The only reason he was still in her training class was because he had come so highly recommended by one of her trainers.

"I had that account nailed!" Marcus yelled angrily.

"Maybe not as 'nailed' as you believed," Kari retorted.

By this time, Marcus was right in front of her

desk. He turned and shoved Avery away, causing the smaller man to fall. Kari's patience snapped.

"You have got two seconds to leave here before I have you escorted out."

"I want that account! I worked hard for it!" Marcus demanded.

Kari stood and crossed her arms over her chest. "You are not going to get anything. In fact, as of right now, you are fired." Not waiting for a response, Kari pressed the button on the intercom system to her left.

"Yes, Ms. Delaney?" Tom responded. Tom Adison was an older wolf shifter who was in charge of the security side of her company and he took his job seriously.

"Tom, I need you to escort Marcus out of the building."

Tom chuckled. "You've got a visitor coming up; I'm pretty sure he'll be able take care of it for you."

"Tom, what do you mean?" Kari asked.

"You'll see." Seconds later, the door swung open, and Kari grinned wickedly.

"Hello, Law."

"Hello, Kari. I heard some yelling as I was coming off the elevator. Is there a problem here?" he asked.

It took everything in her not to laugh. Law literally filled the doorway. Taller than most shifters and virtually all witches, he topped seven feet and was so broad in the shoulders he nearly had to turn sideways to get through the door.

Law was one of the very few people in the world she trusted implicitly. He had taken her in when she was lost and floundering in the human world. For all intents and purposes she considered him a brother.

When it came time to put down roots and start her business, she couldn't think of a better place to be than the small town where she had first met Law.

"No problem here, Marcus was just leaving." Marcus eyed Law. Kari could almost see him weighing the decision. Would it be worth going against the larger man? Probably not. In a fit of anger, Marcus swept everything off the top of her desk on to the floor.

Law took a step forward, but Kari held up a hand. Marcus stormed across the room and out the door.

Kari glanced down at Avery where he was watching everything from his place on the floor beside her desk, his bright blue eyes wide.

"Are you okay?" She leaned down, offered him a hand, and pulled him to his feet.

"I'm fine. I just knew you wouldn't want to talk to him right now; he's such a jerk!" Avery rubbed his bottom.

Law's jaw clenched. He babied Avery to no end. If he had been in the room when Marcus knocked Avery down, they would be scrapping bits of Marcus off the ceiling.

Kari's heart melted just a bit. Avery had a way with words. Somehow he always made her smile. "Avery, why don't you run down to the library? It is almost time for your study session," Kari suggested.

Avery nodded. "Yeah, I just didn't want to leave with him coming through the door, you know?" He and Law exchanged masculine nods, as if she couldn't take care of herself.

"I appreciate that," she said, gently nudging him toward the door. "Have fun. I am sure there are some dusty, musty tomes waiting for you to read."

Avery giggled. “Thanks Kari.” He turned toward the door and paused, looking at Law. “Will you be around later? I can do some more tests for you.”

Law smiled and handed up a small charm. Avery’s face brightened, and he clipped it on his belt. “I think I got the shoes worked out. Shift a few times and let me know.”

“Will do!” Avery gave Law a mock salute and hurried out of the office. Kari knew that he was rushing so that he could catch the afternoon bus.

Kari looked down at the floor. She was glad she didn’t like much on her desk, preferring an open workspace, so there wasn’t much to pick up. She bent down and started to pick up her calendar, phone, desk blotter, and pen cup. Law knelt down beside her, gathering her scattered pens.

“So why are you really here?” she asked.

Law didn’t say anything for a moment. One by one, he picked up her pens and dropped them in the cup before placing the cup on her desk. When they both stood, he looked down at her, his forehead creased with worry.

Kari put the rest of her things down. “It cannot be that bad,” she teased. When he didn’t respond, she frowned. “Can it?”

Law took a deep breath. “You know I travel a bit, taking missions.” She nodded, and he continued. “I get updates from certain active warriors in the pillar cities. They told me to get anyone that I cared about to a pillar city. Outside of my squad and my family, you and Avery are the only people I care about. It’s not safe for either of you to be on your own.”

“But I have always taken care of myself; that has not been an issue before now,” she pointed out.

"Things have changed."

"You are not referring to the notice that Prince Magnus sent out are you?"

Law nodded. "That's the one. There are things going on that they are not telling everyone. It's not safe for you to be by yourself without the protection of a larger family unit, like a coven. So I'm evacuating you and Avery to Noctem Falls. They are taking in another batch of refugees the day after tomorrow."

Kari felt a ball of ice start to form in her stomach. She shook her head. "No way. No way in hell am I going to Noctem Falls! You know how I feel about their discrimination against anyone who was not born five thousand years ago. Ageism. That is what it is: ageism!"

Law rubbed the back of his neck. "I would send you to Lycaonia, but time is of the essence. Noctem Falls is closer."

Kari shook her head again. "No Law, no way. I have worked too hard for too long to establish myself. I have finally got everything up and running; there is no way I can just abandon everything because of some sort of dictate from Prince Magnus."

"Kari, people are dying. Vampires, shifters, paranormals across the country are being murdered." Law's voice was quiet but firm.

Kari blinked. "Why have they not told us? If it is that bad, should there not have been... I do not know, one of those emergency broadcast system alerts or something?"

Law looked at her, sadness and pain filling his eyes. "Kari, paranormals have grown so much since the Great War. There has been no fighting or territory disputes; because of that and our long life span, our population has experienced a boom over the past couple hundred years. The elders that were wiped out in the Great War have been replaced by the younger generations."

The weight of his words was starting to sink in. She collapsed into her chair. "The pillar cities are not big enough, are they?" she whispered in horror.

Law shook his head. "No, they're not. I don't think any of the Founding Families realized how much we would grow. That's why they're evacuating small pockets of people, anyone who would be easy pickings for these guys. I want you to go. Even the large families that are sticking together have more protection than you do."

Kari stared down at her desk. "I just got my business going. Everything is finally coming together. I cannot stop now."

Law smirked. "Don't tell me you can't run this business from that little laptop of yours; I know better. Besides, Tom runs most of the day-to-day operations here. You're more hands on with training and getting new accounts."

Kari pursed her lips. "Maybe," she admitted begrudgingly. She gasped. "What about Avery? He needs to come with me. He is a shifter; would he be welcome? You know he does not do well with large groups."

"The first wave of refugees that went to Noctem Falls was a town of wolf shifters. I don't think Avery being a shifter will be an issue. Prince Magnus is more open-minded than most vampires half his age."

Kari exhaled. "Is Noctem Falls my only choice?"

Law gave her a wolfish grin. "Or you can move in

with me and the guys," he offered.

Kari shuddered. She couldn't think of a worse type of hell than living with a group of bull-headed men. Avery was different; he was more like her. In their condo, household items went back to the places they belonged. Surfaces gleamed; clothes were put in hampers and washed regularly. Even their food was organized in the refrigerator. She couldn't imagine living with a group of rough-around-the-edges alpha males. She swallowed hard. "When do we leave?"

Law smiled. "How soon can you be packed?"

☾

"WHAT DO YOU MEAN, WE have to go?" Avery asked, a panicked look on his face. He had just returned home from the library. Kari rose from the couch and wrapped her arms around him, cuddling him close.

"It is just for a little while. Law says is not safe for us to be out on our own. So we are heading to Noctem Falls. Think of it as a vacation. I have always wanted to show you the vampire city."

Avery raised his head from her shoulder, a skeptical look on his face. "One, you never take vacations. Two, I thought you hated snobby vampires, especially those in the vampire city."

Kari grimaced, she should've known better than to try and sugarcoat this. "Okay, I admit heading there was not my first choice, but if Law says it is dangerous, then it is. Our only other option is moving in with a bunch of Neanderthals, and I do not think either one of us would enjoy it." She gave him a final squeeze and stepped back. With her mind racing around in circles, she began to pace back and forth in their living room. "From what I understand, Prince Magnus is providing housing, and we will be on the market level. There are vendor market stands, wares for sale, food stalls, you name it."

Avery looked down at the floor and scuffed one toe over the other. "Will they like me?" he asked.

Kari straightened her back. "Of course they will, and if they do not, they can deal with me."

Avery looked up, a soft smile on his lips. "They wouldn't want to do that."

Kari winked. "Of course not, but they do not know that yet, do they?"

Avery giggled. "So when do we leave?" he asked.

Kari looked over where three of her suitcases waited.

Avery's eyes rounded. "That soon?"

She nodded. "I took your suitcases out of storage and placed them on your bed. Go ahead and pack." She sighed. "To be honest, I do not know how long we will be there. So take anything you think you may need for a while."

Avery nodded. "Okay Kari." He dropped a kiss on her cheek and immediately headed toward his room.

Kari walked over to the large window and looked down at the picturesque scene their bustling small downtown offered. It wasn't Chicago—hell, it was barely a city—but it was small and quiet, and she loved it.

When she and Avery were house hunting, they had both fallen in love with the location. So they decided to buy two condos in the old brick building in the center of town and had them completely renovated into a huge single condo just for her and Avery. The window overlooked the town square where she could watch people coming and going. It was getting dark, and the streetlights were turning on one by one.

It was still early spring, and the sun was just now starting to stay in the sky longer and longer each day. With an overcast day like this, it still felt like the deepest part of winter. She reached up and rubbed her temples.

"It is just a vacation," she whispered to herself. "We will go, and I will show Avery the city. Things will calm down and we will come home. It is just a vacation."

CHAPTER TWO

DECLAN HELD OUT ONE HAND to fend off the hissing male vampire; with the other, he held back a snarling wolf shifter. He wondered how his day had come to this. His morning had been great. He woke up, got in a good run, ate a huge breakfast, teased Adriel, and was lucky enough to be assigned to Level Six patrol for the day. So how had he ended up between two angry males, looking like he was trying to referee a couple of velociraptors?

"Gerald, you need to calm down," Declan ordered, squaring off to the vampire. Gerald DuBois hissed. "I will when he gives me back my mate!" Gerald tried to reach past Declan, and Declan batted his hand away. Behind him, he heard a snarl.

"She is not your mate!"

Declan looked back at the wolf. "How do you know that?" he asked.

Yellow canine eyes met his. "Because she's mine." The wolf turned back to stare at Gerald. "I'm Peter Hernandez," he said, not taking his eyes off the angry vampire.

Fuck me, Declan thought. He turned to face Gerald. "Okay, Gerald, the wolf here says she is his mate; what do you have to say about that?"

Gerald shook his head. "I have been with her for over five hundred years. Our families arranged our mating. We have a son together; she is mine!"

Declan wished that Warrick was up here. This was his crazy ass uncle. "Gerald, you said it was an arranged mating. As far as I know, we don't have arranged matings."

Gerald looked at him, disgust in his eyes. "Of course not. Arranged matings only happen within the Founding and Noble families, to keep our lines pure."

Declan turned his attention to the small, trembling woman behind the wolf shifter. "Rachelle, honey, you know I'm not going to hurt you. You want to tell old Declan what's going on?"

Rachelle nodded. "It is true, I belong to Peter. We found each other a few days ago. Gerald normally does not let me go up to the market level, but as we were out of some things, and our normal servant has been helping the refugees get settled, I decided to come up here myself." Her face took on a dreamy expression. "And that is when I found Peter. For my entire life, I did not even know what I was missing. I did not know." Her voice broke, and she took a deep breath. Peter wrapped his arm around her. She looked up, tears in her eyes. "I did not know that matings were supposed to be like *this*." From the way she emphasized the word, Declan knew exactly how she'd been treated by Gerald. He turned back to the angry vampire.

"Well, Gerald, Rachelle here says that she belongs to Peter and not you. You know as well as I do that it is against our laws to interfere with matings. You will have to step aside."

Gerald's nostrils flared, and he turned to Peter. Declan had only a second to react. He jumped in front of the wolf shifter as Gerald raked his claws downward, catching Declan across the abdomen. He felt each hard nail rip his flesh open. Rachelle screamed as a crowd quickly gathered around them. Three wolves, including the Wolftown beta, Jorge, tackled Gerald to the floor. Declan blinked, staring up at the ceiling.

I don't get paid enough for this. Wait, do I get paid for this? Damn, I must be hurt worse than I thought. All I had to do was patrol. He reached down to touch his belly. His hand came away covered in blood.

"Well, that's gonna leave a mark," he said before darkness swept him away.

"LOOK KARI! THEY HAVE MEAT kebobs! And are those funnel cakes?" Avery asked. Kari had a new appreciation for his enthusiasm. She had dreaded coming back to the city, but his childlike excitement actually made this somewhat enjoyable. Their escort, a flirtatious witch by the name of Micah Sageson, was pointing out all of the vendors. Micah told her that their luggage had been carried to their new quarters and the only thing she should worry about was learning her new home.

"Everything smells so good!" Avery exclaimed, hopping from one foot to the other. He turned to her. "Where do we start?"

Kari waved her hand pointing to the entire cavern. "Help yourself; just do not come crying to me if you stuff yourself silly and have to be rolled to our new quarters."

Avery was just about to turn and head toward the food stalls when they heard screams. Micah was instantly on alert as wolves poured out of their homes. On the far side of the hall, a small group was forming next to the wall. Seconds later, the smell of blood reached her. She turned to Micah.

"Micah, there is blood, a lot of blood. Someone is close to dying."

His jaw clenched. "You two stay here. I need to see what's happening." He turned and ran toward the crowd.

Avery inched in closer to her and looked up. "I thought we would be safe here," he murmured. Kari felt just as confused; Noctem Falls was supposed to be a safe haven. She was about to walk Avery toward the guest quarters when the scent of the blood changed to her. The more she inhaled and exhaled, the more delicious it smelled. She felt her fangs extend. Avery's complexion turned chalky, his blue eyes were wide, and he trembled.

"Kari? Kari, what's wrong?"

Kari could only shake her head; she couldn't answer. The smell was overwhelming. It was rich and decadent. It smelled like everything that she had ever enjoyed in life combined into one aroma. There was the scents of chocolate, coffee, freshly cut grass, and the crisp smell of linens hanging in the sunshine. She just wanted to roll around in it. She clutched at her chest, breathing heavily.

"Kari, you're scaring me!" Avery exclaimed.

She turned to him and saw tears running down his face. She shook her head, trying to clear her mind. The scent of the blood morphed again, this time tightening things in her lower body and causing her nipples to harden. She became more aroused than she had ever been in her life. Step-by-step she made her way over to the crowd and wedged herself between bodies, pushing them aside. She had to get to the source of that smell. She heard Micah yelling, other men's voices yelling, but her focus was now on the man on the ground. He had red hair. No, not red, strawberry blond, and he was huge. Every bit as big as Law, maybe bigger. He had a square, chiseled jaw and soft, luscious lips. She watched as his breathing became more labored. Something in her snapped; the man on the floor was her mate! She knelt down and brushed the hair out of his face. She looked at Micah.

"Where is the healer?" she demanded.

Micah kept his glowing hands over the man's stomach. "The healer is in Albuquerque. He doesn't live in the city. He stays at the Council Estate."

Micah looked up as two hulking men ran up behind her. "Excuse us," they shouted, pushing her aside. Gently, they lifted the man on to a stretcher. Micah stood and carefully moved with them.

"Let's get our boy down to Broderick's lab. Thanks to Meryn, we have these walkie-talkies, so they're expecting us." Moving as one, they headed toward the back. When she started to follow, one of the men stepped in front of her.

"I'm sorry, but you need to stay here." Kari looked up and up. What was it about these men that they were all so freaking huge?

"That man," she pointed to the stretcher being carried away.

The man nodded. "Declan?"

"Is that his name?" she asked. He nodded. "Declan is my mate."

The man's mouth dropped open. "No shit?"

Kari nodded, her insides shaking.

He grinned. "Then come with me; you're family."

Kari let out a relieved breath. "Thank you..."

"Grant, Grant Douglas." He steered her through the crowd. Looking behind her, she saw that Avery was keeping up with them.

"Family?" she asked as they stepped up to a huge hole in the floor.

Grant looked around frantically. She held out one hand to him and the other to Avery. "I am a vampire; I can take us down. Which level?"

He took her hand. "Level One, and, yes, family. I serve with Declan in the Eta Unit; he is like a brother to me."

Avery clasped her other hand tightly. Through their intertwined fingers, she could feel his body shaking. As one, they stepped into the tunnel, and she quickly lowered them all the way to Level One.

When their feet touched the ground, Grant continued to hold her hand and led her down a long corridor to what looked like a large lab.

"I'm not a surgeon! I don't know what to do!" a frantic male voice bellowed as he cut away her mate's clothing before covering him with a sheet.

"We know, Broderick. Magnus is calling the healer now," a tall, dark haired man explained, pointing to where the Prince of her people paced back and forth on the other side of the room, a scowl on his face.

"Cheryl, that number should be listed at the top of your important contacts. The only reason I do not have it is because we just got cell service; I usually call him from my desk!" he yelled. He took a deep breath and rolled his eyes. "For gods' sakes, stop crying and call the healer!" He hung up the phone and walked over to the side of the bed to stand next to the dark haired man. "Adriel, are you sure you can not convince Bethy to stay? I am about to murder my secretary."

Adriel shook his head. "You will have to take that up with Gavriel."

Kari stepped forward to stand on the other side of the one the Prince called Adriel. She reached down and took Declan's hand.

Adriel blinked, then blinked again. "Hello. Who are you?"

"Kari Delaney. My brother—" she nodded her head over to where Avery bounced from foot to foot nervously— "Avery Therian and I came in with the last set of refugees. Micah was showing us around when I smelled blood. Not exactly the way I wanted to meet my mate."

Adriel looked behind him to Avery and then back to her. "Mate?"

She nodded. "Yes, he is mine."

Declan groaned and opened his eyes. "Gods, what smells so good? Am I in heaven?"

Micah snorted. "No, and don't get any ideas about heading toward the light. I'm busting my balls to keep your wound open for the doc."

Startled, Kari looked at him. Micah had a fine sheen of sweat on his upper lip and dripping along his hairline. "Why on earth are you keeping it open?"

Micah started to answer and Adriel interrupted him. "Concentrate on our brother, I will answer." Micah nodded, looking relieved.

Adriel turned to her. "Micah is keeping his wound open so that we do not have to cut him open later. The doctor will need to make sure that his intestines are not twisted and nothing was punctured. As a shifter, his flesh is healing, which means wounds are closing, but we have learned the hard way that doesn't mean it will untwist itself."

Kari looked down at her mate. He was inching his face toward her belly. Smiling, she stepped closer to the bed, and he buried his nose against her body.

"Declan, quit moving," Micah chided. He looked down, his eyebrows rising. "Well, this is awkward."

Kari looked down the length of Declan's body to what had distracted Micah. To her utter shock, the sheet was tenting, a *lot*. "Oh my."

Avery giggled. "That's impressive."

Kari leaned over to look her mate in the eye. "How do you have enough blood in your system for an erection?"

His eyes were glazed in pain, but he gave her a boyish grin. "Having an erection for my mate will never be a problem. Gods, you're beautiful." He gave her a dopey smile.

Kari looked around and saw that as they had been talking, the man they called Broderick had run an IV, and painkillers were now relaxing her mate. Broderick caught her staring and nodded.

"Thank you," she whispered.

He growled low. "It's literally the least I could do. If I had known I would be called upon for so many medical emergencies I would have studied internal medicine more."

A stunning man walked up behind Broderick and wrapped his arms around his waist. "You have done beautifully, darling. No one here blames you."

"Thank you, Caspian my love, but it is still frustrating that I know just enough to realize I cannot help."

Her hand was squeezed, and she looked down.

Declan stuck his tongue out at her. "You can only think I'm pretty."

Kari fought back her laughter. Her drugged mate was adorable.

"He's blitzed," a female voice said behind her.

"Bethy! Thank goodness, can you please go help Cheryl..." Magnus started.

Bethy held up her hand. "I already handled her. As luck would have it, I was in your office waiting on you when you called. I found the number and sent Etain to the portal to escort Dr. St. John directly to Level One when he arrives. Which should be any moment..."—she looked down at her watch and muttered under her breath—"if he knows what's good for him."

"Bethy lurves me!" Declan declared.

"Is he high?" a male voice asked, a large impressive looking vampire pulled Bethy under his arm.

Kari stared. She had never seen another vampire that huge. She cocked her head and looked from Adriel to the newcomer. "Are the two of you brothers?"

The man looked at her, and a slow smile formed. "In a way, yes, he is my family. My name is Gavriel Ambrosios." He inclined his head regally.

Kari looked from Gavriel to Adriel. The unit leader was related to one of the oldest royal vampire families? When had this happened? She shook her head. "Nope, not trying to figure that out right now." She turned her attention back to her mate. "How are you doing?"

"I'd be better if we were having sex," he admitted, pouting.

Gavriel's eyes widened, then he saw the state her mate was in and winced. "Poor lad."

"We are not having sex! Your intestines are falling out!" Kari objected, her cheeks heated.

Declan smiled. "Take a picture?"

"No!" called nearly every voice in the room. Kari heard the sound of a click and saw that Grant had pulled down the sheet and used his phone to take a picture. She stared at him, and he shrugged. "I'd want one too, if it were me."

Declan tried leaning up to look, and she pushed him back down. "I do not feel the wound yet. I do, however, feel..." He leered up at her.

Kari placed her free hand over his mouth. She yelped when he licked it and wiped her hand on her pants. He licked his lips. "You even taste good."

She looked around the room. "Please tell me this is a side effect of the pain killers."

Adriel shrugged, and Micah wouldn't meet her eyes. Finally, Grant took pity on her. He walked up behind her and placed a hand on her shoulder. "He is usually a perfect gentleman. I think the combination of the drugs and finally meeting his mate is what you are witnessing."

A low growl had them both looking down. Declan's eyes had shifted to a dark, honeyed brown.

"Get your hand off my mate! I licked her. She's mine!"

Avery lost all semblance of control and began to giggle uncontrollably behind them. Grant's mouth twitched as he lifted his hand. "I would never poach on your mate, brother; we all know she is yours."

"Prince Magnus, how far out is that healer?" Micah asked in a weak voice.

All attention was now on the witch who began to sway. Instantly, Adriel was at his side, holding him up.

"You can stop, Micah," Adriel said, sounding concerned.

Micah shook his head. "I can't, not until the doc gets here."

"I'm here, I'm here," a tenor voice called out as a man rushed forward. Frowning, he looked around the room. "Everyone except for the witch and the vampire holding him up needs to leave. Clear the room! Gods only know what debris has found its way into this open wound."

Kari felt her heart stutter. She didn't want to let go; she felt like if she let go, she'd lose him.

"Young lady, did you hear me?" the doctor demanded.

"Yes, sorry." She let go of Declan's hand and patted it gently, placing it on his chest. "You better not die," she tried to joke, wincing when her voice cracked.

Declan looked past her to Grant, who immediately wrapped an arm around her shoulders. "Go with my brother; I'll see you later. We have unfinished business." He wagged his eyebrows, looking down at his groin.

She chuckled, leaned down, and kissed him on the forehead. "I will hold you to that."

He winked, then yawned. Seconds later, his eyes were closed, and he was breathing deeply.

Kari looked over in time to see the doctor drop the IV line. He met her eyes. "He should be fine. Shifters as strong as the Lionharts would never succumb to a small gash like this." Even his comfort sounded condescending.

"You need to work on your bedside manner, Doc." She stepped back with Grant.

He shrugged, turning his attention to Declan. "It's usually not an issue. Dealing with shifters and vampires, I don't get called on much." He shooed them away, turning to Micah. "Can you slowly pull your magic back? I'll let you know when to withdraw completely."

Grant steered her outside the lab, and the door closed behind them.

"I have to do something," she whispered.

"Uh oh," Avery said.

"What? What's wrong?" Grant asked, tucking her closer against him.

"She's about to go ballistic," Avery informed them.

"I am not, I just need..." Kari wracked her brain. They were in Noctem Falls, not her office; there weren't any projects for her to work on. Her gaze landed on Magnus. "You," she said, stepping forward. She was shocked when he took a half a step back, looking suspicious.

"Me, what?" he asked.

"Show me your office. I need your office."

"I see," Bethy said, nodding. "Good, he needs the

help."

"What?" Grant and Magnus spoke at the same time.

Avery smiled. "You're about to get your entire office restructured by one of the most sought after corporate organizers in the world. Come on, Kari; I'll help. I can show that secretary how to set up her desk. You can do your thing and start training Prince Magnus."

"Training? Me?" Magnus' gaze bounced from her to Avery and back.

Kari took a deep breath, focusing on the task at hand to keep her grounded. "Yes, you. Show me to your office."

Magnus, looking out of his depth, turned to Bethy. She shook her head and turned his body to face the door. "You've been begging me to stay since you needed the help. Looks like Fate heard your plea." She giggled at his wide-eyed expression and gave him a gentle nudge.

Bethy turned to her, and Kari could see that Bethy knew exactly why she needed to take over her uncle's office. Bethy grinned wickedly. "Give him hell." Magnus whimpered.

Kari nodded as she and Avery walked behind the prince of the vampire race toward his office where she would systematically break everything down and rebuild it.

Despite meeting her mate with his guts hanging out, it was turning out to be a good day.

"WHAT ABOUT THIS ONE? IT is marked 'Urgent'." She held up a green piece of paper.

Magnus frowned. "Toss it. I only wrote that it was urgent because the person making the complaint was watching. Anything on a green Post-it note can go in the garbage, the truly important notes are always on cream paper."

Kari smiled. So it wasn't that he didn't have a system, he just had his own very unique, impossible-to-understand system that would be a mine field for anyone else coming in. "How would you feel about adopting a new coding system? Not everyone knows your color preferences," she asked, feeling him out.

Magnus thought about it for a moment. "If they align somewhat with what I have, I think I can adapt. If it is too different, I will forget and fall back to what I have always done."

Kari blinked. She had never gotten such an honest answer to that question before. Training Prince Magnus on how to utilize his office might be easier than she thought. His chuckle broke her out of her thoughts. When she looked at him, he winked at her.

"You have to remember, Bethy has been trying to keep me organized for decades. I know my system is a mess, but without someone like her around to keep the changes in place, I backslide," he admitted.

Kari ducked her head. "You are not what I imagined."

"Let me guess. You thought I was an overbearing, egotistical, demanding know-it-all, and who was I to issue such orders impacting so many people?" He raised an eyebrow at her, and she blushed. She had thought all those things.

He sat down in his chair, a thoughtful look on his face. "It is a very fine line to walk. The older generations expect me to act like a royal. If I do not, I lose their respect. On the flip side, if I do, I seem unapproachable to the younger generations." He looked up at her. "I am doing the best I can."

The admission was so unexpected and honest that she dropped the stack of papers she had been holding. Shaking her head at her own ineptitude, she bent down to pick them up. He shocked her even further when he joined her, picking up the scattered pieces of paper.

"Did I shock you, young Kari?" he asked in a teasing manner.

She nodded. "Yes. I was expecting a dictator, but you are..." She hesitated.

"Tell him," a voice said from the doorway.

They both looked over to see Bethy smiling at them. "Tell him what you really think. He needs to hear it," she encouraged.

Magnus handed her the papers as they both straightened, his eyes bright with curiosity. She took a deep breath. "You feel more like a favorite uncle than a prince," she admitted.

Bethy giggled and nodded. "He is."

Magnus blinked and began to blush furiously. "I am demanding when I need to be," he said gruffly, walking back to his chair. He sat down and began to go through his own stack of papers.

"Oh, he is adorable," Kari said, watching the man trying to read notes that were upside down.

"Not many see this side." Bethy walked in and stood beside her.

Kari turned to her, pursing her lips. "You could not get him past color coding his notes?"

Bethy threw her hands in the air. "He was fine when I left him to go live among humans. I don't know how he got so far off track," she said in an exasperated tone.

"I am right here," he muttered.

"It is going to take me weeks to retrain him." Kari handed Bethy the "non-urgent" note.

Bethy winced. "Let me guess, because it was on green paper, it's not urgent."

"Got it in one."

"Oh dear."

"I am still here," Magnus fussed.

"Kari!"

Kari turned around to the doorway as Avery flung himself into the room and into her arms. He clutched his forearm to his chest as blood streamed through his fingers.

"I can't do this anymore! She's a hateful, mean woman!" Avery shook as he buried his face in her neck.

With fury streaming through her veins, Kari gently disentangled Avery from around her neck and passed him to Bethy who cooed at him and ran a hand over his hair. Magnus was at her side as they left his office and headed toward the front lobby where his secretary sat at her desk. She saw them walking toward her and stood.

"Sire, thank goodness you are here. That young shifter brat had the audacity to try and tell me how to do my job."

Kari fought every instinct to throttle the woman. If the prince hadn't been at her side she would have raked her claws across the woman's face for what she had done to Avery. "That shifter brat works for one of the most prestigious training facilities in the world, which grooms personal assistants for the CEOs of the Fortune 1000 companies. He is actually the personal assistant to the owner and CEO of that company; he knows exactly what he is talking about," she fumed.

"Maybe that is impressive in the human world, but this is Noctem Falls. Working for the prince of our people is in a league entirely of its own," Cheryl argued.

"You have disparaged both shifters and humans in the thirty seconds I have been standing in front of you. It leaves me wondering if this point of view has affected the way you do your job," Kari pointed out.

Magnus' eyes narrowed. "Like not passing along complaints from shifter unit warriors or our new refugees?"

When Cheryl paled, Kari knew her guess had been accurate. She turned to Magnus. "In this type of politically charged atmosphere, neglecting to pass on vital information could have disastrous results. If she were my employee, I would fire her."

Magnus nodded. "I agree. Cheryl, you are fired. Please pack your belongings and return to your family level. I will discuss your termination with the head of your Founding Family, Hugo Evreux." Sputtering, Cheryl began to pack up her desk with shaking hands.

Kari looked over at the two unit warriors standing guard just outside the door. "Gentlemen?" she called. As one they turned to her.

"Yes, Ms. Delaney?"

"I am sorry; I have not met either of you yet." Kari smiled warmly at them.

"I am Vindonnus Li'Elearson, Kappa Unit, my friends call me Vin." The fae bowed regally.

"And I am Keegan Basswood, Iota Unit, witch." The blond imp winked at her cheekily.

"Could one of you ensure that Cheryl returns to her Level without issue?" she asked.

Vin nodded. "Of course, it would be my pleasure." His wicked grin hinted that Cheryl would not be missed.

"How could you! You are one of us," Cheryl hissed at her.

Kari blinked. "One of you? You mean vampire?"

Cheryl nodded with a sour expression.

"People like you are the reason I hate Noctem Falls. I do not see you as "my people"; you are the reason I have stayed away," Kari admitted. Magnus wasn't the only one who looked surprised. "It was almost preferable to stay and be cannon fodder for the ferals than return here to face such prejudice. If it were not for my brother, I would have chanced staying on my own."

"That animal is not a vampire; he cannot be your brother," Cheryl sneered.

Kari snapped. She stepped forward and grabbed the woman by the throat and lifted her a foot off the ground. She hissed in her face, showing her fangs. "That *animal* is my family, bitch. It would be in your best interest to remember that. He has more kindness and light in his baby toe than you do in your entire rotting body." She flung Cheryl across the room where Vin caught her easily. He secured both of her arms at her side. "Get her out of here," she ordered.

Grinning, Vin gave a half bow. “At once.”

“My things!” Cheryl protested.

“I will go through your ‘things’. Anything that is truly yours and yours alone will be sent up later,” Kari said, trying to reel in her anger.

When Cheryl opened her mouth to argue further, Kari growled. “I am having a very bad day! I found my mate with his stomach torn open this morning; do not push me!” Cheryl closed her mouth, and Vin practically half-carried half-dragged her down the hall.

Kari took a deep breath and forced herself to turn around. Behind her, Avery, Bethy, and Magnus stood with varying degrees of shock on their faces. “Sire, I am so sorry for my outburst. It was unprofessional and disruptive. I will return to Level Six at once.” She looked down and stared at the floor, feeling more humiliated at her own reckless behavior than anything else she had experienced in her long life.

“Like hell you will!” Magnus shouted.

Kari looked up, eyes wide. “Sire?”

Bethy had one arm wrapped around Avery and a hand covering her mouth as she fought back giggles. “He likes you.”

Magnus crossed the room and took both hands in hers. He shocked her further when he began to spin her around the room in an impromptu dance. “Please, if we are to be working together, call me Magnus.” He dipped her back and brought her upright again. “She is gone! Thank the gods, she is gone!”

Kari laughed as Magnus twirled her around.

"Sire, you are the prince here, you could have fired her ages ago."

Magnus stopped and shook his head. "Not without political fallout. She is an Evreux. It would have been hard to dismiss her without a good reason. If I were to simply say that she got on my nerves, I could have alienated the entire family."

"Well it's a good thing Kari and Avery are moving to Noctem Falls, then isn't it. You desperately need a new personal assistant and secretary," Bethy said slyly.

Avery's eyes were as wide as saucers. "We're moving here?" he whispered.

Kari felt her stomach drop. She hadn't made that connection yet.

Bethy took in their stunned expressions. "Sugar!"

CHAPTER THREE

KARI FELT THE ROOM BEGIN to close in on her. "Declan. Declan is my mate, and he is a unit warrior here; of course he cannot leave."

Avery stepped away from Bethy and wrapped his uninjured arm around her. "It's okay Kari, we can do this! As long as I'm with you, I don't care where we live."

Kari's heart melted a bit. "What about our condo? And your library studies?"

Avery tensed and pulled back. "Where will we live now? I thought the guest quarters were temporary."

Kari could feel the mounting panic threatening to overwhelm her. "I do not know Avery, I do not know." She hated not knowing. She was usually wonderful in a crisis; why was she melting down now?

"It could be because you have had a lot thrown at you this morning," Magnus answered wrapping a fatherly arm around both her and Avery.

Kari winced. "I said that out loud?"

"Yes, but don't worry. If anyone deserves to take a moment to reorient themselves, it's you." Bethy smiled at them.

"Reorient. Right." Kari pushed back the panic and focused on what she should be doing. "We need to finish figuring out how bad Prince Magnus' office is, clean out Cheryl's mess, check in on Declan, grab a bite to eat, then figure out our future plans. I'll break down tasks tomorrow."

Magnus patted them both on the shoulder and stepped back. "I have a feeling that our esteemed doctor will not trust Declan to stay in bed, so I told Adriel he is to be moved to my guest quarters on this level, so we could keep an eye on him. There is more than enough room for the two of you as well."

Kari sputtered. "But Sire, we were supposed to go to Level Six."

Bethy shook her head. "If you were another refugee, that might be the case, but you're not. You're Declan's mate and my uncle's new assistant; that makes you practically family."

Avery scooted closer to her, "I like having more family," he whispered, blushing.

Bethy inhaled. "He's just too sweet!" She pulled Avery into her arms and hugged him. He smiled brightly and rested his head on her shoulder.

Kari looked at Magnus. "Sire, are you sure you would like me as an assistant? To be honest, I will run you ragged."

"Are you sure you want to take this on? From what you said earlier, you run a very successful company training CEO's personal assistants."

"How did you..."

Magnus nodded to Avery. "As if you would let him work for anyone else?"

Avery laughed. "Nope!" He popped his 'p'.

"I can do most of my work remotely," she tapped

her chin. "But I would hate to give up my condo. I love the view, and it is in my hometown."

"I am sure we can arrange something," Magnus said nodding.

Kari turned to Avery who was beaming at her, and he nodded. She turned to Magnus. "I am willing to try this on a probationary basis. If, at the end of the training period, you or I feel like we are not a good fit, I will begin interviewing the paranormal assistants my company has trained for a replacement." She stuck out her hand.

Grinning, Magnus shook it. "Deal."

"Wonderful, now I really get to break you in," she said evilly.

Magnus' grin faded. "What?"

Bethy laughed at his expression, then sobered. She turned to Kari. "Can that wait a bit?" She looked down at her watch. "Adriel should be here any moment with statements regarding Declan's assault, I, for one would like your input."

Kari turned to Avery. "Will you be okay here by yourself?"

Avery rolled his eyes. "Yeeeesss. As long as someone can bring me some antibacterial wipes." He eyed his new desk and shuddered. "And maybe a sage smudge stick."

"Brat." Kari ruffled his hair.

"Don't worry, Ms. Delaney, Vin and I will watch over him," Keegan offered holding up a first-aid kit.

She nodded at him. "My thanks."

Seconds later, Adriel and Gavriel arrived with two men she didn't recognize. Straightening her back, she joined them in Magnus' conference room, unsure of what she was walking into.

☾

KARI SAT BETWEEN BETHY AND the huge bear shifter who had been introduced as Aiden McKenzie, the Unit Commander. She had heard rumors that he and his mate were in the city visiting but hadn't believed them. Shifters, much less a future Elder, hardly ever came to Noctem Falls.

The unit leader, Adriel Aristaios, sat on the other side of Aiden. He was officially introduced when he walked in shortly after they sat down. He told them he had dropped Micah off at the Unit Level before returning to give his report. According to him, Declan would be out of surgery soon, and the doctor hadn't found any issues and was expecting him to recover fully by the next day.

On the other side of Adriel was Stefan Bolivar, the acting Alpha to the wolf pack that had taken refuge here in the city. He reminded her a bit of Avery, in that he was young, but where Avery still had the shine of innocence, Stefan's eyes held a bit of jaded skepticism.

"So, wait. What you are telling me is that Gerald DuBois admitted his mating to Rachelle was arranged?" Magnus asked after Adriel filled them in on the circumstances surrounding Declan's attack.

Adriel nodded. "Yes, for the entire Level to hear. Evidently it is a common practice among the Founding Families to keep bloodlines pure."

Magnus sat back, looking stunned. "But that is not what a mate is."

"Uncle, this concerns me. I grew up here and never heard of such a thing," Bethy admitted.

Gavriel gave an undignified snort. "Because they knew that if Magnus learned of it, he would abolish the practice immediately."

Aiden paled. "Please tell me these women were willing."

Bethy inhaled sharply, looking ill. She stood, placing a hand over her stomach. "Please excuse me." She darted toward Magnus' private bathroom. Gavriel was at her side before Kari could blink. He closed the door as sounds of Bethy retching reached them.

Magnus let out a string of curse words as he stood and began pacing nervously. "She should not be hearing such distressing things in her condition."

Her condition?

It dawned on her what he meant. "She is pregnant?"

Magnus stopped his pacing and turned to her with a smile on his face. "Yes. We found out after she arrived. I am going to be a great uncle." He puffed his chest out proudly.

"A thousand blessings on her and her child; this is wondrous news!" Kari exclaimed, making a mental note to order proper gifts.

Magnus sat back down but stared at his bathroom door. "Maybe she and Meryn should return to Lycaonia. This is not the best environment for them."

Aiden sighed loudly. "I think you know them both well enough by now to know that they wouldn't leave you in the lurch."

"He's right," Bethy said, patting her face with a damp paper towel. She smiled up at her mate. "I'm fine. It was just the idea of being trapped like that with someone who wasn't your mate for years, decades even." Her eyes began to tear up.

Gavriel quickly helped her back to her seat. "So, do we kill Gerald DuBois?" he asked in a calm tone.

Stefan Bolivar nodded. "Sounds good to me."

Kari choked on the sip of water she had just taken. Bethy shook her head and patted her on the back. "No, my love, we don't kill Gerald DuBois." Gavriel simply shrugged.

Kari could understand his line of reasoning. In his mind, Gerald had done wrong, but the most grievous offense, even if it had been indirectly, had been upsetting his pregnant mate. "I like you," she said, nodding her approval.

Gavriel's mouth twitched. "I believe I like you as well Kari Delaney. You were surprised at my suggestion, but you actually agree with it, do you not?"

Kari thought about it for a moment, then slowly nodded. "You are forgetting it was my mate he almost killed. Something tells me that Gerald DuBois is no stranger to violence. Declan may not have been his intended victim, but he clearly wanted to kill someone."

Gavriel's eyes darkened. "Forgive me, I had forgotten Declan nearly died. You are right, a man like that carries a taint of evil. He should be dealt with sooner rather than later."

"He is currently a guest in our detention cells. He will have a chance to plead his case, but I cannot see what he could possibly say to defend himself," Magnus said.

Kari thought it over. "He is losing his 'mate'; that is a powerful argument."

Aiden cursed. "I hadn't thought of it like that. She is right; that could sway people."

"Wonderful," Magnus groused. "We have the dinner with the DeLaFontaines this week. It was already going to be awkward, this will just make it painful."

Stefan groaned. "You can leave me off the invite list. I'm not too proud to admit that sort of dinner is over my head. I stick my foot in my mouth in the best of situations. With a dinner like that, I'd start World War Three."

Kari leaned forward. "Why would it be awkward?"

Bethy chortled, and Gavriel grinned openly. Adriel, on the other hand, was rubbing the back of his neck. Aiden looked resigned. "Well?"

Aiden cleared his throat. "My mate, Meryn, and Adriel's mate, Eva, reenacted the scene from *300* with Ivan DeLaFontaine in the transport tunnel."

Kari frowned, then realized the significance of the tunnel. Eyes wide, she looked from the unit leader to the Unit Commander. "They did not," she whispered.

Adriel nodded. "My Eva delivered a picture-perfect roundhouse kick to the chest, Meryn's squire electrified him with some sort of blue flame so he could not fly. His son had to fish him out of the safety net, tearing it in the process. We still need to get it fixed."

Kari turned to Aiden and Adriel. "I have *got* to meet your mates." Both men winced.

Bethy cleared her throat. "I'll be happy to introduce you to my newest friend, Eva Mae Miller, and my adopted baby sister, Meryn McKenzie."

"You adopted his mate?" Kari asked, pointing at Aiden.

Bethy nodded slowly. "You'll understand after you meet her."

Adriel tapped his clipboard. "I do not care what Declan may say later to try and avoid trouble, I want Gerald DuBois prosecuted to the fullest extent of the law. I will not tolerate anyone hurting my warriors, much less hurting a man who is like a brother to me." He paused. "A bratty, insolent, annoying, and exasperating brother, but a brother just the same."

Kari watched Adriel closely. His voice was even, almost sardonic, his outward appearance cool and collected, but his knuckles were white where he gripped the clipboard nearly to a breaking point. "Thank you, Adriel, for speaking for Declan when he cannot."

Adriel met her gaze and nodded. "I understand that you are to work directly with our prince; however, if you need anything, anything at all, any warrior in this city would drop everything to help both you and your brother. You are one of ours now."

Kari could feel the enormity of his declaration. She understood why Avery had been so happy earlier. It had been a very long time since she felt like she had the support of a family.

"Dear gods! Please tell me no one told Meryn about what happened to Declan!" Bethy gasped.

Aiden stood and shot from the room, Gavriel chuckled with Adriel. Stefan laughed outright, collapsing to one side of his chair.

Kari looked at Bethy. "Why would that make him run?"

Bethy took a moment before she answered. "Since

coming here, I have found myself relying on Declan heavily when working with the city's people. I was raised here, but I am still the prince's niece. Declan, on the other hand, is seen as somewhat of a champion of the people. He strives to remain neutral and will mediate between the Founding Families and the citizens. The people absolutely adore him; Meryn is no different. In Meryn's convoluted mind, the unit warriors belong to Aiden and Aiden belongs to her, so if anyone hurts the warriors, she hurts them."

"And she calls him Simba," Gavriel added, chuckling.

Bethy smiled. "She declared that as his walkie-talkie call sign. When she wasn't feeling well earlier this week, Declan took over guard duty, and they vegged out watching Disney movies and eating Cheetos. I think they watched *Lion King* six times. He spoils her rotten."

"But what could she possibly do that had the Unit Commander running out of here?" Kari asked.

Gavriel, Adriel, and Magnus winced, and Bethy winked at her. "What can't she do?"

"Now I really have to meet her." Kari strummed her fingers on her chair arm. "Is there a way to do interviews with all the mated couples in the city to determine how many of them are arranged and if anyone is being forced?"

Adriel exchanged glances with Magnus, and Magnus nodded. Adriel turned to her. "I think that is a wonderful idea, however, we may have to wait for your mate to heal."

"Why? I understand he is popular, but surely others could get this done."

Adriel tilted his head to one side. "You do not

know who he is, do you?"

Kari began to get agitated. "You mean in the fifteen minutes I was with him, while he was drugged with his intestines hanging out? No, we did not really get a quality chit chat in."

"Oh, I like her!" Bethy said, her eyes dancing.

Adriel made a pained expression. "Forgive me, I did not mean it that way, more rhetorical, I guess," he paused. "Your mate is Declan Lionhart."

She nodded. "That surname sounds familiar; the doctor said something about a Lionhart being too strong to succumb to those type of wounds."

Bethy cocked her head to one side. "Are you familiar with the shifter ruling families?"

Kari shook her head. "I do business mainly with humans and vampires. I try to leave the politics of the Founding Families and goings on of the pillar cities alone."

Magnus leaned forward. "Kari, the Lionharts are as prestigious as the McKenzies. They are considered one of the few shifter Founding Families. His father, Jedrek Lionhart, is the shifter Elder in Eiré Danu. His older brother, Rex, is the shifter Elder here in Noctem Falls, and his younger brother, Ari, is second in command to Brennus Vi'Eirlea, Queen Aleksandra's mate and royal consort."

Kari felt her eyes bug out. "What is he doing here?"

"Ouch," Bethy winced, sneaking glances at Adriel and her uncle.

Kari wished the floor would swallow her whole. She had made more social faux pas this afternoon than she had in the past decade. "My apologies, I did not mean to offend."

Adriel surprised her by nodding. "I understand exactly what you mean. I asked him that myself the day he arrived to act as my second in command. Can you guess what he said?" Kari shook her head. "He told me, 'it looks fun'." Adriel leaned back in his chair. "I believe he appreciated the distance he got from his family."

"But I thought you said his older brother was the shifter Elder here?" she asked.

Adriel nodded. "Yes, but he arrived after Declan."

Kari was nodding her understanding when a thought struck her. "Why is he not here? His younger brother almost died."

Magnus paled and stood. Without saying a word, he left the small conference room.

"Oh dear," Bethy murmured.

"Rex is going to be a bear to deal with. He is very protective of his brothers." Adriel stood. "I will warn our prickly healer. If you will excuse me..." He hurried from the room.

Bethy looked between her and Gavriel. "I'll make an announcement that, starting tomorrow, Declan will be conducting interviews with all the mated couples."

"Will he be healed by then?" Kari asked worriedly.

Bethy nodded. "Lions tend to heal faster than most shifters." She looked around. "Uncle will be back soon. Did you want to wait here?"

Kari nodded. "Yes, that is fine. After he returns, we will head back to the office. I want to go over past reports to see if I can find anything that may indicate issues between couples."

Stefan stood when Bethy and Gavriel did. "Can

I tell Rachelle and Peter that the wolves have the support of Prince Magnus?"

Bethy rubbed her temples. "Stefan, I'm so sorry, I completely forgot that this affects one of your pack members. Yes, of course, tell them my uncle supports them one hundred percent. If any of your people discover mates, please advise them to alert us immediately so that we may avoid another scene like today."

Stefan nodded. "Of course. If I may make a suggestion?" He hesitated, as if his opinion wouldn't be welcome.

Gavriel looked kindly at the young wolf. "Please."

"If you want some of the women to open up, include Micah. I haven't been here long, but I see the way he treats them; they trust him."

Bethy smiled at the young wolf. "I'll have Adriel add his name to the assignment. That's a very good suggestion, Stefan. Please know that your input is vital. We're relying on you to let us know how things stand with your people."

Stefan blushed. "Thanks. I know I'm young, but sometimes that can help people see things more clearly."

Aiden stamped through the doorway. "Drones! Where in the hell did she get drones?" Aiden roared, waving a small device in his hand.

Bethy's eyes widened. "Oh Meryn."

Grinning, Kari stood. "Change of plans. I need to meet Meryn McKenzie."

Aiden set the drone down on the table. "I'll take you to her. Maybe *you* can keep her out of trouble."

Kari laughed. "No promises."

"Great, just great," he muttered.

As they left the conference room, they passed Magnus' office. She leaned down to Avery. "Come on, there is someone we have to meet."

Avery sprang from his chair excitedly. "Is it the crazy human?"

Vin and Keegan chuckled then gulped when Aiden turned to them with a sour expression. Vin gave a weak smile. "Sorry sir, but we saw the drone."

Aiden shook his head. "She means well."

Keegan coughed. "I'm sure she does. What did she have attached to it? Usually, they can hold a camera or weapon..." Keegan trailed off, taking in his commander's expression.

Aiden froze. "Attached?"

"Shit," Vin whispered.

Aiden turned to her. "Follow me."

Avery hurried behind Aiden. After the Unit Commander left the room, she quickly turned to Vin. "Snag the drone in the conference room and bring it by when he is not looking," she whispered.

"Are you trying to get me killed?" he whispered back.

"Two questions. One: Do you really think she has only the one? Two: Would you not try to get on her good side by returning it?"

Keegan swallowed hard. "Good point. We'll get it back to her."

Kari grinned at them. "Thanks." She ran after Aiden who was walking quickly toward the living quarters.

She caught up to Avery and snagged his hand. Laughing, they practically had to run to keep up with the grouchy bear.

Avery turned to her. "This place is fun!"

She winked at him, and they both giggled when Aiden began to grumble.

Maybe this won't be too bad after all.

☾

"WHERE'S MY DRONE?" THE SMALL woman demanded.

Kari exchanged glances with Avery. This woman was less than half Aiden's size. Her short brown hair seemed to have a mind of its own, curling in every direction.

"Meryn, were you going to attach anything to it?" Aiden asked.

Meryn froze and looked down at her feet. "No."

Aiden exhaled. "Baby, this isn't home. You can't just do whatever you want."

Meryn's head popped up; she looked genuinely confused. "Why not?"

"We're visiting dignitaries."

"So?"

"We could cause Magnus problems."

"So?"

Exasperated, Aiden threw his hands in the air. "Because one day, I'll be an Elder."

"And?"

"Just tell me this: Are you working with dangerous chemicals or explosives?"

Avery's eyes widened at the question.

Meryn tilted her head to one side, thinking about her answer. "Hmm no. I think."

Aiden's head snapped to the handsome Asian man standing behind Meryn. "Ryuu?"

Ryuu had a faint smile. "What she is handling is in no way a danger to her."

Aiden turned back to Meryn. "No more attempting to go after Gerald DuBois."

"I make no promises," Meryn said, crossing her arms over her chest.

Aiden looked over at Kari and scowled. "Where have I heard that before?"

Kari widened her eyes, giving him her best innocent look. "Who me?"

Meryn peeked past her mate. "Who are the new peeps?"

Aiden turned so that Meryn could see them. "Meryn, this is Kari Delaney, Declan's mate, and her younger brother, Avery Therian."

Meryn stared at her then nodded before turning to Avery. Her eyes narrowed, and she tilted her head again. "He's pretty."

Avery blushed. "Thank you."

Kari sighed. "I wish I had his eyelashes."

Meryn shook her head. "He is pretty like that too, but I mean his..." she waved her hand around her chest. "I don't know, his heart maybe. I've never seen anyone so kind. He gives off good vibes."

Aiden frowned and walked over to his mate. "When did you start seeing vibes?" He rubbed her back.

Meryn shrugged. "I think I always have, but I've created a classification system for what I see now; it's helping me identify more." She pointed to Kari. "Like she's all boxes and clean lines like Beth. I'm guessing that means she's organized."

"You have no idea," Avery muttered.

Kari bumped him with her hip.

Meryn pointed to Avery. "He's fluffy. Light and fluffy and sweet. Like cotton candy." Her eyes became unfocused, and even though he was standing behind her and couldn't see her expression, Ryuu reacted by reaching down and circling one of her wrists. She shook her head as if to clear it. "Fluffy means nice."

Aiden and Ryuu's eyes met over Meryn's head. Meryn elbowed them both. "I know when you do that."

Aiden leaned down and nuzzled her neck. "Just worried about you baby."

"I'm cool. I'm getting better at using my Jedi powers." Meryn beamed at them.

Avery turned to Kari with puppy dog eyes. "Can we keep her?" he pleaded.

Kari laughed. "I think Bethy has dibs. She adopted Meryn as her sister."

Meryn nodded. "Yup! But you can join me for *Doctor Who* in the afternoons." She looked at Kari. "I got Declan hooked."

Avery began to bounce from foot to foot. "Who's your favorite Doctor?" he blurted out.

Meryn's eyes lit up. "I love Ten, but Eleven has his moments, you know?"

Avery bobbed his head up and down. "I had such a crush on Eccleston," he admitted shyly.

Meryn began to nod energetically. "It was totally the jacket."

Avery pointed to her then turned to Kari. "She gets it!"

Kari watched as the two of them jumped down the geek rabbit hole. She didn't care if Meryn McKenzie blew up half the city; she understood Avery and was treating him as a friend. For that reason alone, Kari would defend the small women unconditionally.

Aiden's eyes began to glaze over when they began chattering away about favorite episodes. He shook his head. "Okay baby, I'm heading back out to help Magnus field the shit storm Rex Lionhart will stir up with Declan getting hurt." He turned to Kari. "Staying?"

Kari nodded. "For a bit."

"Meryn has a walkie-talkie. If you need us, let her know." Aiden gave Meryn a final kiss then left.

Meryn rubbed her lower back, and Avery immediately became contrite. "Ohmygosh! I'm so sorry. I'm nattering on like a geek, and you should be sitting down."

Meryn waved off his concern. "I needed to walk around. I've been working with Nigel and Neil creating the perfect revenge for Declan. Then Aiden had to go and steal my drone."

Kari waved her finger back and forth. "Vin and Keegan will be bringing it back soon. I hate to admit it, but I want to see what you can do. Declan is my mate, after all."

Meryn threw her hands in the air and hopped around. "Yes! Yes! Kari, you rock!"

Avery moved his hands as if trying to get her to calm down. "Please, don't bounce!"

Meryn giggled. "It's not like the baby is going to fall out or anything." She grabbed his hand. "Come on! I'll show you my secret lair."

Kari raised an eyebrow to Ryuu. He cleared his throat. "The communication hub."

Meryn and Avery began going back and forth about the latest *Doctor Who* special as they walked down the hall. Meryn used her hand, and the door opened to a large room. “My bat cave!”

CHAPTER FOUR

KARI LOOKED AROUND THE ROOM. Long tables lined three walls with piles of boxes, electronics, and cables organized in small piles. Meryn hurried over to a table and removed a large cardboard box covering what looked like a small helicopter.

"I told them you had more than one," Kari murmured.

Meryn turned to her and grinned. "I actually ordered three, so that each of us could practice."

"Us?"

"She means us," a male voice piped up.

Kari looked to her right and blinked. She was seeing double.

One of the men chuckled. "There's nothing wrong with your vision; we're twins."

Avery moved to stand beside Meryn. "Could you teach me how to use this?"

Meryn shrugged. "I'm not too good with them yet. Nigel is the best pilot of the three of us."

Nigel snorted. "That's not saying much; we're all kinda terrible."

Avery picked the small drone up and turned it over. "What were you going to use it for?"

"Revenge," the other man said, dropping his voice an octave. He held up his hands in front of him like a zombie. "Muwahahaha."

Meryn tapped on her lips with her finger a thoughtful expression on her face. "You still need to work on your evil laugh, Neil, it still sounds kinda cute."

Neil rolled his eyes. "I'll get it eventually."

"I thought it was scary," Avery said, trying to be kind.

Neil's face brightened, "Really?"

Avery nodded. "Totally."

Nigel looked from her to Avery before turning to Meryn. "Introductions?"

"Hmmm?" Meryn said, preoccupied with the small clear crystal in her hand.

"Earth to Meryn." Neil stood and leaned over to wave a hand in front of her face.

"Right. Introductions. Kari Delaney, Simba's mate, boxy. Avery Therian, awesome *Doctor Who* fan, fluffy. Kari, Avery, these two are Nigel and Neil Morninglory, witches in two of the units here in the city. My charming shadow is my squire, Ryuu Sei." Meryn frowned and picked up another crystal, this one clouded. "Did it take?"

Kari walked over to Meryn and looked at the crystal. "What is it?

Meryn looked up at her beaming. "My Baby Keelans have been working on a way to affix a spell to crystals."

"Baby Keelans?" Kari asked.

Meryn's excitement dimmed. "They remind me of someone back home, younger versions."

Avery laid a head on Meryn's shoulder. "Is that person okay?"

Meryn nodded, still looking sad. "Yes, but he's not in his body right now."

Avery's brows snapped together. "Huh?"

Neil shook his head. "Don't bother, we can't get an answer outta of her about it."

"It's complicated," Meryn argued.

"Obviously," Kari drawled.

Avery lifted his head. "Is that a spell?" he asked, pointing to the crystal.

Meryn's head bobbed. "Yup. When we heard what that dickhead did to Declan, we decided to move the drone project up on our 'To Do' list. We're going to fly this baby to the detention cell and hit him with the spell."

Avery's eyes widened. "Is that legal?"

Meryn shrugged. "To-may-toe, to-mah-to. It's not like it'd kill him, well, not this spell." Meryn waved the brown crystal around.

Kari pulled Avery back. "What *does* that one do?"

"Diarrhea," Meryn said, grinning wickedly.

"And some nightmares thrown in for fun. The whole point is to try to get him to shit himself," Nigel explained.

Avery looked between the three proud looking mad scientists. "Can I play?"

They all nodded. "Of course," Neil said, patting the seat next to him.

"Avery dear, what about your new position?" Kari asked, not really comfortable leaving him with this nutty trio.

Avery turned his face crestfallen. "I can start tomorrow. We weren't really planning on working anyway; this was our vacation. Besides, I know it will take you a couple days to get Magnus sorted.

All I need are industrial strength anti-bacterial wipes and maybe a bonfire to clean out that horrid woman's desk."

"Bonfire?" Meryn asked, looking interested.

"Horrid woman?" Neil asked at the same time.

Kari smiled. "I may have choked the life out of Magnus' secretary before throwing her across the room and getting her fired. Avery is her replacement. I will be working with Magnus to get the funnel of information he has been receiving organized, especially since it looks like we will be moving here since I am mated to Declan."

"Kick ass!" Meryn giggled. "You'll get along great with Eva."

"Is she the one with the perfect roundhouse kick?" Kari asked.

"Yup. She's awesome."

"Did you get an update about Declan?" Neil asked.

Kari shook her head. "I want to head there after checking in with Prince Magnus. So far I have not received any updates about his condition."

Nigel ground his teeth together. "Declan is a great guy. We love playing pranks on him, but only because he treats us like bratty younger brothers. I can't believe that jerk tried to gut him."

"From what I was told, he was actually aiming for a wolf, but trust me, that does not justify what happened," Kari shared.

Meryn opened her mouth to speak when a ringing noise started. Everyone looked around at each other before checking their phones.

"*Denka*, I believe the computer is ringing," Ryuu said, pointing at the computer in the middle of the room.

Meryn hurried over and opened the flashing program. "It's my minions!"

"I'm afraid to ask." Kari winked at Avery.

Seconds later, two handsome men were waving at Meryn on the screen.

"About time you got up and running! We've been waiting to Skype with you for days," the blond complained.

"Someone has been going stir crazy," the dark haired one jerked his head toward his friend.

"I miss you guys so much. I never liked people before finding Aiden, so this is new for me." Meryn rubbed her breastbone.

"We miss you too, you nut. Everything is so quiet around here," the dark haired one complained.

"You have company?" the blond asked.

Meryn huffed. "Okay, introductions again." She waved to the screen. "Everyone, the pretty one is Noah Caraway, the dashing one next to him is Jaxon Darrow. They are my minions. I am training them in my Jedi computer ways." She turned and pointed behind her. "Guys, the red headed twins are Nigel and Neil Morninglory; they are unit warriors here. The adorable one with the big expressive eyes is Avery Therian, and the woman behind him is his sister, Kari Delaney. She just found out that her mate is Declan, the cool lion shifter I texted you about."

Kari waved at the two 'minions' as everyone said hello. She noticed that Noah looked a bit sadder than when they first connected.

"So what world domination plans have you created since you left?" Jaxon asked.

"Well, I completely set up the wireless and cellular network for the city, and today, we started working with flying drones. I hope to use them as weapons and as our eyes in the sky to help the warriors," Meryn babbled.

The twins cracked up. "That's the responsible answer; the truth is she wanted internet to play Farmville and watch Netflix. The drones are part of a plan to send a diarrhea spell to the detention cell to get back at the guy that nearly gutted Declan," Neil explained.

Jaxon's eyes widened, and a low growl was heard. "I thought you were supposed to be safe there. How did Declan end up gutted?"

Everyone turned to Kari, and she spread her hands. "I only have the barest of facts. He was acting as a mediator on Level Six between a Founding Family vampire and a wolf shifter. They were fighting over a woman, and Declan stepped between them." Kari didn't know how much information had been released, so she decided to err on the side of caution when it came to revealing facts.

"Exactly why that fucker needs to pay," Meryn said vehemently.

"Yeah," the twins agreed together.

Noah began to look more uneasy. Meryn frowned. "Noah, are you constipated? You look like something is bothering you."

Jaxon groaned and buried his face in his hands.

Noah's mouth opened and closed like a guppy. He finally shook his head and looked down.

"Not the right thing to say?" Meryn asked, looking around.

Avery shook his head and Kari shrugged. She had no idea why the young blond was upset.

"Noah, you know that *denka* is at a disadvantage

not being in the same room as you; she can't sense how you are feeling. I'm afraid you will have to be very direct with your concern," Ryuu advised, smiling gently.

"Concern?" Meryn's head whipped back around to the screen. "What's wrong?"

"Are you replacing us?" Noah blurted, the color draining from his face.

"Huh? No. Why?" Meryn sputtered.

Kari looked from the twins to the two men on the screen. "Ah."

Ryuu looked at her and nodded.

"What!?" Meryn demanded.

Avery took pity on her. "Noah is worried now that you have Nigel and Neil, you won't need them anymore."

"That's ridiculous. Noah and Jaxon are my minions. I found them; they're mine. Nigel and Neil are my Baby Keelans..." Meryn paused. "Oh. I can see how that can be confusing. But I feel the same about all four of you."

"How?" Noah asked, biting his lower lip.

"Hmm. Not like Aiden, because we don't have sex."

"Thank the gods," Noah whispered.

"Not like Ryuu, because y'all don't feed me..." Meryn scratched her head, looking truly confused.

"*Denka*, do you care about them?" Ryuu asked.

"Yes, of course."

"Worry about them?"

"Yes."

"Want them to be happy?"

"Duh."

"Then what type of family member do you care

about, worry over, want to be happy, that are usually close in age and male?" Ryuu prompted.

Meryn frowned. Kari could imagine the wheels turning a mile a minute in her brain. Finally, Meryn's face lit up. "They are like male versions of Beth and Amelia. That would make them my brothers!" Meryn announced happily. Her eyes narrowed, and she grinned. "I have brothers now; brothers are cool."

Kari took in the four men's faces and smiled. She could see how Meryn's words affected them.

Noah dissolving into tears broke the silence. Jaxon rubbed his back gently, his own eyes shining brightly. Nigel and Neil were clutching each other's hands so hard Kari was afraid they were going to snap off each other's fingers.

"Now how did I break them?" Meryn groaned. She laid her head on her crossed forearms on the table. Avery rubbed her back. "I don't think they are broken, Meryn. I think they are just fine," he whispered.

"We are. We are. We are. We are!" Noah sobbed.

Meryn lifted her head, looking angry. "You stop that! No crying, Noah, I can't help you from here!" Meryn twisted her hands together anxiously.

A sniff then a giggle escaped Noah. "Like you would know what to do even if you were here."

Meryn's face relaxed at his laughter. "Probably not."

"Meryn, I understand Noah and Jaxon, you've known them longer, but you've only just met us." Nigel pointed between him and his brother.

"So?"

"We just met."

"Yes, you said that."

"How can you possibly love us enough to call us brothers?" Neil asked. His eyes were hopeful but leery. As if he was afraid to believe that Meryn could possibly care for them that much.

Kari understood his concern, but knew exactly where Meryn was coming from. She knew the moment she laid eyes on Avery that he was going to be someone special to her. She was willing to bet that Meryn had known that the four men were important to her the moment she met them as well.

"Do I or do I not have this empathy, feeling thing?" Meryn demanded.

They both nodded.

"I just know." She looked them both in the eye. "I know what it's like to have no one. No one to share things with or to care if you eat Hot Pockets for a month straight." All four men shuddered. "So, when I see someone as amazing as the two of you, who stuck up for me and see the fun in the dreariest situations, I want to give you what I didn't have." She shrugged. "No one should be all alone, not ever." Her last few words were pain filled whispers, but everyone heard them clearly.

"I accept!" Noah blurted out, startling everyone.

Jaxon swallowed hard. "I do too. Gods only know what the four of us would do without you around." He looked at the twins. "It would be four right?" The question hung in the air.

"Of course!" Nigel practically shouted.

"Try to send us away! We're like two bad pennies, we'll always turn up," Neil said, wiping his eyes.

"So my minions and my Baby Keelans are my brothers; that's awesome!" She pursed her lips.

"Should we get tattoos?"

"That would be totally badass," Noah nodded.

Noah's eyes widened. "Won't that hurt?" Nigel exchanged worried looks with Noah. Jaxon and Neil shrugged.

Meryn tilted her head and then looked back at Kari. "What do brothers do? Beth is my Yoda and keeps me from making too many political blunders, and Amelia hugs me a lot. What do I do with them?"

Kari blinked. "Did none of your friends growing up have brothers?"

Meryn shook her head. "I never had any friends."

Kari's heart turned over. "Well..." She glanced at Avery. "Brothers are there for you when no one else is. They are always on your side, even if you are wrong, and they bring you the best snacks when you are upset."

Avery giggled. "I don't think I should be used as a universal template for brothers, Kari."

Kari sniffed. "Why not? You are perfect."

Avery rolled his eyes and turned to Meryn. "What about just continuing on doing what you have been doing?"

Meryn shook her head. "No, because that is minion and Baby Keelan stuff. We need to do brother stuff now."

Jaxon chuckled while Noah and the twins exchanged looks. Finally, Neil spoke up. "Actually Meryn, your minion and Baby Keelan stuff is brother stuff, you just didn't know what to call it at the time."

Jaxon nodded. "He's right. Playing Xbox, designing tech toys, implementing world domination plans, and binge watching shows on Netflix while eating junk food are practically essential brother-like activities."

Neil turned to the screen. "What shows are you watching?"

Noah practically began bouncing in his seat. "Well, ever since Netflix dropped *Doctor Who*, we've been watching *Supernatural*."

"What?" Meryn whispered.

"We're three seasons behind. Our cable was spotty before Meryn arrived," Neil said.

"*What*?" Meryn gasped low.

Kari became concerned when Ryuu hurried over to his charge's side and began rubbing her back. "It will be okay, *denka*."

"Oh shit! She didn't know," Jaxon hissed.

"All is lost!" Meryn wailed loudly, throwing her hands in the air.

Neil turned to Jaxon and Noah. "What do we do?"

Noah's eyes were wide as he shook his head helplessly. "I don't know. This is major! Find her some chocolate, coffee, Cheetos, anything!"

Avery looked back at Kari, worry on his face. "Kari, help her."

Kari walked over and unclipped the walkie-talkie from Meryn's geek bag. "Hmm hello?"

"This is Adriel. Kari, is that you? Is everything well?"

Kari took in Meryn's epic breakdown. "Not really. Meryn just found out Netflix dropped *Doctor Who*."

After a second of silence, Bethy's voice came across the walkie-talkie. "Oh my gods! Kari, can you please get her back to my uncle's quarters? I'll meet you there. I'll have Sebastian whip up some Magic Pudding for her. I think I have some Classic

Who on DVDs in storage. We'll get her settled, and I'll look for them."

"The world is a darker place. How could this happen! It's a conspiracy! Evil has taken root in the world!" Meryn ranted.

"Right. I will get her there." Kari lowered the walkie-talkie. "Avery, Ryuu get Meryn back to Magnus' quarters. Neil, Nigel, go find Bethy and help her go through storage. She is pregnant, and some of those boxes may be heavy." She looked at Noah and Jaxon. "You two find out if *Doctor Who* is available through any other online streaming source, if not, get Aiden's credit card and buy every season they have available on iTunes." She placed her hands on her hips. They just stared at her. "Today, gentlemen!"

At once, the six men began to move. Ryuu inclined his head. "You have my thanks."

Noah and Jaxon disconnected from Skype as they got to work. Nigel and Neil left at a run to help Bethy, and Avery and Ryuu were gently coaxing Meryn back to Magnus'.

Kari walked behind them, smiling at the way Avery soothed his new friend. He was the sweetest soul she had ever met. As far as Kari was concerned, the second he'd connected with Meryn she became family. So she was willing to do whatever it took to make the crazy human happy, if only to keep Avery smiling.

Bethy met them at the door. An anxious looking man peered out from behind her.

"You poor thing! You're having a rough week aren't you?" Bethy said in a sympathetic voice.

Meryn stopped in her tracks and looked at her

adopted sister. Her bottom lip began to quiver, and Bethy's eyes widened. Before anyone knew what was happening, Meryn went into a full blown nuclear meltdown.

Bethy was immediately at her side, wrapping her arms around her. "Shsssh, honey, it's okay."

Meryn just shook her head. "It's dark! And I hate it here! Now I can't watch *Doctor Who* and that was my escape! I miss Noah and Jaxon and Penny and Amelia, even though she hugs me!" Meryn's barely coherent wailing echoed through the stone halls. A tiny light began to buzz around her head. Ryuu stood close to Meryn's side, his hand on her wrist. A faint blue light glowed from his circled fingers.

Bethy sniffled as her eyes began to tear up. "I know; I miss home too."

Kari watched in disbelief as Bethy began to break down right along side Meryn. Avery wrung his hands as he bounced from foot to foot, panicked.

Kari walked to the doorway. "Your name?"

The man blinked. "My name is Sebastian, I am the Rioux squire."

"Good. Let us get these two somewhere warm and comfortable. Where would be the best place?"

He tore his eyes away from the upset women. "Meryn has been using the guest quarters' media room to relax in. I will take them there and turn on the fireplace."

"Fireplace?" Kari asked.

"Ventless gas fireplace. Does wonders to knock the chill off when it gets cold." Sebastian was about to step toward his two charges when Gavriel appeared behind him.

He took one look at the two women, his eyes

turned red, and his body began to expand. "If another one of these idiotic, parasitic, sycophantic vampires have upset them, I will rip them apart limb by limb."

Avery turned and winced. "Meryn found out Netflix dropped *Doctor Who,* and Bethy started crying when Meryn did."

Gavriel took a deep breath and slowly began to relax down to his original size, though his eyes remained red. He walked over and pulled both women to his body. Bethy and Meryn buried their faces in his chest.

"Hush now *zain'ka moya, solnyshko moya,* I have you now. Let us go warm up and partake of Sebastian's Magic Pudding; things are not as dark as they may seem." Gavriel gently kissed both women on the tops of their heads and steered them inside, Ryuu close behind them. Avery walked over to stand with Kari; they looked at each other, unsure if they should follow.

Sebastian reappeared at the door, smiling. "Please come in. I have put on a fresh pot of tea, I am sure that the two of you could use a cup."

Avery nodded, but Kari shook her head. She gently pushed Avery out in front of her, handing him the walkie-talkie. "Take care of your new friends. I still have work to do in Magnus' office, plus I would like to actually speak with my mate sometime today without him being drugged to the gills."

Avery took a step, then spun on his heel and threw himself at her. She hugged him tight. "Love you, Kari," he whispered.

"Love you too, kiddo. Go relax and help those two smile again, yeah?"

Avery pulled back. "Right!"

Kari met Sebastian's eyes. He winked then nodded. Feeling better now that the squire was watching out for her brother, she began to retrace her steps, heading back to the office where she would be spending most of her time.

KARI OPENED THE DOOR TO Magnus' office; both men looked absolutely exhausted. When they started to rise, she waved them back into their seats. "So I take it from your expressions that the phone call with Rex Lionhart went well?" Kari stepped into the room and shut the door behind her.

Aiden groaned and rubbed his hands over his face. "He handled it about as well as I would have if it had been my younger brother who'd been hurt."

Magnus nodded. "I cannot imagine receiving a phone call like that about Caspian."

Kari cocked her head to one side. "Is your walkie-talkie turned off?" she asked Aiden.

Aiden's eyes narrowed. "Why?"

Kari took a deep breath. "Meryn had..." she paused, unsure how to explain what happened. "An episode earlier. She found out that *Doctor Who* is no longer on Netflix and didn't handle it well." Kari watched as every ounce of color drained from Aiden's face.

He stood suddenly. "I have to go to her." His eyes darted around the room. "I need Bart! Bart would know what to do."

"Who is Bart?" Magnus asked.

"He is an old human that runs the store near Lycaonia. He is an expert in all things female."

Magnus smiled. "He sounds like an extraordinary human."

Aiden stepped from around the desk and headed toward the door. He stopped then turned to Magnus. "Is there a place to buy chocolate here?" he asked.

Magnus nodded, pointing a finger up to the ceiling. "Level Six, look for Pierre. He deals strictly with imported chocolate."

Aiden exhaled in relief as the air whooshed from his lungs. "Chocolate fixes everything," he said seriously and then opened the door and left.

"I truly think he believes that," Kari said, more to herself than anything. Magnus chuckled. "Chocolate will help a man like that go a long way," he joked.

"Magnus, I hate to ask, but is there any way that I could visit Declan?" Kari did not want to give the impression that she did not want her new position, but everything in her had been fighting to go see Declan from the moment she had left his side. Surely, by now, he had to be out of surgery.

Magnus stood. "Of course, you are not a prisoner here. In fact, if you can wait a moment, I would like you to come with me to greet Rex when he arrives. The three of us can visit Declan together."

Kari let out the breath she didn't know she was holding. "That would be wonderful."

Magnus walked over to her and placed a hand on either shoulder. "Kari, I know that a lot has been thrown at you today, and you have handled it beautifully. Whatever you need, do not be afraid to ask. I know exactly how large a gift you are from Fate, not only to Declan, but to me as well. I believe that you are desperately needed in the city, especially now."

His sincere praise had her smiling. "Thank you, Magnus."

Magnus lowered his hands and smiled. "It is the least I could do for someone who is going to help me run the city."

Kari gave him an evil grin and wagged her finger back and forth. "Oh, I am not going to be running the city." He looked at her, puzzled. "I will be running you." She patted his cheek when he groaned. "Buck up, I have not killed anyone...yet." She winked at him.

He threw his head back and laughed. He straightened and offered her his arm. She accepted, and they left the office together before heading to Level Six.

Kari could've picked Rex Lionhart out of a thousand people; he looked that much like his brother.

Rex walked right up to them and greeted Magnus. "Prince Magnus," he said shortly.

Magnus nodded "Elder Lionhart," he replied just as brusquely.

Rex growled low in his throat, his impatience belying him. "I don't have time for niceties; I'm here to see my brother."

Magnus inclined his head, a small grin on his lips. "Of course, but allow me to be the one to introduce you to your new sister." He stepped back and motioned to Kari. "Rex Lionhart, I would like you to meet Kari Delaney, Declan's mate." Rex's head snapped to her so quickly she thought he'd hurt himself. A wide, warm smile changed his face completely, and without hesitation, he pulled her into a huge hug, squeezing her so tightly she thought her spine might snap. He swung her around, laughing before he lowered her to the floor. "A mate? My brother? By the gods! It's about time. I can't wait to get to know you better, but if you're like me, I bet you're just dying to see him too."

Kari nodded. "Yes. Yes, actually, I am."

Rex bowed regally and offered her his arm. "Well then pretty lady, if you would escort me to Level One to where my brother is, maybe we could both see him."

"I guess I am just chopped liver now," Magnus mused.

Rex's expression became puzzled. "You normally don't speak like this. You're usually so formal I fight the urge to stick you with a pin. What has changed you?"

Magnus glanced around and then indicated the transport tunnel. "I have much to tell you, maybe later, once we are in my office."

Rex nodded his understanding, and the three of them made their way down the tunnel back to Level One. Kari was so nervous she didn't know what to do. She hadn't even thought about in-laws, and here she was standing next to a new brother. Magnus knocked on the door, and they walked in.

The doctor sat in a chair beside the bed making notes on a form on the clipboard in his lap.

Declan opened his eyes and smiled. "My mate. You're just as beautiful as I remember. For a moment I feared I had dreamt you." He jerked his thumb to the healer. "The doctor assured me that you were real, but I wanted to see for myself."

Kari blushed. "It is nice to be able to speak with

you when you are not drugged."

Declan winced and rubbed his stomach. "I'm getting better," he joked.

Kari rolled her eyes. "You would be a Monty Python fan."

He shrugged. "Blame Colton Albright; he introduced me to the movies. Why don't you come over here and sit next to me," he suggested, patting the bed.

Kari walked over to him, and instead of sitting on the side of the bed, she sat in the chair on the other side of the bed opposite the doctor. Declan practically turned onto his side to face her. His whole face was lit up with a smile that hadn't diminished since they'd walked through the door.

"I can't believe the gods have given me such an angel."

A throat cleared.

"And gods, the smell!" he continued, taking a deep breath.

The throat cleared again.

"So tell me all about yourself," Declan asked, ignoring Rex.

Rex stepped to the foot of the bed. "Nice of you to welcome your brother," he criticized.

Declan gave his brother a sidelong glance. "Hello Rex, how are you?" he asked dutifully. When Declan turned his attention back to Kari, Rex put his hand under the sheet. Seconds later, Declan yowled loudly.

The doctor dropped his clipboard, and he stood, fuming. "What are you doing to my patient?" he demanded.

Rex brushed off his fingers on his suit, and in the

light, small golden hairs drifted toward the floor. "Just getting his attention," he informed the agitated healer.

Declan pulled his leg up and began rubbing it. "You ripped out my leg hairs."

Rex gave his brother the evil eye. "Not all of them; quit being such a baby."

Kari covered her mouth with her hand to hide her smile. Even if their looks didn't announce to everyone that they were siblings, their actions definitely would. "Is that all you have to say to your brother who came here to see how you were doing?" Rex asked.

Declan lowered his leg. "I'm fine."

Rex crossed his arms. "I heard you almost died. Did you call Father? Mother?"

Declan shook his head. "I was kinda unconscious, then in surgery, then unconscious again. I am just now waking up, so no, I haven't called Father yet."

At the mention of surgery, Rex's eyes softened. "Are you really okay?"

Declan nodded, ducking his head. "Yeah, Bubber."

"Okay." Rex smiled at the term Bubber.

Kari turned her mate. "Bubber?"

Declan grinned evilly. "I couldn't say brother when I was a child."

"That is so cute!" she gushed.

Though he pretended to be indifferent, Rex wore a smile. She could tell that he liked the affectionate term.

"Try not to agitate my patient. He needs to lie still for the next couple of hours," the doctor huffed, picking up his clipboard before sitting back down.

Rex ignored the doctor. "You know an Elder seat may be opening up in Storm Keep," Rex began.

"No," Declan said, shortly.

Rex scowled. "You haven't even let me finish."

"I don't need to. I know I don't want to become an Elder; I've never wanted to become an Elder. I hate politics, yet somehow I always seem to find myself in the middle of these situations."

"Maybe if you became an Elder, you wouldn't be getting cut up mediating disputes between two factions that should know better," Rex said, biting off each word.

Declan crossed his arms. "I like what I do here. I help people. That's all I've ever wanted to do."

"I just want to keep you safe, little brother," Rex admitted.

Declan nodded. "I know, but keeping me safe and running my life are two separate things."

"I don't want to run your life, Declan. Just ensure that you're happy."

Declan looked over at her and winked. "Something tells me I'm going to be real happy," he leered at her.

She raised an eyebrow. "We will see," she said, noncommittally.

Rex chuckled. "Sounds like you got yourself a smart woman there, Declan." He stopped and tapped his chin. "You know what, as a mating gift to both of you, I'll call Father and let him know what happened. I'll run interference for as long as I'm here."

Declan's his face became a mask of disbelief. "Really? You'd do that for me?"

Rex flicked Declan's big toe causing him to flinch again. "Of course. I have a feeling that I'm going to be here for a few more days." He raised an eyebrow at Magnus. "Someone still needs to explain to me how this entire debacle happened."

"I suppose that is my cue to invite you back to my office for an explanation," Magnus said.

Rex inclined his head. "That would be most welcome."

Kari didn't know what to do. She should be there with them to help document anything that was said or any agreements made, but she was loath to leave Declan's side.

"Kari?" Magnus called her name softly.

When she looked up at him, he winked at her. "You do not have to start for a few days. Take some time to get to know your mate."

"We will, however, expect you both at dinner," Rex threw out over his shoulder as he walked out of the room.

Magnus met her eyes, and he rolled his slowly. "Yes, of course you are both welcome to dinner." He waved and walked out behind Rex.

The door closed, and Kari looked over at her mate. "So?"

"Yeah," he rubbed the back of his neck.

"Well, this couldn't get anymore painfully awkward," the doctor said, standing.

Kari and Declan smirked at each other.

"Well, if my services are no longer needed..." The doctor stood.

"Just a moment, Doctor, if you have a moment. I was wondering if there is a treatment for homesickness?" she asked.

He blinked. "Forgive me, I never introduced myself, things were so chaotic earlier. I'm Dr.

Nathaniel St. John." He frowned, considering her question. "Do you mean actual homesickness?"

She nodded. "Meryn, the Unit Commander's mate had something of a meltdown earlier, and I am concerned for her, as she is with child."

The doctor's eyebrows snapped together, a frown overtaking his face. "Any kind of heightened emotion can raise blood sugar and blood pressure; neither are good for a woman when she carries. We must do everything possible to make sure that she stays healthy for the baby." He chewed on his lower lip for moment. "I'll swing by and make sure she's okay. At the very least, I could possibly give her low dose sedative. I have a feeling that she is being affected in the same way that the shifter children are."

"Shifter children?" both Kari and Declan asked at the same time.

The doctor nodded. "Like Elder Lionhart, I'll be staying here few days as well. As Declan was recovering, I had a few concerned wolf-shifter parents find their way down here to me to ask if I could look in on their children. Some of the shifter children are lethargic, despondent, and weepy. I have a feeling that they, like your Meryn, are just missing home."

"It could be from being underground for the shifter children," Declan volunteered.

The doctor snapped his fingers "Of course. I had forgotten all about that."

Kari looked from one to the other. "What am I missing?" she asked.

Declan winced as he adjusted his pillow before answering. "Most shifters and fae have a hard time in Noctem Falls. The lack of daylight, plants, sun, and wind affects them greatly."

The doctor tucked his clipboard under one arm. "The fae and shifters are very much creatures of the earth. I'll make recommendations to the parents to find a way to get the children to the surface for an hour so."

Declan nodded at the idea. "Find the unit leader Adriel Aristaios; he can make arrangements with the other fae and shifter unit warriors for topside time with the children." He turned to Kari. "Even we unit warriors need to take turns doing topside patrol. Being underground for so long can take a toll on us, I can't imagine what it's doing to the babies."

"I had no idea," she said.

"Thank you for your suggestion, Declan. I'll check in on you tomorrow." He grinned. "I know you're a new mating, but no funny business until I clear you for extracurricular activity. There are no food restrictions, so enjoy yourself at dinner." He wagged a finger at her. "And no feeding from him until I give the okay."

She looked down at her hands, blushing. Declan chuckled. When she heard the door close, she peeked up at him. "I meet the man of my dreams, cannot feed, cannot have sex, and our first date will be a horribly awkward, politically charged dinner with your brother and my new boss." She closed her eyes and tilted her head back. "Lovely."

"Man of your dreams, huh?" her mate said, sounding smug. There was a brief silence. "Wait...boss?"

CHAPTER FIVE

KARI KEPT HER HANDS IN her lap. "When I was freaking out about your injury, Avery suggested I help organize Magnus' office to center myself."

"Who's Avery?"

"My younger brother."

Declan scratched his head. "The little guy with blond hair and blue eyes? Kinda adorable?"

Kari laughed. "That is him, and please, do not let him hear you say that; he would be devastated."

Declan grinned. "You were upset?"

Kari poked him in the arm. "I saw your intestines, Declan. How would you have felt, had it been me?"

As her words registered, she watched as his eyes melted to a tawny gold color. When his lips pulled back, his canines were peeking out. She raised an eyebrow. He grunted and took even breaths.

"Anyway, yes, I was perturbed by your injury, so I started dismantling Magnus' office."

"Magnus, huh?" Declan asked, referring to her use of the prince's first name. She shrugged. "He gave me permission to use his name; he likes me." Feeling playful, she stuck her tongue out at him. He stuck his out at her in retaliation. They both laughed. Declan brought his arms up, with only a slight wince and rested them behind his head. "Do you rip apart the offices of rulers for a living," he asked flippantly.

"Actually, yes I do," she confessed.

"Seriously?"

"Yes. When I was younger, I took work as a secretary at first and then as a personal assistant. The one thing I hated the most was, just as I was learning the system, I would have to change jobs. So I started a company that not only trained personal assistants, but also the men and women who would employ them. They would both be trained in the same methods; that way there was never any miscommunication or differing expectations. More than half the time, bosses had no idea what to ask of their assistants. To them, personal assistants, secretaries, and gophers were the same thing."

"That is brilliant! I'm surprised no on has ever thought of doing things that way before," Declan shook his head in disbelief.

"Needless to say, we were very successful. I started by training my core team of personal assistants in varying methods of organization, deportment, business, economics, communication, language, business law, and foreign policy."

"Is that all?" Declan joked.

She winked. "They became the ones who would go in first and train company presidents and CEOs. While they were busy drumming up business, I took on a group of candidates that were taught mostly the same things, except I added on items like, event planning, fundraisers, charity work, and so on. They were groomed to blend into any professional environment. By the time the CEOs were ready, we had personal assistants waiting for them. The core group then branched out and took on new contracts while a few stayed in our home office to take over training."

"Gods, the prince needs someone like you desperately."

"I know," she shuddered. "You should see his Post-it Note stack."

He dropped his arms and reached over to take her hand. "My poor little general."

She smiled at his endearment. "Am I supposed to call you Simba too?

He grimaced. "I did that to cheer Meryn up. She's been kinda down lately. Did she really have a meltdown?"

"Yes, poor thing."

"She got to you already?" he asked, understanding her sympathy.

"She gets Avery. He lights up around her and is pulled into conversations."

"Why would it be important that she gets him?" Declan asked.

"Because Avery is special. He has a genius level IQ, but the naiveté of a child. I have had to protect him ever since I found him ten years ago."

"Protect him from what?" Declan growled.

"When I first met Avery, he was being pressured, against the wall of an alley in Chicago, into taking a job as a prostitute." Declan began to growl even louder. Kari smiled. "Needless to say he has been with me ever since."

"So you take care of him?"

"Yes and no. He has a photographic memory. There is a reason why I kept him on as my personal assistant. He is a whiz with numbers; he does all my book keeping and payroll. Plus he is like a walking talking Rolodex and Google. He takes care of me just as much as I take care of him.

Declan whistled low. "That's impressive."

Kari smiled. "Yes he is. So, you are second-in-command here?"

"Yes, I help Adriel run the units here in Noctem Falls."

"Magnus told me about your brothers. It must be nice to have such a large family," she commented wistfully.

"It has its moments. Rex is the oldest, then me, then Ari. My father is the elder at Éire Danu, and Ari stayed behind with him to serve as second in command to Brennus, the queen's consort. I came out here to Noctem Falls. At the time, Rex was up for promotion to work with the queen, but after I transferred, he put out feelers and became the Elder here instead. I think he just wanted to spy on me."

Kari rolled her eyes. "Or it could be that he is your big brother, and he cares about you."

Declan shrugged. "Could be."

Kari eyed her mate. "You have a very typical middle child syndrome. That is why you are a natural mediator."

Declan thought about it. "I can see that. It makes a lot of sense when you put it that way."

"Do you have any friends here in the city?" she asked.

"A few. I hang out mostly with the warriors from the Eta Unit and some of the warriors from the other units. Before Aiden, Meryn, Gavriel, and Bethy came to the city, our job consisted of a simple patrol and then we would be free to pursue our own hobbies. Since they've arrived, it's a bit different. There's been more camaraderie, looking out for each other, and talking amongst the warriors. In Eta, we were always kind of tight; we just never knew how to talk to Adriel.

"I knew he was a good guy because I work with him the most, but it's almost like he kept up this mask because he felt like he had to, and I can see why. Politics in the city dictate, if you are a vampire of any rank, you can't rub elbows with the plebes. That was the way Adriel was raised. The Founding Families believe because he is the Unit Leader, he should keep a distance from his men.

"I knew he never wanted that, but it wasn't until Eva arrived that his shell began to crack. I swear to the gods, yesterday, he made a joke," Declan said excitedly.

Kari smiled. "Is it really that big a deal that he cracked a joke?"

Declan nodded enthusiastically. "Yes, he tries so hard to keep his emotions to himself that, every time he slips up by smiling, laughing, or getting angry it's kinda like he's letting us see him. I think the guys have come together more in the past week than they have in the past decade."

"Is it true that you all live in separate houses on the Unit Level?"

He looked at her strangely. "Is this an interview?" he asked wryly.

She winced. "Sorry, I tend to revert back to authoritative mode when I get nervous. And conducting interviews is usually how I get to know people."

"People? You mean employees, what about your

friends?"

Kari just looked down. "I have never had many friends except for Avery and Law."

Declan's eyebrows snapped together. "Law? Law? How do I know that name?"

Kari shrugged. "Law is the one who made me evacuate to Noctem Falls; he was worried that something might happen because Avery and I live on our own."

Declan nodded his approval. "That sounds like a good idea. I'm glad he sent you to us. Pretty soon, we won't be able to take in many more refugees."

Kari nodded. "That is what he told me too."

Declan was nodding, and then he stopped. "Wait a minute, do I make you nervous?" he asked.

She looked at him flatly. "You know you do."

Declan opened his mouth to speak as the door opened. They both turned as Magnus and Adriel walked through.

Adriel looked from Declan to her. "I am sorry to interrupt, but we were heading to the living quarters now and we would like to help you get him settled." Behind them, Etain and Grant walked in. Once again, Kari was reminded how extremely large the warriors were.

With Etain on one side of Declan and Grant on the other, they very gently began to lift him from the bed. They wrapped his arms around their shoulders and carried him forward.

Grant grunted. "Man, you need to lay off of old man Richter's meat pies," he teased.

Declan shook his head. "No way, they're too good."

Etain shifted his weight. "You're heavy."

"It's all muscle," Declan protested.

Magnus looped his arm through hers, and they walked behind the men heading out of Broderick's lab and infirmary toward the living quarters.

Sebastian met them at the door and nodded. "We moved the ladies to Aiden and Meryn's room so that little Meryn could lie down."

"Thank you Sebastian," Magnus said nodding.

They walked past a very elegant looking antechamber before turning down a long hallway.

Magnus pointed. "These are the guest quarters. Meryn and Aiden are in the guest room to the right. We have put you and Avery in the one first on the left and we have set it up so that Declan is in the last room on the left, next to yours."

As they walked past the room Meryn and Aiden were sharing, people began to file out. Gavriel, Dr. St. John, Kuruk, and Aiden came out of the room to stand in the hallway.

"How are they?" Kari asked.

The doctor rubbed the back of his neck. "Bethy and Meryn are doing better. Bethy more than Meryn since she was raised here. But Meryn is exhausted, depressed, and experiencing mood swings not only due to her pregnancy but also because of the lack of sunshine. I think she's experiencing what humans call SAD, seasonal affective disorder."

Gavriel looked up. "I believe that Meryn is not used to dealing with so many emotions. In Lycaonia, all of the housing is spread out, but here, the levels are stacked on top of each other. She is getting no relief, especially given that the children are also being affected by the caves. It is safe to say that she is experiencing everything multiplied."

“She hasn’t been sleeping much either,” Declan added.

The doctor nodded. “Like the children, she may just need some open air and sunshine.”

Magnus stepped forward immediately, looking concerned. “What is wrong with the children?”

Dr. St. John turned to him. “They are experiencing the same symptoms as Meryn, low-level depression, listlessness, being tired but unable to sleep. For children that are used to running and playing outside, who have animals that share their bodies, these caves are not the best environment for them.”

Magnus turned. “Adriel, please arrange a field trip for the children and their parents. I am opening up the Royal Gardens on Level One to them so they can play there as much as they like.”

Adriel nodded. “That is a great idea. I will pull warriors together to assist. I will make sure all the families are assigned warriors.”

Declan cleared his throat. “Hey Doc, is it okay for me to shift to heal? My brother is requesting my presence at dinner, and I would like to be able to sit upright.”

Dr. St. John nodded. “Yes, that is fine. Now that you’ve healed a bit, your shifter abilities can help you from here.”

Declan turned to her. “If you ever get cold, my lion has very warm fur.” Kari laughed.

“What about Beth?” Gavriel asked, concerned for his own mate.

Declan stepped from between Etain and Grant and tugged on her hand. “Hey, I want to check on the little menace before I lay down.” He whispered before yawning wide.

"Okay," she agreed. They stepped away from the group as the healer explained how Bethy was just tired from the pregnancy, which might have been compounded by the mounting stress.

Kari helped Declan hobble into the bedroom. Meryn was laying on her stomach, face down, with her head in the pillow. Ryuu was by the bed as Meryn began to toss and turn grumbling.

Bethy apologized when she saw them. "I'm sorry. I'm usually not so emotional, but I hate seeing her like this." Nigel, Neil, and Avery were sitting at a table holding teacups and looking worried.

Declan turned to Kari. "Can I help her?" She raised an eyebrow, and he winked. Raising his hand, he shifted it to a claw. Kari realized that he was asking if it was okay for him to shift and lie down with Meryn, and she nodded her agreement. Declan shuffled over to the bed and sat down. He pulled Meryn out of her pillow, and she looked up at him her eyes rimmed in red.

"How are you here? Your guts were hanging out," she asked bluntly.

"Yup, Grant took pictures for me; I'll show you later."

"Cool." Meryn saw that he was sitting on the bed with her in his hospital gown. Her eyes grew wide with a hint of excitement. "Will you please sleep with me?" she asked.

Kari watched her mate peek over his shoulder. Out of the corner of her eye, she saw Aiden pop his head back in the room. Kari could almost hear him thinking.

Is it worth poking the bear? I could get mauled or worse, but it would be worth it.

“I don’t know, Meryn. Your mate is right outside, and you know how I’d have to get naked. Are you sure?” he asked, seductively.

Meryn gave a weak smile. “Please, I need you,” she said, playing along. Growls and snarls snapped behind them. Declan ignored Aiden and then shifted, letting the hospital gown shred. He began to flex and stretch. Kari could tell that he was feeling much better.

Meryn’s eyes were wide as he hopped back up onto the bed. She buried her small face in his fur, her tiny hands clutching at his mane.

“Just so fluffy!” Kari heard her mumble.

“I’m fluffy too, Meryn,” Aiden said, pouting. He stood beside the bed scowling down at his little mate.

Meryn shook her head, pulled back and turned to her mate. “It’s not the same, you’re not cuddly.” Meryn tucked herself practically under Declan. She was barely visible as she wiggled around getting comfortable. She turned her face back to the room. “Felix, you need to get in on this; he’s so warm.”

“Felix?” Kari asked. Seconds later, a small sprite appeared. His green eyes were red from crying.

“A sprite? Here?” Kari asked, completely astonished. From everything that she had heard, sprites never left Éire Danu.

Meryn patted the bed. “Felix, you better stay visible, you don’t want to get squished.” Kari watched as Felix walked across Declan’s long body and chose a spot in his mane. He patted down some fur and then very carefully folded back part of the mane like a blanket and got comfortable.

“Not cuddly? I’m a bear!” Aiden protested beside

them.

Gavriel chuckled. "Get over it, Aiden; Meryn appears to be a cat person." Bethy leaned against her mate. "She likes Colton, too, when he shifts," she added with a sly smile.

"Not cuddly?" Aiden looked around the room. "What about teddy bears? They are made to look like bears!" Nigel and Neil giggled. Meryn's head popped up, and her eyes landed on Avery. "Come on, you know you're tired."

Avery's eyes cut to Kari, and she nodded at his hesitation. He stood up and walked over to the bed. Like Felix, the air around him shimmered before he shrank down to the form of a tiny fox. However, unlike other shifters, his clothes shrank with him. The tiny fox was wearing a sweater, trousers, and shoes. Avery hopped up onto the bed and then curled up around Felix. Bethy's eyes were practically bugging out of her head. "How'd he do that?"

Kari pointed to the tiny charm attached to Avery's pants. "It was a gift from my adopted brother. He spoils Avery terribly."

Bethy's eyes were full of wonder. "I could have used that so many times when shifting."

"I'll see if he can make another charm," Kari offered.

With no one speaking, the sound of purring and tiny snores filled the room. Ryuu smiled. "She's out."

Aiden slumped forward. "Thank the gods! She was able to sleep with Eva, too." He looked up. "Speak of the devil."

A tall blonde woman leaned against the doorway. "Looks like I'm not needed here after all Ryuu," the woman said walking over to the bed.

Aiden smiled. "Eva, thank you for coming. It seems like the only time she can sleep well is when she is with you. I didn't know Declan was helping," he growled at the lion.

Adriel pointed to the newcomer. "Kari, this is Eva Mae Miller, my mate. Eva this is Kari Delaney; she is Declan's mate." Eva nodded at her, smiling.

Dr. St. John walked over to the bed and looked down. "This is interesting. It has been proven that the decibel level in the domestic cat's purr has healing attributes for humans. I wonder if any studies have been done with larger cats?"

Bethy shook her head at his curiosity. "We better leave before we wake her."

Ryuu smiled. "All four of them are sleeping so hard I doubt an explosion in the next room would wake them."

Magnus laid a hand on her shoulder. "You should rest as well."

She shook her head, declining. "My mind is still racing. I will let them sleep for a couple of hours then I will help Declan get ready for dinner."

Magnus groaned. "I had forgotten that Rex is here." He looked around the room. "Where is he anyway?"

Sebastian cleared his throat. "I settled him in the Council quarters here on Level One." He turned to Kari. "It is at the opposite end of the tunnel from here," he explained, mostly for her sake.

Bethy yawned. "I could use a nap," she eyed the pile longingly.

Gavriel pulled her to her feet and gently nudged her toward the door. "I am all you need." He steered her out of the room. He paused at the doorway, looking over his shoulder. "We will see you at dinner."

Aiden turned to Adriel. "Let's get the guys ready for the kiddos. Maybe they could do training drills like we do back home with Penny," he suggested.

"Who is Penny?" Magnus asked.

Aiden's face brightened. "Colton Albright's adopted daughter. She's my godsdaughter. She's only four and has kicked the butts of the guys in some of our training drills," he said, beaming as if he were the proud papa.

Kari turned her face away so Aiden wouldn't see her smiling; he was such a softie.

Magnus chuckled. "I would love to meet her."

Aiden's eyes clouded. "Maybe we should let the city calm down a bit first."

Kari placed a hand over her mouth. Aiden was in protective papa bear mode. "You are so adorable!"

Aiden blushed. "I am a fierce warrior."

"You are cuddly," she teased.

"Humph," he said gruffly.

Eva spread her arms to herd everyone to the door. "I'll watch over pint-size; y'all get." She turned to the twins. "Go get your books. You can use this time to study." They groaned and lay their heads down on the table.

"What subject are you studying?" Adriel asked.

"Battle tactics and maneuvering," Neil answered. Nigel's face brightened as he turned to Aiden. "Maybe you can help us, Commander?"

Aiden smiled. "There are only two people who have ever scored better than I have in that practical."

"Who?" the twins asked together.

"My father, Byron McKenzie, who is currently the

shifter elder and former Unit Commander." Aiden paused smiling.

"Who's the other?" Nigel asked.

Aiden pointed to Meryn.

Adriel's mouth dropped open. "You are not serious."

Eva chuckled. Placing her finger under his chin, she closed his mouth. "Better close that darlin', you're gonna catch flies."

Aiden nodded, a thoughtful look on his face. "She is ruthless and practical. She is willing to make the sacrifices needed to win the endgame." He stopped a moment. He looked like he was choosing his words carefully. "Witches, in particular, have always had a hard time doing these practicals. Everything about your gifts revolves around helping others, but Meryn is able to set aside emotion and make decisions that save lives."

"But she's nice," Neil protested.

Aiden's eyes turned sad. "It would be easier on her if she was heartless. She pays for every choice she makes; they weigh on her greatly."

Adriel frowned, looking at Meryn. "She may be small, but she has the heart of a giant."

Magnus clapped his hands together softly. "Okay everyone, clear out."

"I'll wake them an hour before dinner," Eva said, once again trying to get everybody to leave the room.

Adriel and Aiden headed to their mates and gave them each a soft kiss before leaving. Nigel and Neil rose and ran for their books.

Magnus turned to her wincing. "More paper-work?"

"Always paperwork," Kari said, laughing.

CHAPTER SIX

"OKAY, EXPLAIN IT TO ME again, why is this one chronological?" Magnus asked, holding up a stack of files.

Kari looked up from her desk or what she had commandeered to be her desk. "Because in the long term, paranormals will remember *when* something happened, not who, where, or what. It is just how we think. Humans remember people and faces."

"How do you know this?" he asked.

"I did a study to help better organize things."

"Why are humans better with faces?" he wondered.

"They have shorter lifespans and usually interact with significantly less people over the course of their lives than paranormals. Most humans live in the same place where they are born, surrounded by familiar things, people, and family. The only thing that changes for them are the people in their lives.

"Paranormals, on the other hand, can live up to fifty times longer. Cities rise and fall, religions are born, family and friends become strangers, but time is a faithful companion. Time never changes, it is why a vampire can tell you when he came to America, but not who was on the boat with him, the weather the day the boat landed, or even who they were traveling with." She stood up and went to his desk. She looked through a tall stack of manila folders before she pulled out a single file. She flipped it open. "When did you begin the Royal Gardens?"

"Six hundred and forty years ago," he answered almost immediately.

She smiled. "And who was the powerful witch that set the crystals?" Magnus' face went blank, and then slowly, understanding began to dawn on his features. She continued. "This is why timelines are better for you than personnel files. A file for the witch Louis Tournesol would be useless since you can not remember who he was."

Magnus sat back. "That is impressive."

"I am glad you think so. Those eight stacks need to be divided by decade." She pointed to the stack leaning against the wall.

Magnus paled. "Those are all of my daily reports from the day I took over as Prince."

"Yes, I know."

"Why are you not doing it?" he asked.

Kari raised a brow. "What good would it do if I organized them? They are your files; you are the one who will have to use them. You will need to know what is there and how to get to them. I may be an excellent organizer, but I cannot think for you."

Magnus nodded, looking properly chastised. "That is fair enough. Your methods have already helped me change how I think. That alone will make things easier."

"And we are just getting started," she said smiling wide.

Magnus was about to answer when the phone rang.

He went to reach for it when she popped his hand. "Never answer your own phone," she admonished.

"But Cheryl..." Magnus started.

"Cheryl is not here and for a good reason." Kari picked up the phone from its cradle. "Prince Magnus' office, how can I assist you?"

"This is Ivan DeLaFontaine; I demand to speak to Magnus at once!" Magnus, overhearing the conversation, reached for the phone again only to have Kari bat his hand away.

"I am sorry, Mr. DeLaFontaine, Prince Magnus is not available at the moment. I can review his upcoming schedule to see when he has an opening." There was a brief moment of silence.

"This is not Cheryl," Ivan stated.

"No it is not."

"Do you know who I am?" he asked.

"Of course."

"Then I demand to speak to Magnus at once," he insisted.

"No," she answered shortly.

"No? No? How dare you?" he sputtered.

"I dare because it is my job to do so. You are so angry that you have forgotten to call our prince by his proper title twice. You are demanding he come to the phone like an errant schoolboy. My job is to not only assist Prince Magnus but to assist you as well. I know you are a member of one of our esteemed Founding Families. What kind of impression do you think you would make if you were to speak to Prince Magnus now?

There was more silence from his line. "I see your point. I wish my assistant had half of your political savvy." She heard him take a deep breath. "I suppose this matter can wait until our dinner. Do you know if that has been scheduled?"

Kari picked up the calendar and cringed. "I am going to be very honest with you, Mr. DeLaFontaine. I, as Prince Magnus' new assistant, and Avery Therian, as his new receptionist, have only been here a few hours. I am still trying to make sense of his former assistant's notes and calendar. Would it be at all possible to have Avery call your office tomorrow with an update?"

There was a harsh laugh. "That I believe. Cheryl Evreux is useless, and I told Prince Magnus that on many occasions. Thank you for your assistance; I look forward to young Avery's call." The line disconnected.

Magnus looked up at her. "That was amazing. It would have taken me hours to calm him down."

Kari placed the phone back on the cradle and began tapping it. "Really? That was all bluster; he was not truly angry. He was just testing your new gatekeeper."

"Gatekeeper?" Magnus asked.

"Yes, me, and later Avery." She tapped the phone lightly. "He knew Cheryl had been fired probably within minutes of her returning to her level, and he said 'young Avery'. He knows who we are and our new positions. He backpedaled very quickly when I reminded him of his insolence in forgetting your title. He is up to something."

Magnus snorted, going back to his files. "All of them are usually up to something all of the time. The entire lot of them should take up hobbies and leave politics alone."

Kari tilted her head. "What fun would that be?"

Magnus just looked at her flatly. "If you feel that way, you rule. I will go fishing."

"Poppycock," she said, flapping her hand at him. "The people need you."

A crackle heralded an incoming call on the walkie-talkie. "Uh... Magneto? You just received a large number of boxes on Level Six." Adriel's familiar voice informed them.

"Professor, this is Magneto, can you bring the Eta and Mu Units to Level Six for a special training exercise?"

"Of course," Adriel replied. Grinning, Magnus returned the walkie-talkie to his belt.

"Magneto?" she asked.

"Meryn's idea of call signs," he said, his eyes twinkling. He looked younger caught up in his excitement.

"Professor?" she asked.

"Adriel: it is the clipboard," he explained.

She nodded. "I can see the relation."

He looked up at her, his eyes brightening. "Would you like to take a break with me?" he asked.

"Of course, but you have to tell me why you have a devilish look in your eye."

He stood and extended his arm. "I do believe you will enjoy my delivery. Stories of Meryn's arrival at the Alpha estate have motivated me."

Kari accepted his arm. "I cannot wait to see what she has inspired."

Magnus escorted her to the transport tunnel and they flew up to Level Six.

Eta and Mu Units arrived, and they made their way over to the large pile of stacked boxes. The warriors took up positions around the boxes, their feet spread, and their hands clasped behind their backs. Silently, they waited for Magnus to begin.

Curious groups of children edged closer as their families began to circle around.

Magnus turned to face the group, with a stern look. The children inched back, looking apprehensive. Magnus cleared his throat. "It has come to my attention that we have some fierce shifter children staying here on Level Six," he began.

Their eyes widened, and their lips started to quiver. Kari knew they were seconds away from tears. She leaned in toward Magnus. "You might want to tone it down; they will be crying in a moment."

Magnus looked around shocked and instantly looked contrite. He knelt down on one knee and indicated for them to crowd around. In a whisper that could clearly be heard by everyone, he continued. "I am sorry if I have frightened you. I have to look scary to keep these warriors in line so you do not have to worry." He ducked his head down closer to the children. "Can you help me keep a secret?" he asked. They all nodded eagerly.

"They are not as scary as they look." The children chortled, looking up at the large warriors.

He winked at them then stood. In a louder voice, he pointed to the boxes. "These are my new weapons. Our warriors need to be trained in the use of them, and I was hoping you all would be able to help." It was now the parents' turn to look concerned.

Magnus opened a box, reached in, and pulled out a Nerf Gatling gun. "Where are my cadets?" he asked. The children swarmed forward, grabbing the toys. Magnus laughed as the children excitedly began to play with their new weapons. He turned, and Kari watched in slow motion as a tiny little girl came running up to the boxes only to trip over her own feet. Magnus moved without being seen and easily caught the child before she hit the floor. She giggled when Magnus set her on her feet. "My niece Bethy taught me how to do that. She is constantly falling." Magnus turned and reached into the box behind him. When he turned back around, he handed the tiny child one of the largest guns Kari had seen being passed around. The toy was bigger than the little girl, but the child refused another. She stuck her tongue in the corner of her mouth as she struggled under its weight.

Once all of the toys had been distributed, Kari realized that Magnus had made sure the warriors received tiny little handguns, while most of the children got bombs, grenades, and Gatling guns. The warriors were looking at the children with envy.

Boys and their toys, she thought to herself.

Magnus clapped his hands together. "Okay kids, let them have it!"

Kari had to step back as chaos ensued. She was sure that Magnus had envisioned a war between the children and the warriors, but that quickly changed as one of the largest vampires she'd ever seen reached for the tiny girl with the biggest gun and placed her easily on his shoulders. Squealing at her new vantage point, the girl turned the gun on the other warriors. The warrior holding her pointed to the Eta Unit. "Get them!" he encouraged.

The war quickly became a battle between the Eta and Mu Units. The children shrieked as they were carried by the large warriors and laughter filled the air. Adriel stood in the center, directing the three other warriors from Eta. From behind the boxes, another warrior popped up, a small boy at his side. Kari watched as the warrior helped the child to aim. Seconds later, small foam missiles rained down on the Unit Leader. Adriel tried to block the projectiles with his clipboard but could not keep them all at bay. Dramatically, he fell to the floor in defeat. The small boy jumped up and down, and the warrior ruffled his hair.

Kari laughed at the men's antics until she heard something that didn't fit in with the joyous afternoon. A faint sniffle had her looking over to her right. She saw a woman standing there, tears in her eyes. The woman saw her staring and wiped her cheeks quickly. "I'm sorry, it's just the children have been so down lately. I had so many apprehensions coming here, but look at them." She pointed to the room and the game Magnus had orchestrated. "We had no idea he was so kind."

Kari nodded. "I have not been here very long, but even I can see that he loves children." Kari looked around the room; the earlier apprehensive looks the parents had worn were gone, replaced with admiration and respect. Magnus clearly earned their trust and their gratitude.

A loud burst of laughter had her turning her attention back to the room. Magnus was on the floor covered in children. He reached a hand up begging for help from either the Eta or Mu Units; the men just laughed.

"How is your mate?" a quiet voice from her left asked. She turned to see a small, pale vampire standing partially behind a wolf shifter.

"Rachelle?" Kari asked, guessing the woman's

identity. The woman nodded. Kari patted her shoulder gently. "He is perfectly fine. He was able to shift and is currently napping like the big old cat he is."

All around her, the people began to look relieved.

"Thank the gods!" someone behind her whispered.

Kari looked to see that most of the Level Six vampires along with the shifters looked thankful.

"You seem surprised," Rachelle stated.

"I suppose I am," Kari admitted. "I never thought a shifter would be so highly regarded here in Noctem Falls."

Rachelle's eyes softened. "Declan is different."

"He does not play power games; he just likes to help people," a male vampire in the crowd said, speaking above the group.

A female vendor leaned against her stand. "I would have expected something like this from Declan." She pointed to the children. "I did not know Prince Magnus had it in him."

The man sitting at the stall next to her waved his glass. "He is always happier when Bethy visits, and now that she is expecting and out of season, it is no wonder he can not stop smiling. His house has been touched by the gods."

"We are lucky to have him as our Prince," another voice said warmly.

"I wish I could be so blessed," the female vendor said wistfully.

Rachelle ducked her face down, blushing. "I am with child," she announced quietly. Around them everyone became silent. The children, picking up the shift in mood, also stilled their motions. Everyone turned to where Rachelle stood. Her mate stepped closer.

Kari smiled at the timid woman. “I am so happy for you!”

Magnus walked up and took Rachelle’s hands in his own. “Is this true?” he asked intently.

She nodded, her face now red from embarrassment from all the attention. Her mate wrapped an arm around her.

Kari was shocked at the tears streaming down Magnus’ cheeks. He swallowed hard. “The first child to be conceived here in nearly two centuries,” he whispered, practically choking on the words.

“Why is everyone crying?” the girl asked from her perch on top of the warrior’s shoulders.

The warrior shook his head. He had tears in his own eyes. “Because they are so happy,” he explained.

She frowned. “They should be laughing then.”

He reached up and tickled her, and she squealed. The crowd began to laugh.

“We need a celebration!” one of the men yelled.

“A party!” one of the wolves suggested.

“Excellent idea,” Magnus agreed. He patted Rachelle’s hands before releasing them and turning to the crowd for ideas.

Rachelle shook her head. “You do not need to make a fuss. Your own niece is also pregnant. I am not the first.”

Magnus smiled softly. “She will return to Lycaonia with her mate. Her child will be born there. I will still spoil my future niece or nephew horribly, but your child was conceived here. Regardless if you leave with your mate when they return home, your child will always be able to claim Noctem Falls as their home.”

"What about another barbecue?" a vendor suggested loudly.

"Think bigger!" Magnus challenged.

Kari watched as the little boy who had taken down Adriel walked up to Magnus and pulled on his pants leg. "Can we have cotton candy?" he asked. Magnus' eyes grew wide, and he snapped his fingers. "What about a fair? We could have games, toys, food, contests, games, food..." Magnus suggested.

"Sire, you said games and food twice," one of the girls said giggling.

He winked at her. "Those are the most important things."

"When could we have it?" the boy asked.

Magnus looked at her. She mentally added up transport time needed for food orders and equipment needed for the fair. "Three days," she replied. "That should give us plenty of time to order things and get the city estate set up for deliveries. We will have to let the fae at the Albuquerque portal know that we will have a lot of things coming through."

The woman to her left turned to her friend. "I want to make my famous peanut butter pie."

Kari turned to Magnus "This woman needs supplies to make pie." Everyone chuckled at her serious expression.

Magnus smiled. "I take it you like peanut butter pie?"

"It sounds heavenly!" Kari groaned.

Magnus turned to Adriel. "Adriel, you are in charge of Noctem Falls' First Annual Spring Fair."

Adriel's mouth opened and closed wordlessly. Grant and Micah began to laugh at their Unit Leader's expression.

"Come along, Kari; I have papers to go through," Magnus said pompously. Adriel shot her a panicked look, and she nodded to assure him that of course she would help. That poor man looked a bit out of his depth. She waved goodbye and followed Magnus back down to Level One.

After a few more hours in the office, organizing decades of reports, Kari called it a day. Magnus left an hour earlier to meet with Rex before dinner. She found her way back to the living quarters and to her mate. She was now staring down at her lion.

She sighed. "They are too cute to wake up."

"I know," Beth agreed. In her hands she held a steaming cup of coffee.

"It *is* his brother," Aiden reminded them.

Kari walked over, gently picked up Avery, and cuddled him close. He opened one eye when she kissed his nose. She handed him off to Ryuu before extracting Felix from Declan's mane. When Felix opened his eyes and stared up at her drowsily, she felt as if she lost a bit of her heart. He looked around, locking in on Ryuu. The squire held out a hand, and Kari carefully set the sprite down in his open palm. Felix yawned and climbed Ryuu's shirt, heading for his vest. He lifted Ryuu's jacket and disappeared in the fabric.

"I just adore that sprite to pieces," Bethy admitted smiling softly.

Aiden stepped forward to get Meryn, but when he went to lift her, he discovered she was wrapped around Declan like an octopus. He practically had to pry her off of him.

"No," she protested reaching for warmth.

It took Bethy's gentle coaxing with the promise

of coffee to get Meryn to let go. When they finally had her disengaged, he carried her out of the room, kissing her forehead.

Ryuu nodded and gave her a half bow. “I will settle young Avery in his room.” He and Bethy walked behind Aiden. The entire time, Bethy assured Meryn that she had another cup of coffee waiting for her in the dining room.

When the room was finally quiet, Declan opened an amber eye and the air around him shimmered. When he shifted back to human, Kari felt her mouth go dry. He was all golden skin and muscle.

He stretched his body, easily touching the head and footboard. “You keep looking at me like that and we’ll miss dinner.”

He sat up and looked around. His eyes went to where a robe was draped over the chair at the end of the bed. Smiling he swung his legs over the side and stood in front of her in all his naked glory.

Her eyes went to his stomach. She reached out and began to trace his abdomen. “There is no scar,” she said, and his eyes softened.

“I’m okay. You know us shifters are hard to take down.”

He pulled the robe on and held out his hand. “Hopefully someone left clothes for me in my room, otherwise dinner will be a drafty affair.” He winked at her saucily.

“All I kept thinking when I saw you hurt was that I had only just met you; losing you and not even knowing you would have been too much.”

Declan took her hand. “You’re stuck with me now.”

She couldn’t meet his eyes. She didn’t know how

to react. She had been scared to death, and he was acting as if he had stubbed his toe.

Hand in hand they walked across the hall to his room. Unfortunately there were no clothes in sight. She chuckled at the thought of him going to dinner in his robe.

He smirked at her. "You think I'm kidding? I'm starving!" He waved his hands wildly causing the robe to gap in the middle. She licked her lips at the sight of his tawny skin.

Growling, he suddenly picked her up and tossed her on to his bed. He carelessly let the robe fall to the floor and strode up to the edge of the bed. In a flash he had pulled her down onto the mattress and slid her underneath him. When his lips met hers, she couldn't hold back. The desperation and fear she'd felt came forward. She wanted to stay like this with him forever. As he deepened the kiss, she let her hands move across his skin. It was hot and smooth under her touch; she couldn't get enough. When they broke apart, Kari was breathing hard. "That was the best kiss of my life," she admitted.

He leaned forward and began to kiss his way down her neck. "Mine too," he whispered. "We definitely have chemistry."

Grinning, she shifted her hips, and he hissed in pleasure as his hardening bulge began to rub against her mound. Even though she was still clothed she could feel the heat of his skin and it was maddening. She started squirming, reaching for the pleasure that seemed just out of reach. "Looks as if the little guy wants to meet me again."

He stopped and looked down at her frowning. "Little?" His eyes narrowed. "I'll show you little," he threatened darkly.

There was a knock at the door seconds before it swung open. Grant walked in, and his eyes widened. Looking shocked, he held up a bundle. "Your clothes."

Declan hissed. "Mine!" he growled, before he bit down on her neck. All at once, pleasure exploded throughout her body. It was as if his bite was connected to every erogenous zone, igniting them all at once. She arched her back and wrapped her legs around him, pulling him close to the juncture between her thighs. She rode out the uncontrollable orgasm as long as she could before she collapsed back onto the bed, barely able to catch her breath. When she turned her head toward the door, poor Grant look shell shocked. "Shit! I'm of course... I'm just... I'm good... going...I meant going!" he rambled. Dropping the clothes he ran from the room.

Kari rotated her head to stare at her mate. "Okay, what was that?" she asked, still panting.

He groaned and buried his face where her neck and shoulder met. He gently began lapping at the bite mark. She moaned at each pass of his tongue on her neck, feeling it tease her clit. She pushed at his shoulders to get him to stop, any more and she wouldn't leave the bed... ever.

He pulled back, looking a bit guilty, though his eyes held a deep sense of satisfaction. "Sorry about that. Lions are very possessive, and they like to show others that their mates belong only to them. You belong to me, and my lion didn't like the fact that Grant could see you flushed with pleasure from our kiss. The bite was to show him that you are mine, and I can make you happy." He looked down at her concern showing on his face. "Are you okay? Did it hurt?"

She cracked her neck. "I so needed that. It took the edge off. Evidently I was more stressed than I realized." She pushed his chest until he rolled to one side. She sat up and stretched her arms overhead.

Despite her words, he still had a worried look on his face. She swung her legs to the side and got up. She walked over to the door and picked his clothes up off the floor. "Declan, I am a vampire. I like to bite and to be bitten." She could almost see the light bulb going off over his head.

He leered at her. "Come back here, sexy."

She shook her head. "You need to clean up. I am going to see if Bethy needs help with Meryn." She stretched again. "I feel fantastic!"

Declan whimpered, and she shot him a sultry look. "My poor lion. I will not leave you hanging. Doc said no extracurricular activity, so try not to move." He nodded eagerly. "Lay back," she ordered. His eyes grew wide, and he immediately complied. She walked toward him, swaying her hips. He watched every single movement, his eyes shifting to a dark honey color. She slowly got on the bed and settled between his legs. Without warning, she leaned over and swallowed him completely down.

"Oh gods!" he shouted. She continued to work his long length in her throat. Using her hollowed cheeks to create suction, she worked his shaft. When she pulled back, she teased the slit at the tip of his cock and then swallowed him back down. Out of the corner of her eye, she could see him twisting the sheets in his hands. When she reached up and pulled on his sac, she heard a ripping sound and saw that he had sent his claws through both the sheets and the mattress.

Reveling in the power she was wielding over his body, she took a chance. She turned her head and sunk her fangs into the thick vein that snaked its way up the side of his cock. Shouting incoherently, he came. The taste of him was amazing. It was unlike anything she'd ever had before. It was tart at first, then sweet. The creamy mixture as satisfying as melted chocolate and just as addictive. She knew she would never get enough of him.

Declan was still breathing hard when she closed the bite with a swipe of her tongue and sat up on her knees. With her thumb, she captured a bit of his come from the corner of her mouth. With the twist of her wrist, she licked it.

"Thank you, my mate," he said between pants.

"My pleasure. You taste incredible."

"Do we have to go to dinner?" he asked pitifully.

"It *is* your brother," she reminded him.

"I know. That's why I'm asking."

Laughing, she got off the bed. "When you are able to move, get ready for dinner," she teased.

"Heartless woman," he muttered to himself.

She winked at him and left feeling better than she had in decades.

CHAPTER SEVEN

KARI SAT NEXT TO DECLAN at the large dining room table. Everyone else had changed for dinner, and even though their clothes were far more formal, they looked considerably more relaxed than when she met them after Declan's attack.

Kari watched Rex as he sat across from Declan and beside Meryn. Meryn kept looking up at him as if trying to determine what she thought of him. Rex turned his head very slightly and glanced down at the small human, and as everyone was talking, he gave her a slow, long wink and then went back to his wine. Meryn nodded, her opinion seemingly cemented. She picked up a butter knife, sat it on the plate, and began spinning it. Ryuu and Sebastian walked around serving the appetizers.

Rex took another sip of wine and looked over at Declan. "I don't understand why you are second in command when you are clearly more suited to an advisory role." Rex tilted his wineglass back and forward, the red liquid shifting in the glass.

Kari could hear Declan's teeth grinding. "Because I'm tired of the game," Declan admitted. "If Father wants to play keeping up with the McKenzies, he can. I want no part of it."

Rex looked shocked. "What do you mean, keeping up with the McKenzies?"

Aiden's eyes widened as he looked from one brother to the other. "Yes, what about the McKenzies?" he asked.

Declan scowled at his brother. "As if you don't know."

Rex shook his head. "I have no idea what in the gods' names you are talking about."

Declan "We almost lost Mother because of his games."

Rex's eyebrows shot to his hairline. "Declan, we almost lost Mother when she gave birth to Ari; Father had nothing to do with that."

"And why did she get pregnant?" Declan asked. He continued without waiting for an answer. "Because Adelaide McKenzie had just given birth to her fourth son and Father wanted another to keep up."

Rex shook his head. "That is not..." he cleared his throat and looked around the table. "Maybe we should have this discussion later."

"Awkward," Meryn piped up, looking thoroughly entertained.

Declan gave a harsh laugh. "Why not now? I think everyone here has heard enough already. Why not hear the rest?"

"If that is what you would like." Rex set his wine glass down. "Mother had another child for you."

Declan tensed beside her. "What?" he demanded.

Rex looked at his younger brother. "You were older of course, an adult, but the way you were raised, Mother was always regretful of it. Father and

I spent a lot of time away from home, and Mother was always busy with societal demands. She wanted you to know how a family should be. So she begged Father for another child. When Ari was born, she knew she had done the right thing. Father returned home, and I took a position in Éire Danu to be closer to you and our new little brother so that I could take care of you both. You were finally able to experience what I had growing up with Mother and Father before he became an Elder. After Ari, we celebrated Winter Solstices and birthdays. For the first time in centuries, we sat down at the dinner table and listened to one another. It wasn't until Ari was older that I realized you were the only one who never had that growing up. I'm sorry I failed you, little brother. I'm sorry Father and I were too busy to give you the home you deserved."

Declan slumped back in his chair, and Kari reached for his hand. "For me?" he asked.

Rex nodded. "For you," he confirmed. "We are a political family, and yes, we have our fingers in many pies, but it has never been about keeping up appearances. Politics is what Father is good at and what he raised me to be good at. You learned watching us, and Ari is learning watching Father now. I said that you would be a good advisor not because of your blood, but because of how you were raised. What you gleaned from us growing up cannot be taught. Declan, you have the most important thing required to be a successful leader, and it isn't the Lionhart name."

"What then?" Declan asked.

"You have the people's trust." Rex sighed. "They respect me, and that's good; I am an Elder here, but they trust you. They care for you. That is why I get frustrated that you are being underutilized. You could do so much more for them in an advisory role instead of just being a grunt."

Aiden and Adriel cleared their throats at the same time. Rex nodded his head in their direction without looking their way. "My apologies," he said in an obligatory fashion before continuing. "Declan, do you do anything during the day that challenges you?" he asked. "Patrolling here can't be that stimulating. You may have these people fooled, Declan Lionhart, but don't ever forget that I am your older brother. I watched your mind take shape, and I know exactly how smart you are. Why you felt it necessary to become a warrior I'll never know. When did it become shameful to help your people as an Elder?" He raised an eyebrow at Declan.

Her mate shrugged. "When did it become permissible for the Council to live outside of the pillar city they served?" Declan challenged in return.

Rex winced. "That wasn't entirely my decision. The fae elder brought the idea forward. He could live here if he were on his own, but he has a mate and children. At the time, their firstborn needed the sun, and we did not want to separate the family. Magnus obviously could stay here as a vampire and their prince, so yes, we set up the council estate. It has helped the city in ways the city's founders would never imagine. We have access to the human city for commerce and supplies, but we can be here in a matter of moments through the portal."

"But it does set you up away from them," Bethy interjected. "The people feel like you don't care."

Magnus rubbed his jaw. "I understand why the fae

and even the witches like to be above ground, and I agree that having a council estate is probably a good idea. There have been many times when having the council separate from the city has played in our favor." He paused a moment. "What if we created something like the Royal Gardens in the council quarters here on Level One. We could install crystals in the ceiling to mimic the daytime sun and the nighttime stars. We do not have the fresh air you would get being topside, but they could get some sunshine."

Rex blinked. "You would be willing to do that?"

"Of course. I am willing to do anything that would help create a united front for the people to see. I would have done so ages ago, had it come up."

"But it did," Rex said, looking confused. "I wrote up the proposal myself suggesting something similar and left it with your office."

Magnus turned in Kari's direction. "Cheryl strikes again?" he asked, his voice tight.

Kari thought about it. "Magnus, I do believe there is a fine line between incompetency and sabotage. One is deliberate, but both can result in disaster."

Magnus cursed under his breath. "Thank the gods you found your way to us, Kari." He turned his attention to Declan. "So what exactly have you been trained in?"

Declan said nothing, and Kari elbowed him in the ribs. "There is no shame in who you are, Declan. I am finding this political side of you very sexy," she admitted.

His head snapped around as he turned to look at her. "Really?" he asked.

She nodded. "Smart is very, very sexy." She lifted

her hand from his and tickled his upper thigh.

Declan turned to Magnus. “I have several degrees that may help.”

Rex gave such an exaggerated eye roll that his head tilted. “Declan has degrees in political science, criminal justice, business law, and he speaks at least 25 languages. Recently, he received his MBA, a degree in foreign law, and for fun I believe, he challenged himself and studied human history.” He turned to his brother. “How is your project going on documenting paranormal history as it clashed with the human world?” Rex gave Declan a sardonic salute.

Magnus and Adriel exchanged looks. Adriel tapped the table; even Kari could see he was becoming agitated. “You mean to tell me you have been running patrols for the past gods knows how many years when you have that education?” Adriel demanded.

Magnus scowled blackly. “I could have used your expertise! Do you know how many times I wished for at least one competent person around me?” he ranted, throwing his hands up in the air.

Declan winced. “I don’t like politics. I have always enjoyed learning, so sharing what I have studied would be no hardship.” He looked at Adriel. “And I like patrols. I like getting out and talking to people and getting to know their problems.”

A little bit of understanding filled Rex’s eyes, and he smiled. “When was last time you went home?”

Declan shrugged.

“Home?” Meryn asked.

“Ever since the end of the Great War, the Lionharts have called Éire Danu our home. Lions do well in the sun, so it is a very good fit for our pride. My father serves as the Shifter Elder, and our youngest brother Ari serves as second in command to Royal Consort Brennus Vi'Eirlea. Our family seat has always been in Éire Danu.

Meryn snapped her fingers. "That's why you came here. Declan went from Éire Danu to Noctem Falls, and you knew he would be have issues adjusting."

Rex shrugged. "He is my little brother; of course I had concerns, though he did adjust admirably well for a shifter," he said proudly.

Magnus eyed Declan. "Would you consider an advisory role?" Magnus asked. "You could stay with the Eta Unit and assist Adriel as he will be taking on more responsibility."

Adriel blinked. "I will?" he asked. Eva chuckled at her mate's expression.

Magnus ignored him and continued speaking to Declan. "I do believe that you will be better utilized in that capacity. It would be a waste of your intelligence not to do more."

Kari gave Declan's hand a gentle squeeze. She gave him a look as if to say it was up to him.

Declan nodded. "I would consider an advisory role, though, advisory only."

"Excellent!" Rex exclaimed looking much happier. "Father will be ecstatic when I call him later. Though you should call them yourself. Mother, more than Father, has a thing or two to say to you," he teased.

The color drained from Declan's face. "What did she say?" he asked.

Rex shrugged. "You know Mother. You almost died, got mated, and you never called. Yes, she's most eager to speak to you," he said diplomatically. Declan buried his face in his other hand, groaning, and Rex chuckled.

Mention of the attack reminded Kari to ask what would happen to her mate's attacker. She turned to Magnus. "What are we going to do with DuBois?"

Rex growled. "The rest of the council members will be coming in tomorrow. We will be deciding what to do with him.

"Will he be moved?" Meryn asked.

Aiden shook his head. "No, Meryn."

Magnus eyes narrowed. "What are you up to?"

"Two words," Meryn said holding up her fingers. "Plausible deniability."

Rex gave her an evil grin. "I like the way you think. I wish I could just skin that man alive and mount his head on my wall.

Eva gasped. Adriel wrapped arm around her shoulders. Rex, along with everyone else, looked on in confusion. "Was it something I said?" he asked.

Eva swallowed hard repeatedly, unable to speak. Adriel rubbed her back. "Eva lost her parents when she was young. As you know, she is a tiger shifter; her parents were hunted in tiger form and killed for their skin."

Around the table there were gasps. Meryn frowned and turned to Aiden. "When I thought Colton was killed, you said that shifters turn back to humans when they die."

Aiden nodded. "That's true for the most part. It's very rare to encounter a shifter that stays in animal form after death." He turned to the table. "Father and I are finding that the more endangered the species of animal the shifter is, the more likely it is that they remain as an animal upon death. With the sky-rocketing number of endangered species now, more and more shifters are staying in an animal form when they die. It's making it very difficult to find people if they're killed while shifted."

Rex turned to Eva. "You have my deepest and sincerest apologies. I did not mean to bring up such horrible memories."

Eva shook her head. "No, it's okay; you didn't know. Besides we have happier news to discuss. Did I hear that someone else is pregnant?" she asked smoothing over the painful subject.

Meryn laughed. "Someone else is preggo? Sweet. Who else is joining the bloated, cranky, and crazy team?"

Adriel turned to Declan. "Rachelle," he informed him.

Declan smiled wide. "Get outta here! Are you serious? That's freaking awesome." Kari could see the wheels turning in her mate's head. Declan was now twice as glad he was hurt instead of either Rachelle or her wolf mate. Rex groaned and put his face in his hands at Declan's language.

Kari smiled. "Yes, darling, I can see politics is definitely not one of your fortes."

Meryn flashed Declan a thumbs up. "I've been trying to tell Aiden that sometimes you guys act too stuffy."

"Stuffy?" Magnus asked incredulously.

"Yes, stuffy," she said, pointing to his suit and tie. "Would it kill you to wear a pair of sweatpants?" she asked.

Magnus and Bethy's eyes widened, and they shuddered in unison. "Sweat. Pants?" Magnus asked, enunciating each word.

Bethy leaned over and looked down the table at Meryn. “You just stop that crazy talk. The Prince of Noctem Falls in sweatpants?”

Meryn looked confused. “Don’t you have sweatpants? Doesn’t everybody own sweatpants? They are the most comfortable things ever.” Her clothes began to shimmer, and then right before her eyes, Kari watched as Meryn’s normal t-shirt and jeans morphed to sweatpants and a hoodie.

Kari turned to Declan. “How did she do that? I thought she was human.”

Declan chuckled. “She’s also the person who inherited the Gown of Éire Danu.”

“You are kidding me. That gown is famous. She was just wearing a t-shirt.”

Bethy groaned. “Yes, t-shirts. There have been zombie t-shirts and Care Bear t-shirts. T-shirts, grungy sneakers, and jeans: That is what the Gown of Éire Danu has been reduced to.”

Meryn shrugged, stretching the fabric of her hoodie out in front of her. “This is so comfy, Bethy. You should really try this. I mean especially when you start showing. Your belly won’t fit in those fancy dress pants of yours.”

Bethy gasped and looked behind her.

Sebastian was already moving “Do not worry. I will take measurements and make you a whole new wardrobe of fashionable maternity clothes. You will be comfortable and beautiful.”

Bethy exhaled. “Thank the gods!” She looked at Meryn’s hoodie and shuddered again.

Meryn looked Magnus dead in the face. “Stuffy.”

Magnus chuckled. “Maybe we are a bit formal.”

Adriel looked over at Kari. "Kari, how is your brother doing?" he asked conversationally.

She nodded and then looked at Meryn. "He has made friends here, and I cannot tell you what a gift that is. Even now he is having dinner with Nigel and Neil. He normally just spends his time by himself or reading. He has never been able to make any friends on his own, never mind a paranormal his own age. I was already so grateful to find my mate after coming here, but the second blessing is for Avery to have friends."

"Avery's good peeps," Meryn said. She tilted her head. "I can't adopt him as my brother like I did the others because he's yours, but I can tell he is definitely going to be good friend.

Aiden blinked. "Brothers?" he asked.

Meryn nodded. "Yep! So they are still my minions and Baby Keelans, but Ryuu helped me figure out that that means I care for them like brothers. So they are my brothers now."

Aiden, Adriel, and Magnus blinked. Adriel leaned forward to look at Meryn. "Wait, have you formally adopted them?" he asked.

Meryn frowned and looked up at Rex. "How can I make it official? Can you help?" she asked.

Rex nodded. "Of course."

Aiden scowled at him. "Don't help. She needs to stay out of trouble."

Rex leaned down and whispered to Meryn conspiratorially. "Come see me later, and I'll help you with the paperwork."

"Nice!" she said and held out her tiny fist. He just looked at it. She sighed. "Hold up your hand." He held up his hand. "Now make a fist," she instructed.

He made a fist. She took her little hand and bumped his. "Like this. It's a fist bump."

Rex looked down at his hand. "Fist bump. Declan, we can fist bump," he said, looking excited.

Declan just shook his head. "No, we can't."

Kari could see the stubborn look on Rex's face. She was willing to bet that Rex would not leave the city until he had gotten his fist bump from Declan.

"Meryn, we need to talk about this," Aiden began before a light vibrating noise interrupted him. He looked confused for a moment and then pulled out his phone. When he saw the incoming number, he stood and looked around the table. "My apologies, I have to take this. I'll be right back." He walked out of the room.

Meryn turned in her chair to look at Ryuu who shrugged. Meryn sat back down and began chewing on her thumb.

"Guilty conscience?" Eva teased.

Meryn shook her head. "No, that's why I'm confused. I haven't done anything yet."

"Yet?" Adriel asked.

Meryn shrugged. "It can't possibly be a bad idea if my future self hasn't traveled back in time to stop me."

Eva's mouth twitched. "Is that the basis for your decision making?"

A few seconds later, Aiden stormed into the room, his face like a dark thundercloud. He stopped beside Meryn and looked down at his mate. "How could you!" he roared.

Even Declan flinched at Aiden's ire. Meryn on the other hand looked undisturbed. Kari had a feeling she had been roared at before.

Meryn's eyes widened. "What did I do?" she asked.

"Don't act like you don't know," he seethed.

She shook her head. "I, no shit, have no idea what you're talking about." Aiden looked at her face and saw her confusion. "Well, if you didn't, who did?"

"Who did what?" she demanded.

Aiden took a deep breath and looked at Gavriel. "It seems as though Sascha Baberiov, Gamma's unit leader, was arrested today."

Bethy gasped, covering her mouth with her hands. Gavriel just stared before he looked at Meryn. "What did you do?" he asked.

"I am finding the lack of faith in me disturbing," Meryn protested.

"Why was he arrested?" Bethy finally asked.

"Things," Aiden said, a flush working it's way up his neck.

"Things?" Meryn prompted.

Aiden swallowed, his face becoming redder by the second. "It's personal," he stuttered.

"Personal?" A wicked grin crossed Meryn's face. "Now I have to know. Either you tell me more, or I will text Colton," she threatened.

Aiden began rubbing his hands over his face. When he stopped, he stared at the floor. "The local sheriff received a complaint from one of the farmers that a man was seen on his property doing something with one of his animals."

"Oh my gods," Beth whispered with a horrified expression. Gavriel's face was unreadable.

"Animal?" Meryn asked. "Did he kill a cow or something and was, like, eating?"

Aiden shook his head slowly. Kari watched the

Unit Commander, wondering if he became any redder, would he pass out.

"The... the report says..." Aiden paused. "Um something else."

"Oh for gods' sake, Aiden, just say it!" Meryn ordered.

"Sascha was arrested as a person of interest in the ongoing investigation regarding indecent liberties taken with livestock. The culprit was seen masturbating on the farmer's pig."

Kari was afraid to breathe; the silence in the room had become unbearably thick.

"What?" Meryn whispered.

"I can see why you thought Meryn was behind this," Gavriel said, his lips twitching violently.

Aiden looked down at his mate. "Are you sure you didn't have anything to do with this?"

Meryn held up a hand as she stared, unblinking. "Give me a second; I'm enjoying this." She slowly shook her head "I'm not saying it's not a hella cool idea, but I..." Her eyes grew round. She pulled out her phone, and her small fingers flew over its surface. She looked up, smiled at Aiden, and giggled nervously as she waited for a reply. Seconds later, her phone vibrated, and she looked down. Her eyes widened, and she began to laugh. Soon, she was laughing so hard she could barely breathe. When she almost toppled off one side, Rex reached over and grabbed her, securing her in her seat. Everyone stared at her in shock. She waved her phone around, laughing hysterically.

"Meryn, what is it?" Bethy asked. Meryn just shook her head. Finally, Ryuu stepped forward and plucked the phone from her hand. He looked down, and a smile crossed his lips. "Young Master Noah evidently is the one that submitted the report on the Sheriff's system," he informed them in a conversational tone.

Aiden blinked. "Can he do that?" Meryn nodded. "Why would he do that?" he asked. "I thought he was one of your minions."

Meryn wiped her eyes. "Exactly."

Aiden collapsed into his seat, looking exhausted. "As usual, I have no idea what you're saying."

Ryuu cleared his throat. "I believe she is referring to the inference that in the movie *Despicable Me,* the minions were actually the ones responsible for helping to carry out the nefarious deeds."

Aiden looked adorably confused. "I thought they were just the little yellow guys in overalls."

Meryn shook her head. "I told you they were helping me take over the world."

Aiden ground his teeth together and, with a clenched jaw, asked, "Why would Noah do something like that? Does he understand the implications of one of the unit leaders being pulled into a human law enforcement environment? What would happen if Sascha had to shift?"

Meryn held up a hand. "He did it in retaliation."

"Retaliation for what?" Aiden asked.

"Sascha set up a fireworks display in the center of town."

"And?" Aiden asked, looking confused. "That sounds festive."

"All the fireworks were purple," Meryn informed him.

Kari watched in fascination as Gavriel lost all sense of composure. He leaned back so far in his chair, it tipped backward. Bethy stared down in shock. Adriel was laughing openly, and Declan wheezed at her side, pounding the table.

"What?" Kari asked. She would have felt like a total outsider, but she noticed that neither Eva, Broderick, Caspian, nor Magnus looked like they knew what was going on.

Declan caught his breath first. "There's been an ongoing prank war between Sascha and Keelan. They, of course, pulled in their units to assist as the years went on. Alpha Unit warriors would electrocute the members of the Gamma Unit, and the Gamma Unit would find ways to turn the members of the Alpha Unit purple.

"How could they possibly do that?" Eva asked.

Meryn turned to her. "Well, one time they put purple dye in the shower head after setting up fireballs in the house. Keelan ended up looking like a plum." She giggled. "Then there was the time that they dropped purple glitter on Keelan during the Midwinter Solstice ball; he complained he had glitter in his unmentionables for days."

"But why fireworks? Would that not be for everyone?" Kari asked.

Her question seemed to kill the laughter. It was as if someone had just turned off the faucet, and the joy dried up.

Meryn looked at Aiden, who shook his head. He turned to Kari. "Members of the units know what has happened to Keelan, but for the most part, his sacrifice and what he has done remains a secret. Let's just say that Sascha's fireworks was a huge display taunting the Alpha Unit."

"So why did Noah get involved?" Eva asked.

"Even though no one has officially been assigned as Alpha's sixth man yet, Noah has been living at the Alpha estate. So when Sascha set up the fireworks display, I'm sure he felt like it was his responsibility to react."

"I see," Kari said.

"Man, I can't wait to get home to talk to Sascha." Meryn rubbed her hands together in glee.

"Can you please get him released?" Aiden begged.

"Fine." Meryn hopped off her chair and looked back at Ryuu. "Can you make me a plate with some pudding and bring into the communications hub? I have to up my game to make my minions proud." Whistling, she walked past Kuruk and left the dining room.

Aiden sighed. "At least she is feeling better."

Magnus shook his head in disbelief. "She is so little."

Adriel nodded. "She is too little to cause so much trouble."

Eva met Kari's eyes and winked. Kari felt a sense of camaraderie with her. There was just something about being mated to one of the warriors and keeping them on their toes that seemed to bring people together.

"Well, I am sure you gentlemen can help keep her in line," Kari said magnanimously. All the men looked at her, their gazes shooting daggers. Beside her, Declan chuckled. "No one can control the menace."

Everyone was in high spirits for the rest of the dinner except for Aiden, who poked at his food, looking slightly ill. When dinner was over, she thanked Sebastian, and she and Declan walked hand-in-hand to the telecommunications hub to get Avery. Declan told her that her and Avery's things were forwarded to his house when it became general knowledge that they were mates, so if they needed anything to settle in for the night they would have to make a trip to the Unit Level.

When they opened the door, Avery and the twins were laughing, and Meryn was pointing at the computer screen. Kari caught a glimpse of a wanted poster before Meryn was able to minimize the screen. Meryn looked at her and smiled. Kari shook her head. "Try not to kill your mate; he already looks slightly ill."

Meryn shrugged. "He'll get over it; he always does," she said an upbeat manner.

Ryuu chuckled where he was standing off to one side. Kari looked at him, and he nodded. "*Denka* is correct, he usually does."

Avery looked at her. "Did you need me?" he asked.

Kari nodded. "Our things were sent to the Unit Level, to Declan's house. We are about to head there now to grab clothes and some toiletries for tonight, and I was wondering if you would like to come with us."

He stood, nodding. "Yes, please. I need to get my books too," he said, reaching for his backpack. He turned to his new friends. "Be right back."

Together, the three of them walked toward the transport tunnel. One in each hand, she held onto Avery and Declan and flew them up to the Unit Level. Stepping away from the entrance, they looked around. To Kari, it looked as if someone had taken a tiny village and put it underground. Off to the left she could see individual stone houses and, to the right, other larger buildings stood.

Declan tugged her hand "This way," he said, guiding her down the wide street that separated the houses. At the end of the road, a larger house stood. Declan pointed. "That is where Adriel and Eva live. Ours is the one next to it on the right."

She stopped and stared. "Declan, it looks like a small castle."

Declan nodded. "There was all the stone to work with when the witches were remodeling for me. A castle was the first thing I could think of when they asked me how I wanted the house styled."

Avery's eyes were bugged out. "Is that a draw-bridge?" he asked.

Declan nodded. "Ostentatious, I know, but I couldn't have a castle without one.

Avery looked down. "There's no moat."

Declan shrugged. "I couldn't get everything."

"How do you get in?" Avery asked, running to the walkway.

Declan went to the back of the mailbox and punched in a code. Slowly, the small drawbridge opened and lowered. Kari was feeling as excited as Avery looked. They walked across the bridge and looked around. Just inside the building was the foyer.

"Is this secure?" Kari asked taking in the design.

Declan looked at her funny. "Who in the hell would break in?"

"Good point." Right by the stairs was a stack of suitcases. Kari turned to Declan. "Who brought them here?"

"Probably Grant, he's one of my closest friends after Adriel. He has access to the house, and he knew you'd want your things. He probably just took it upon himself to make sure they got delivered."

"He is very sweet, quiet, but sweet."

Declan nodded. "He is very much like Meryn and doesn't do well with others. But he is very loyal. It took me a long time to get to know him after we were assigned to Eta."

"Why?" she asked.

"It's hard getting to know someone when they don't talk much."

"I bet that was not a problem for you," Avery teased.

Declan grinned. "It's true, I like to talk, and that's what I did. I talked, and kept talking and finally, he started talking back. We've been friends ever since."

Kari and Avery opened their suitcases right there in the foyer and dug through their things to get what they needed. When they both stood with a set of pajamas in one hand and toiletries in the other, Declan nodded. They walked outside and he had just closed the drawbridge behind them when they heard a low growl.

"Mine!" a voice called. Kari stood back in shock as the large warrior she had seen earlier with the children lifted Avery up and crushed his lips to her brother's. That was when Kari found her breaking point. So much had happened in the past day, and this was something she simply couldn't handle. Screeching, she launched herself at the warrior trying to steal her brother away.

Declan wrapped his arms around her to keep his mate from attacking Warrick.

"Put him down!" she screamed.

"Can I get some help?" Declan yelled out. Up and

down the road doors opened, and men began to pour out. Seconds later, another set of hands helped to hold Kari still. Declan nodded his thanks to Goddard.

"Kari my love, calm down," he said in a gentle voice.

"Get away from him! Get away from my brother!" she yelled before breaking down into sobs.

Avery, in Warrick's arms, looked terrified and torn. Kari's crying had him stepping away from his newly discovered mate and racing over to his sister.

"Goddard, can you get her and Avery back down to Level One?" Declan asked.

Goddard nodded and steered Kari back toward the transport tunnel. Avery scooped up their things and followed his sister closely.

Declan turned to Warrick who stood there looking stunned. He watched Avery disappear down the tunnel, a look of wonder on his face. "He is mine," he whispered. "I could smell his blood from the bandages on his arm, he is mine."

"That remains to be seen." Declan crossed his arms over his chest. He looked at the gathered warriors. "Thank you for coming so quickly; I've got it from here." The men nodded and headed back to their homes.

"Declan, you are standing between me and my mate," Warrick said in a low voice.

Declan held up a hand. "And your caveman stunt just drove my mate over the edge."

"But he is mine, Declan," Warrick protested.

Declan shook his head. "Kari needs her brother. She's been through so much; she can't lose him."

Warrick looked confused. "Why would she lose

him? I am not taking him away."

"She will no longer be the most important person in his life."

"But she has you," Warrick pointed out.

"We only just met this morning," Declan reminded him.

Warrick began to pace back and forth. "If I had just been with you on patrol on Level Six this morning, I would have had your back. You would never have gotten hurt, and I could have met my mate."

"And Kari would've killed you then. She is super protective of Avery. I have no idea how to make this right," Declan ran a hand through his hair in frustration.

"How do you think I feel?" Warrick entreated. Declan just looked up at him. Warrick exhaled. "Declan, I am not gay."

"Oh. Oh! Wait, you don't want him?" Declan demanded, feeling angry. There was nothing wrong with his new little brother. "He is absolutely adorable; how could you not want him?"

"Of course, I want him. I kissed him, did I not?

"Oh yeah. Well, you have plenty of time to figure all this out. He's not of age yet."

Warrick groaned and buried his face in his hands. "You are kidding me, right?"

"Nope, he's only ninety-nine."

Warrick blushed. "I would not press my claim on him right away."

Declan cleared his throat. "Do you know how to claim a man?" he asked delicately.

Warrick scowled at him. "Of course I do. I have fed from men before. I have been with men before; I just prefer women."

Declan rubbed the back of his neck. "Are you sure he is your mate?"

Warrick gave him a flat look. "Are you sure Kari is your mate?" he asked in response. They stared at each other in silence.

"Shit," Declan exclaimed.

"I agree."

"Okay, I'll go talk to them, but you have got to give them time. They just found out today that they have to move to the city, and Avery is special. You need to take time to get to know who he is."

Warrick got a goofy look on his face. "Yes, he is special. He is so beautiful." Declan chuckled. Warrick looked at him. "Could you tell him I would like to see him tomorrow? I could bring him lunch," he offered.

Declan eyed him. "Don't push my mate."

"And how would you feel if I tried to keep you from Kari?"

"Good point. All right, I'll talk to Kari and tell her that you're willing to wait to claim Avery, and you're willing to take it slow. You will take it slow, right?" Declan mustered up the best 'fatherly' look he could.

"I swear to you, Declan, on my honor, I would never do anything to harm Avery," Warrick vowed.

Declan nodded. "You are a man of honor, and I'll hold you to your promise."

"You are very protective of him," Warrick observed.

Declan rolled his eyes. "He's my little brother now."

"Thank you for your help. I appreciate it. I know you have a lot on your plate," Warrick said, looking worried.

Declan waved a hand at him. "You are one of my closest friends, and it looks like we're about to become family; it's the very least I can do."

At the mention of family, Warrick groaned. "My family is going to shit purple dinosaurs."

Declan racked his brain but couldn't find a reason why they would be upset. "Why would they care?"

Warrick's shoulders slumped "My uncle just lost his mate to a wolf shifter, he is in jail, and I am about to come out as not only gay but mated to a shifter as well."

"Dammit!" Declan exclaimed. "We really didn't need this right now."

"What is the alternative?" Warrick asked. "Should we have left my poor sweet aunt with a man who treats her like a slave? Should I give up Avery and live the rest of my existence alone?"

"Of course not; if we had, you wouldn't have a new baby cousin on the way," Declan said smiling.

Warrick's entire face brightened. "Can you believe it? I cannot wait to help. It has been so long since any babies were born here we are all going to have to take classes on how to care for infants. And to have Avery at my side for these moments, it is almost too much happiness for one person. Now I understand the dreams I have been having."

Declan swallowed hard remembering the flames from his own dreams, suddenly he was fearful for Avery. "How bad were they?"

Warrick blinked. "Bad? No, they were wonderful. An amazingly beautiful woman hands me a gift. It is a box wrapped in gold paper. She tells me the gift is rare and precious and that I must care for it always. Then I wake up. I know now that Avery is that gift, one I may not deserve."

Declan exhaled in relief. "You more than deserve it my friend. Now, if you could do me a favor?"

"Anything," Warrick replied.

"I haven't gotten one of those floating stones that the twins made for Meryn. Can you float me down to Level One?"

Warrick nodded. "Of course. Do not forget to tell my mate about lunch."

"I won't," Declan promised.

Now he just needed to figure out what he was going to tell his mate.

CHAPTER EIGHT

DECLAN WALKED DOWN THE HALL of the living quarters. He hesitated at Avery's door and then knocked. He heard a light voice say, 'Come in'. He stepped into the room. Avery was sitting cross-legged on the bed looking even younger than Declan knew him to be. Declan walked over and sat on the edge of the bed. "How are you doing?" he asked.

Avery stared down at his hands. "I'm okay, I guess. I am excited, scared, and nervous too," he admitted. When he looked up, Declan could see the weariness in his eyes. "What is he like?" Declan knew Avery was referring to Warrick.

"Warrick is the biggest softie I know," Declan said.

Avery's eyes widened. "Really? He's so big." Avery blushed.

Declan chuckled. "That's all that people see, and I think that makes him sad. Plus, his family are kind of assholes, well except for his aunt."

"I'd like to see him," Avery admitted, twisting his fingers together.

"He wants to see you too. Tomorrow in fact."

"Tomorrow?" Avery asked, looking excited.

"He's going to bring you lunch. He is really looking forward to it."

"What about Kari? I've never seen her cry like that." Avery asked looking scared.

"Don't worry about your sister. I'll talk to her. As soon as she realizes that Warrick will never hurt you, she should calm down."

"What about *you know*?" Avery asked, giving him a look. It took Declan a moment to realize that Avery was referring to sex. He stood quickly, clearing his throat. "Well, it's late. You need to get some sleep now." Declan turned to the door then back Avery. "Hey, if Warrick tries 'you know', tell me so I can kick his ass."

"I thought you said he wouldn't hurt me?"

Declan gave him a wry look. "Oh, he wouldn't be hurting you, Avery."

Avery covered his mouth, giggling, then sobered. "Why would you fight your friend? You don't even know me."

"Because you're my baby brother now, and it will be a cold day in hell before I let someone hurt you."

Avery looked at him shyly. "Thank you."

Declan cleared his throat again. "Okay then, good night," he said gruffly stepping into the hallway. He closed the door, leaned against it, and exhaled. When he looked up, his mate was standing next to him. It was evident she had been listening in. He met Kari's eyes, and she simply held out her hand and led them to their bedroom.

"So I guess we're staying in this room together," he said as he shut the door. He'd have to thank the Doc for putting him on observation for the night. Level One's guest quarters were impressive. He turned back to him mate and blinked.

She was staring at him with tears in her eyes. "He is all I have," she admitted brokenly.

His heart hurt for her. He pulled her into his arms and held her tight. "Not anymore. You have me and my idiotic brothers now."

She snorted through her tears, the beginning of a smile on her lips. "If Warrick even breathes on him wrong, I will..."

He stopped her threat with a kiss. He put both hands on her shoulders and began rubbing her arms. "I will run interference until Avery is of age. Listen, I know Warrick seems intimidating, but he really is the biggest teddy bear I have ever known. I even got him to agree to wait until Avery is one hundred before pressing his claim. He would sooner rip off his own arm and beat himself with it than allow Avery to get even a paper cut. I don't think anyone will be more beloved or spoiled in the city, except for maybe you."

She wiped her eyes, looking less afraid. She started to say something and yawned.

"Let's get into bed," Declan suggested.

Kari nodded and walked over to the large guest bed. Declan realized with disappointment that she'd already changed into a pair of pajamas. They were silky to the touch, but unfortunately, they covered a lot of her skin. Declan simply stripped to his boxers and then climbed into bed behind Kari. He wrapped an arm around her waist, and they yawned at the same time. "I can't believe I'm too tired for sex," Declan admitted.

She reached back and poked him in the ribs. "You have not been cleared for sex yet," she reminded him.

Declan nuzzled his nose over his bite marks and noted with satisfaction that she shivered at his touch. "Best day of my life. I almost die, I meet my mate, she gives me an amazing orgasm, learned my family isn't as dysfunctional as I thought, kind of get promoted, get a new baby brother who ends up mated to one of my best friends, and end the day with snuggling."

She chuckled. "I met my mate with his intestines hanging out, he almost died, I took a new job, found out I have to permanently move away from my beloved condo, met my in-laws, receive an amazing orgasm, realize the city is more disturbing than I thought, lose my baby brother to a huge warrior..."

"You didn't lose him," Declan said, interrupting her.

"Whatever," she refuted. He licked her bite mark, and she moaned. "No extracurricular activity," she said.

"Tomorrow, all bets are off," he promised darkly. He waited for her response and then realized she was already lightly snoring in her sleep.

She has got to be the most exquisite thing I have ever seen.

It wasn't long until he too closed his eyes and went to sleep

☾

THE NEXT DAY, KARI SAT in Magnus' office going over his files from the past two decades. Most of them had been organized, and they both decided that anything older could be gone through at a more leisurely rate. The most pertinent information had been catalogued.

Rex had called Magnus early that morning and advised him that the council members had arrived. They were settled and would be arranging the trial soon.

"Gods, what a morning," Magnus complained. "As much as I want DuBois to pay for what he has done, I absolutely loathe the idea of having a trial." He sat back in his chair, looking worn out. "Even though I hated the man, it seemed like things were so much easier when DuSang ruled. He would have just pronounced DuBois guilty and dealt with it."

Kari walked over to where the electric kettle was plugged in at a makeshift coffee bar. She poured the steaming water over a couple of tea bags and started them steeping. "Yes, sometimes it is easier to be a dictator, but not in the long run. I know what you are doing seems thankless and impossible, but you have to know that you are doing the right thing. Your people need to feel like they are being heard, and you are doing a wonderful job of doing what is best for them."

"It is disheartening to do so much and still find yourself falling short." Magnus closed his eyes.

Kari carried the teacup over and set it in front of the prince. "Magnus, I have heard you on more than one occasion say that you did not want to rule. Are you okay?" she asked.

He looked at her and shrugged. "I am tired, Kari. I have been doing this for hundreds of years, and you are right, it is a thankless task. I am trying to bring these people into the twenty-first century and give them the freedom to do what they wish. And after seven hundred years, I realize that they have been arranging matings behind my back. They do not tell me anything; yet expect me to instinctively do what they want. The weaker ones simply want to be told what to do, and I seem weak if I am not the dictator they want me to be. Sometimes, I wonder if I am doing any good at all."

Kari went back over to the stack of the more recent files and slammed them on his desk. He looked up at her, startled. "If you ever doubt that you are doing any good, look at that."

He opened the folder and his breath caught. With trembling hands, he went over each picture. Each file held the snapshot and profile of one of the Wolf-town refugee children.

"Look at the children, Magnus. Those children have a future because of you. I am sorry; it may sound callous, but your seven hundred years of thankless tasks is worth it for those little faces."

Magnus looked up at her, his eyes bright. "Thank you. Thank you for being my assistant and for being more than a mindless drone. Maybe if I had some-body like you at my side over these long years, it would not have been so bad."

"That is what a true assistant is for, someone to reach into the blackness and help you shoulder the burden and to remind you that you are doing a good job. I am sorry you have not had the support you needed in previous years, but I am here now and I will do anything I can to help."

Magnus smiled. "Anything?" he asked.

"Why?" she asked suspiciously.

He reached into his desk, pulled out a file folder,

and handed it to her. "Leif Grassfield and Travis Hickory are two witches that recently left Noctem Falls to return to Storm Keep for testing; that is how we got Nigel and Neil."

"What about them?" she asked.

"I want them back," Magnus answered.

Kari blinked. "Excuse me?"

"Storm Keep knew that Nigel and Neil were untrained and were pretty much walking disasters. They may be pranksters and tricksters, but they are good boys. I took them in because I did not want them to be separated. As it turns out, they are actually very powerful, so it was a good decision on my part. The problem is they are just not suited to Noctem Falls. There is way too much politics swirling around here, and they are too young. I want to see if I can get Leif and Travis reassigned to Noctem Falls."

"What about Nigel and Neil?" she asked, concerned for her new young friends. "They belong here, Magnus. They are happy with Meryn and..."

Magnus held up a hand. "You do not need to go mama bear on me. I have a soft spot for those boys, and I know Meryn would not give them up either. She has done so much for the city; I would like to keep her happy."

She grinned. "And you would like to stay off any of America's Most Wanted lists."

"I have to admit, she does scare me a bit with that laptop of hers."

Kari looked over the files. "What exactly would you like me to do?"

"I would have you call Storm Keep and make a complaint about the twins recent behavior. But tell them I very magnanimously have decided to offer to train the boys and keep them here. However, due to the current refugee situation, I need more experienced witches. Maybe let it be known that I will not hold it against them for sending the twins."

Kari took a deep breath "That is an iffy leg you are trying to stand on. It is wobbly and could be knocked out from under you."

"The suggestion came up during the dinner we recently had with the Bellerose and Géroux families, and I think it is the best chance we have."

"How badly do you need them?"

"I needed them here yesterday."

"Right. Let us see what happens." Kari reached for the phone and dialed the number that would connect her to the training academy the witches ran at Storm Keep. A bright voice answered. "Thank you for calling the Storm Keep training academy, this is Angelica, how can I help you?"

"Hello Angelica, my name is Kari Delaney. I am the personal assistant to Prince Magnus of Noctem Falls." Kari deliberately paused, waiting for a reaction; it would determine her course of action.

"Oh my goodness! How can I help you?" Angelica replied tittering nervously.

"I am hoping you can do something for me. You see, Prince Magnus has brought it to my attention that the two newest recruits from Storm Keep, their names are—one moment..." Kari ruffled papers as if she were looking for the names.

"Do you mean Nigel and Neil Morninglory?" Angelica asked.

"Yes, those two. They were not quite... How can I put this delicately? Ready to leave Storm Keep.

Now, I am not saying that your trainers knew this, but it really did not leave a very good impression with Prince Magnus."

"Oh no! Did something happen?" Angelica stuttered.

Kari eyed Magnus and raised an eyebrow. He nodded, quickly jotted something down, and handed her the legal pad.

Kari read what he wrote and had a hard time not laughing out loud. "Yes." She cleared her throat. "As it so happens, those two pulled down the pants of the second in command to the Eta Unit, in the middle of a team meeting."

"Oh my! Oh dear, why would they do such a thing?" Angelica asked, panicking. "Ms. Delaney you have our most profound apologies. Is there anything that we can do to rectify this for Prince Magnus?"

Kari fought to keep her voice even. The image of the two redheaded imps de-pantsing Declan kept replaying in her mind. "Prince Magnus, as you know, is very busy right now dealing with refugees. He is taking in not only local shifters but also fae and witches to keep them safe. Despite being buried in new responsibilities, he is offering to continue Nigel and Neil's training here in Noctem Falls, so that, when they leave here, they will not only be more advanced in their magic, but they will also have a better understanding of how politics work."

"He is willing to do that?" Angelica asked, sounding amazed.

"Yes, but unfortunately every warrior here is busy with the refugees. I think it would be in Storm Keep's best interest to send Leif Grassfield and Travis Hickory back to Noctem Falls where they can resume their positions here as warriors and act as mentors to both Nigel and Neil." When Angelica didn't respond, Kari decided to go in for the kill. "Let us be honest with each other, Angelica. We can keep those two troublemakers very busy here helping with the refugees, and they will get the training and the discipline they need in the process." Angelica was quiet for a moment before speaking.

"If you could just give me a few minutes, I'm sure I can get this approved, considering all Prince Magnus is offering. Are you able to hold?"

"Yes, of course." Kari muted the phone when hold music started.

"They did what?" she asked, laughing out loud.

Magnus chuckled. "Adriel had a very hard time reporting that one with a straight face. They were right in the middle of introductions when those two pulled down Declan's pants, evidently to see if he had wet himself."

"Why would he do that?"

"Evidently from laughing so hard."

It wasn't a minute later and Angelica came on the line "Ms. Delaney, I'm so sorry, we would love to help, but..."

Kari un-muted the phone. "But what exactly?" she asked.

"We don't know where Leif and Travis are. They never reported in for testing."

Kari looked over at Magnus who shrugged. "If we find them, can we let them know that their assignment has been changed and that they are to report to Noctem Falls?"

"Yes, of course! We are changing their orders now

and will send you an updated copy via fax. But how are you going to find them?" Angelica asked.

"I have no idea. Thank you for all you have done. I will take it from here."

"No, thank you, Ms. Delaney. This takes a lot off our plate. If you ever need anything in the future, please let me know."

"Thank you, Angelica." Kari hung up the phone and then just stared down at the legal pad.

"What?" Magnus asked.

"That was too easy. Way too easy. I wonder what is wrong with Leif and Travis," she mused.

"There is nothing wrong with them. They are seasoned warriors and wonderful witches that have served faithfully for centuries," Magnus asserted.

"Exactly. And yet Storm Keep was willing to give them up so easily."

"I know that they were both very vocal about coming back to Noctem Falls regardless of what their scores were. Maybe the academy just realized that since they were going to come back anyway, might as well send them back now, especially at my behest," Magnus hypothesized.

"Okay, so how do we find Travis and Leif?"

"We will start with Leif's Unit Leader, Dimitri Romanov." Magnus pulled out his walkie-talkie. "Tree Beard, come in, over."

"Yes, sire."

"Would you happen to know how to reach Leif or Travis? Storm Keep is advising me that they have not arrived there yet."

"Yes, sire, I can call their cell phones. We all maintain cell phones and numbers given just to unit warriors. They took a slight detour on their way to

Storm Keep. They are in Vegas."

"They have been in Vegas since they left?"

"Yes, sire. I call and check in on them every couple days to make sure they have not drowned themselves in booze or accidentally married a human."

"Can you reach out to them to let them know their assignment has been changed? They are now to return to Noctem Falls?"

"Sire, are you serious? What about Nigel and Neil?" he asked.

"They are to stay as well. Travis and Leif will act as their new mentors."

"Hot damn! I mean thank you, Sire!"

"You are welcome; call our boys home."

"Yes sir!"

Magnus was about to clip his walkie-talkie back on when they heard a new voice.

"Magneto, come in, over," a piping voice blared.

"Magneto here, Menace."

"Cool, I just wanted to let you know that the cameras are done, over."

"Thank you, Menace; we will be right there." Magnus looked up at her. "Would you like to go and check them out?"

"Sure, but what cameras is she talking about?" she asked.

"Meryn installed security cameras at specific points around the city. We are hoping they will help to track the killer."

"You still have not found him?"

"No. When the murders stopped, our leads disappeared."

"I am more interested in how they will be organizing the recorded footage."

They left the office and walked the short distance to the communications hub. They opened the door to see that Nigel, Neil, Avery, and Meryn were crowded around a computer monitor. When they walked up behind them, Kari felt her mouth drop.

"Meryn McKenzie!" Magnus exclaimed. All four of them jumped. "What on earth is that?" he asked, pointing to the screen.

"I'm calling it the porn channel," Meryn answered cheekily.

"Are those the cameras?" Kari asked, unable to take her eyes off the two figures moving against each other on the computer screen.

Avery tilted his head. "I didn't know you could do it like that." Kari reached around his face and covered his eyes with her hands.

Magnus frowned. "Meryn, I am very disappointed in you. Those cameras were meant to be put in places to watch for our killer. They were not meant to compromise the privacy of the citizens of the city."

Meryn shook her head, laughing. "They are in public spaces."

Magnus' mouth dropped. "Where is this?"

Meryn looked at the computer screen then pointed to a small number. "The backside of the transport tunnel on Level Five."

"They're doing that in the air?" Avery asked, trying to move Kari's hands.

"Yup. I'm envious; Aiden and I haven't even mastered shower sex yet." Meryn informed them, giggling.

Magnus sat down in one of the chairs. "There has not been a dull moment around here since you arrived." He frowned. "Meryn, do the people know that the cameras went up?"

"Yes, the warriors let them know that was the next step after Wi-Fi was established."

Kari gave up on trying to cover Avery's eyes and simply leaned forward and turned off the monitor. "Meryn, where is all of this footage being stored?"

Meryn stood and walked over to a large black box on the table next to the monitor. "This is a network attached storage unit. It has about thirty-two terabytes of storage, which, after our RAID configuration, gives us sixteen terabytes of usable space. We will be able to recycle and store video here. One of the unit warriors will come in daily and fast-forward through the footage. Any movement or anything out of the ordinary is stored and all the rest is deleted."

"Is there a way to keep it all?"

Meryn winced. "Why keep thousands and thousands of gigabytes of boring footage?" Kari gave her a flat look. "I guess we could keep it. We will definitely need a set-up that will move the video to tape storage and we'll need more hard drives."

Kari nodded. "I think that is a good idea. You never know if the warrior reviewing the footage is having an off morning. He may miss something or delete it by accident. It is better to keep the footage intact."

Meryn nodded. "Yeah, I could totally miss stuff without coffee." She looked at Magnus. "That kind of set up can get expensive," she warned.

Magnus waved a hand. "Do what you have to do to arrange for the storage capacity for the next couple years."

Meryn rubbed her hands together gleefully. "I get to order new technology! I love it!"

"Magneto." A voice came over the walkie-talkie. Magnus looked at Meryn "These walkie-talkies are worth their weight in gold." She gave him a thumbs up. Magnus picked up the walkie-talkie. "Magneto here, what is it Professor?"

"Sire, I just wanted to let you know that we are ready to start the field trip. I was wondering if you would like to attend?"

"Of course, Kari and I will be there shortly."

She waved at Meryn and kissed Avery on the top of his head before following Magnus down the hall to the other side of Level One.

Declan was waiting for her at the entrance to the rarely seen sections of Noctem Falls Royal quarters. The doors to the gardens were larger and grander than the ones in the living quarters. The entire section where Magnus lived was modern compared to the doors in front of her. They looked like they belonged in a castle. The door itself was wooden, and the rounded stone arch had symbols and words carved into it in a language she could not read. Around her, excited children jabbered to each other, pointing at the door; parents smiled at their children's excitement.

Declan walked up to her and took her hand. "Are you ready to see the Royal Gardens?" he asked. She nodded, and in truth, she was. Noctem Fall's Royal Gardens, which coaxed living plants to bloom out of season and underground, was as nearly impossible to be invited into as the Fae Gardens.

Just then, a very exuberant Magnus made his way to the front and greeted the children. "Well, I see all my fierce little cadets are here." The children giggled. "I understand that some of you are not feeling very well, so I have made sure that you can spend time here in the Royal Gardens. So without further ado..." He turned, placed his hand on the door, and as if by magic, it unlocked. They all heard the tumblers turn, and slowly the doors cracked open. Magnus pushed them forward and opened them wide.

Immediately, Kari could smell the flowers, the earth, and the leaves that lay just beyond. Declan took her hand and walked her forward. The children took off at a dead run, screaming in excitement. Their parents had a hard job trying to keep up with them. Everywhere they turned, there was something else to look at.

Huge trees grew impossibly tall, and above them, the sky was a bright blue. She'd never seen daylight in a cave before, but here it felt real, as if she were standing topside. She looked around in wonder. Vine flowers grew out of control. Water fountains gurgled and bubbled, giving the entire scene a beautiful background murmur that harmonized with the gently swaying wind chimes caught by an artificial breeze that swept through the cavern.

Magnus cleared his throat, and the children stopped to look at him. He pointed, and Kari realized that there was now a new addition to the Royal Gardens. The witches had been very busy.

Magnus had them create a playground. Every piece of play equipment imaginable had been created for the children. There were teeter-totters, swing sets, monkey bars, and a carousel. For the older children there were multiple courts to choose from including a foursquare, a basketball, and a badminton court.

Magnus worked with Adriel and a lot of the other warriors to ensure that each child was watched over carefully. Declan wrapped his arm around her shoulders and steered her off to the right. They followed a tiny brook and moved deeper into the forest. "This is impossible," she whispered, looking around. She was almost afraid that if she spoke too loud, the magic would end.

"No, not impossible when you combine the magical efforts of hundreds of witches over hundreds of years, each one adding something different."

"What about Nigel and Neil?" she teased.

Declan smiled. "Who do you think recommended the playground?"

She stopped dead in her tracks. "I thought Magnus had that ordered."

Declan shook his head. "He ordered it built, but he didn't think of it. When the twins learned that Magnus and Adriel were planning a field trip in the Royal Gardens, they came up with the playground idea for the kids. They knew the children wouldn't be entertained for long with only plants to amuse them. Of course, Magnus agreed. He told them it was a brilliant idea. Evidently the twins were very involved in taking care of children when they lived in Storm Keep. They grew up in an orphanage, so they understood the way the children think, plus they are youngest here besides Bethy, Meryn, Stefan, and your Avery."

"Where exactly are you taking me Declan?"

He smiled. "We're on our way to Grandma's house, better be careful that a lion doesn't come along and huff and puff and blow you."

Kari laughed at his mangled version of Grimm's

Fairy Tales. His face lit up at her laughter. "It's someplace private where we can get to know each other better."

"You still have not been cleared by the doctor yet," she teased.

"I'll take my chances," he whispered, nipping at her neck. They walked until they reached the top of a long stone staircase. She looked down; at the bottom of the stairs was an open meadow with tall, sweet smelling grasses and beyond that more open space.

"One of the witches Magnus called in about a century ago used their magic to simulate the sky complete with clouds. I've heard that if you lay in the field, you can pick out different shapes. Wait here for a second. The orchard's about a quarter-mile away. I was thinking we could snag a few apples for a snack before lunch while looking up at the clouds."

"I think that sounds perfect."

"I'll be right back." He pulled her hand to his lips and kissed her gently.

"Hurry back." Kari wrapped her arms around her waist, hugging herself. She'd never been so happy in her entire life. Of course, work was ridiculously busy, and she had a feeling that Prince Magnus in the long run would be a challenge that she would never quite master. But wasn't that what you're supposed to do? Find something to dedicate your life to? Work that would be satisfying and rewarding? What could be better than helping the Prince of her people?

Out of nowhere, she felt a cold breeze. She rubbed her arms, looking around. The plants around her were still, neither their leaves nor petals swayed.

She looked out all around her. It was as if she knew that if she turned fast enough, she would see something—something terrifying.

She gripped the handrail as a wave of dizziness swept through her. She shook her head, trying to clear her vision. When she started to turn away from the stairs, another wave hit her; seconds later, she knew she was falling, and there was nothing she could do to stop it.

CHAPTER NINE

"KARI! KARI! OPEN YOUR EYES, please!" She felt a warm hand on her cheek, and slowly, she tried to blink. When her eyes opened, she saw Declan standing beside her.

"Declan?" she asked, looking around. She was no longer in the Royal Gardens. Instead, she was lying on a firm bed in the fluorescent-lit room of the infirmary. She tried to get up and groaned; her head was pounding.

"You just lie there. You've had quite a spill," Dr. St. John said, walking up on her other side. He flashed a light in her eyes, and she blinked.

"I don't think you have a concussion, mostly thanks to your accelerated healing, but I'm afraid that your arm, being non-critical is still mending."

"Arm?" she looked down, her arm was wrapped tight, and a dull throbbing ache radiated from her wrist. "What happened?" she asked.

"That is what I would like to know," Declan growled. "When I came back, you were at the bottom of the stairs looking broken." He took a deep ragged breath. "I never want to see that again."

She looked beyond Declan to see Avery pale, trembling, and crying softly. "Hey," she whispered.

That was all it took. Avery began to sob hysterically. She could only understand about every third or fourth word.

Kari met Warrick's eyes, and for the first time, they had an understanding. They both cared for Avery and wanted him to be happy. She gave him a sour look and then nodded. He very gently wrapped an arm around Avery and scooped him up and into his arms.

"Come on, sweetheart, it looks like Declan can take care of Kari."

Avery shook his head back and forth. " I want to stay with her," Avery cried. "She needs me."

Warrick cradled Avery's head to his chest. "She will be okay, love. Declan brought a snack for Kari. We will see her after lunch."

"Avery, I heard Warrick brought lunch for you. Go enjoy it so you can tell me about it later."

Avery sniffled and wiped his nose on his sleeve. "Are you sure?"

"Yes, I am fine. I'm feeling better already."

Avery wiggled until Warrick put him down. He walked over and kissed her forehead. "You can't leave me. No one can ever leave me again." His tears dripped onto her cheek, and she felt her own eyes began to fill.

"No matter what, you will always have me," Kari promised.

Avery took one deep breath and kissed her forehead again. "I'll hold you to that." Warrick took his hand and they left.

"All right, Warrick is not so bad," Kari admitted begrudgingly.

"He does care, and he is very gentle with him. I

told you he was in good hands," Declan insisted.

She looked over at the healer. "Doc, is my arm broken?"

"Yes, in two places. I wrapped it tight, though; if you feed, you should be healed in an hour."

Declan began to purr in his chair. The Doc rolled his eyes and looked at Declan. "You're cleared for extracurricular activity." He turned to Kari. "You, however need to take it easy. No extracurricular activity for you. The back of your skull was crushed. It was so soft, I was afraid your brains were going to leak out. So, just to be clear, don't let him pound you into the mattress."

Kari smirked. "So just not on my back then."

The doctor threw his hands up in the air. "Fine! Fuck your brains out, literally. Don't come crying to me when you're dead." He crossed the room and opened the door. He was about to shut it behind him when he looked over his shoulder and winked.

"He is an odd little man." Declan looked over to her and sighed. "So still no extracurricular activity."

She shook her head. "No, he just said you could not fuck me on my back where my head could be bounced around on the mattress."

Declan tapped her nose. "Behave. I am not having sex with you for the first time in infirmary bed while you have a broken arm and cracked skull." He took out a knife and began peeling an apple.

Kari's mouth began to water as she sniffed the air. "Is that what you went to get? I have never smelled anything like it."

He smiled and kept peeling. "It's a hybrid apple." He began to turn the apple in his hand slowly. It was dark red which faded to a light pink and then into a golden yellow and finally into a bright green.

Declan ate the peel; his eyes closed as he hummed his satisfaction. "It's called Forbidden Fruit. Some say it's the world's first apple."

Unlike every other apple she had ever peeled for herself, instead of cutting from top to bottom he cut it around the apple making a ring. He ate the first ring, almost testing it to make sure it was good before he peeled another ring and then handed it to her. She looked at it and took a bite. "Oh my gods! It is so juicy and sweet!"

He nodded "Take another bite," he encouraged.

She took another bite. This time there was a hint of sweet before a crisp tart flavor exploded across her taste buds. "It is sour, just like a Granny Smith. This has to be the most perfect apple I have ever tasted.

He chewed then swallowed. "I can't get enough of them and the pies! Gods, the pies you make with them," he sighed happily. "There's a vendor on Level Six that knows she can get me to promise just about anything for a few pies."

Kari stared at him. "Anything?" she asked.

Declan paused popping another piece of apple in his mouth "Well, almost anything," he winked cheekily at her.

She smiled and leaned back against the pillows. Together, they ate the apples he had collected. There was silence between them, but it wasn't awkward, and she didn't feel like she had to speak to fill it.

He lazily cut and peeled apple after apple for her, as if doing so made him the happiest man in the world. As they ate together, they shared hundreds of glances and brief touches. It had to be one of the most comfortable yet intimate afternoons she'd ever spent.

"Declan, thank you," she said quietly.

"You're welcome. Know that I am sharing these apples with you because you're my mate," he joked, eating another ring.

"No, thank you for being my mate. For worrying about me and spending your afternoon with me just so I would not be alone."

A frown creased his forehead. "How long were you on your own?" he asked.

"Over one hundred years, until I found Avery ten years ago."

"I thought you said you had an adopted brother."

"I do. He checks in on me from time to time. He did not like that I was all alone, but I was stubborn." She felt her eyelids get heavier.

He set the knife and apples aside. "I'll let you get some rest," he stood.

"Do not go," she said, practically pleading. "Stay with me and keep the nightmares away."

He froze before immediately moving toward the bed. He walked around to the other side of the bed and lifted the covers. He got in carefully, taking care not to hurt her arm, and spooned their bodies together. "You would heal if you fed," he offered in a husky voice.

She hesitated. "Feedings can be very sexual when it is right from the source. Given the way I feel about you—" she turned slowly, wincing a bit at the pain in her arm. She looked up at him "Are you sure?"

"You need blood, and I've got plenty. I'm a big boy, my love; I can handle you," he assured her.

She licked her lips, and he swallowed hard. "You

are a very big boy."

He preened at her words before his look became serious. "Kari, it is my right and my duty to provide for you; I offer all of myself to you."

She inhaled sharply. She had never expected to hear those words. In truth, she had never thought she would ever find a mate. "I am so thankful to Fate. I do not know what I have done to deserve such an honorable and kind man like you, but I will always be thankful for Her gift."

She heard his breath catch. "You're wrong, my love; it is I who does not deserve you. I can only pray I live up to whatever expectation Fate may have of me to have been paired with you for eternity."

She tried to pull herself up to reach his neck. When he saw her struggling, he simply scooted down. She licked his neck, and his body shuddered. Moving swiftly, she bit down at the same time she shoved her uninjured hand down the front of his pants. She felt blood fill his cock, hardening it under her touch. He shouted out her name, and she rubbed her thumb over the sensitive head. He blew like a geyser, and for a moment, Kari regretted that she wasn't able to taste it, but his blood was more than enough to satisfy her. His blood on her tongue was even better than chocolate covered cherries with coffee.

The potency of it tantalized her senses like a fine, aged liquor. She drank until she felt her bones begin to mend, and then regretfully, she pulled from his neck. She licked the holes and then sat back. Declan's eyes were wild and his breathing erratic. "What did you just do to me?" he asked.

She looked at him confused, but then realized her other hand was still down his pants. The entire front of his groin was covered in that sticky substance she had enjoyed earlier. "Have you been coming this whole time?" she asked bringing up her fingers to lick them clean. She sighed happily, it tasted better than she remembered.

He swallowed hard; his lips were dry from where he'd been breathing through his mouth. "Yeah," he said, his voice hoarse.

Fighting back a giggle at his befuddled expression, she rolled on to her back and pointed across the room. "You should go wash up," she suggested smiling.

He shook his head. "I can't move, don't want to move, want to stay here forever," he panted.

"Well, at least get your pants off. When that dries, you will be one big itch."

Groaning, he swung his legs over the bed. When he started to stand, his legs didn't support him, and he fell to the floor.

"Are you okay?" she asked, laughing. Before she could get up to help, he was already pulling himself up.

"Don't you dare move out of that bed," he threatened. "Doc said you were to stay there until lunch."

"I fed. Look." She undid the sling and flexed her arm.

"Wonderful, now stay in that bed." On shaky legs he went into the attached bathroom, and she heard the water run for a few moments. A minute later he came out and gave her a flat look.

"What?"

"I've never had a mess like that before."

"You are welcome," she said and then yawned. Declan smiled and climbed back into bed with her.

He dug out his phone from his pocket set an alarm.

"You must like naps," Kari said, closing her eyes. "This is your second one in two days."

He grunted. "We've had an eventful two days," he protested. He pulled her close, his nose rubbing the back of her neck. Smiling, she knew she wouldn't be awake much longer when he started to purr. She could see why Meryn liked having Declan to sleep with; he was better than any chamomile tea.

☾

WHEN THE ALARM WENT OFF, they smiled at each other as they got ready for lunch. She washed her face and made sure her hair wasn't sticking up in every direction. They left the laboratory infirmary and headed to Magnus' living quarters.

"Are you sure it is okay for us to eat lunch here? I mean, I know that he is my boss, but I thought only royals were supposed to be on Level One."

"Well, there's a lot going on right now, so he's been meeting with Adriel, Aiden, and Bethy. I think he'd want you there to help with planning, which means I get invited since I'm your mate." He looked down at her with a boyish grin.

"You seem particularly happy about that. You also seem to be forgetting you have accepted an advisory role, so they may want you there too."

"Have you tasted Sebastian's cooking? I think I've eaten better in the past two days than I have in probably the past six years."

They walked in, and Magnus jumped up out of his

chair. "Thank the gods you are well! When I heard what happened, I feared the worst."

Kari held up her hand. "I am doing much better. Declan allowed me to feed." Magnus nodded his understanding and kissed her cheek. "Please sit. We were just going over what we have lined up for the rest of today."

She watched as Rex looked over at his brother. Seeing Declan's goofy smile, he began to visibly relax.

Magnus opened up his portfolio and looked down his at his legal pad. "Kari has lined up a few interviews later for Declan. I have been called into a meeting with the full council, and I have asked Aiden to join me." He paused and looked up. "Kari, I think it would be a good idea if you were to sit in on the interviews with Declan."

Beth nodded. "That is a wonderful idea, Uncle."

"Why?" Declan asked.

"It might make some of the women more comfortable to speak if another woman is in the room," Magnus explained. "Plus, it will fulfill a sense of propriety about them being alone in a closed room with a man. Some were reluctant to leave their mates with Micah in the room, but were comfortable with the idea of a mated pair asking the questions."

Declan snorted. "That's archaic. Are they afraid Micah being in the same room would besmirch their mate's honor?"

Adriel shrugged. "That is the world we live in right now, the one we are trying to change."

Aiden turned to Magnus. "What can I expect from the council?"

"There is me as the vampire Elder of course,"

Magnus began. “Then we have Rex here as shifter Elder. Dagda Vi’Ilsimir is our fae Elder, and Alastair Primrose is the witch Elder. Dagda is a good man; we get along. He has a mate and a young child. His eldest, and the reason why the council moved to the city, is training to be a warrior in Éire Danu. I know Dagda expects great things of him.”

Aiden nodded. “I’ve heard of them both. I know that they’ve worked with my father on many occasions.”

Magnus flipped a page and was about to begin speaking again when the door flew open, and a tall, lanky man with dark brown hair and wild expression entered the room. His hazel eyes zeroed in on Bethy. “You’re pregnant!” he screeched.

Her face lit up, and she jumped up out of her chair. “Tarragon!” She raced around the table, and just as she was about to reach him, her foot caught one of the chair’s legs, and she lurched forward. Both Tarragon and Kuruk caught her before she hit the floor. Tarragon began to shake uncontrollably. “You’re pregnant! What are we going to do?” he howled in despair.

Tarak walked up behind him to help prop him up. “It will be okay. We can get through this,” he said encouragingly.

Bethy wrapped her arms around the twitchy man’s neck and hugged him close. “It’s so good to have you home, Tarragon.”

He returned her hug, a gentle smile on his face. He pulled back and looked her in the eyes. “You’re well?” He looked over her, confused. “You’re not in the process of healing, there’s no bruising?” Perplexed, he looked around.

Gavriel cleared his throat, and all eyes went to him. He waved at Tarragon.

Tarragon's face cleared. "Ah, yes. You're mated now, I remember. He looks like the kinda chap that can keep you from harm. Maybe this won't be so bad. I've learned a lot more healing spells, but if I had known you were pregnant..." his voice trailed off.

Tarak chuckled. "We would have never seen you again. You would have been holed up in some dusty library in Storm Keep, looking up spells for infants."

Tarragon paled. "We need a NICU."

"And why would we need a neonatal intensive care unit?" Bethy asked.

Tarragon just gave her a look as if to say 'why wouldn't we need one with your child?'

Magnus waved a hand at him. "Arrange for whatever you need or whatever you think you may need or whatever you think you could ever possibly need for any and every worst-case scenario you can imagine," Magnus ordered. Tarragon looked relieved.

"You can add the NICU to my laboratory. Evidently, it's becoming this city's infirmary," Broderick said sourly.

Magnus winced. "We have never really needed an infirmary before. The only person who ever got hurt was Bethy."

"Maybe we should have one," Bethy suggested. "I mean we have shifter children here now; I'm sure they will get into tumbles. Plus, you never know what may happen. Declan and Kari both needed the facilities recently, and Dr. St. John has expressed an interest in maintaining an infirmary here."

Tarragon swayed looking ill. "What if her child is

like her? What if we have to do it all over again?" he asked. Kuruk paled and started shaking his head. He looked over at his brother. Tarak wrapped an arm around Tarragon and steered him out of the room. "Let us go enjoy a celebratory drink," he suggested.

Tarragon's eyes were still unfocused. "Yes, right, celebrate. A drink would be lovely, thank you." He was still trembling and shaky as the door shut behind them. Kuruk, with one hand on Bethy's shoulder, steered her toward her chair.

Magnus continued as if the poor healer hadn't just had a nervous breakdown. "Next, I have a surprise for Meryn."

"A surprise?" Meryn asked, perking up.

"Yes, I heard you refer to something, and I realized I do not think we have one here. I believe you, Nigel, and Neil were talking about an Xbox." He grinned.

"You didn't?" she whispered.

Magnus nodded enthusiastically, and Sebastian came into the room with a wheeled cart. Stacked high were three unopened Xboxes. Meryn squealed and launched out of her chair. She ran over to Magnus and began peppering his face with kisses. He began to blush furiously and tried to fend off her affection. But to anyone watching, it didn't look as if he were trying very hard.

"Thank you! Thank you! Thank you!" She raced to the cart and began looking over the boxes. "We can play online now, and you got us headsets and extra controllers. We can kill zombies all we want!"

Magnus chuckled. "I am glad that you are feeling better Meryn."

Declan saw her eyeing the Xboxes and raised

an eyebrow, she shrugged. They'd find out soon enough.

"Are you feeling better?" Bethy asked Meryn.

Meryn stayed facing the games. "I'm okay. But, like, your city sucks."

"Meryn!" Bethy exclaimed.

"It does. I thought it would be all *Lord Of The Rings*, but it's more like *Resident Evil*.

"*Resident Evil*?" Aiden asked.

Meryn pushed the cart so it was behind her chair and sat down. Smiling, she patted the boxes. "Yeah, it has this evil corporation zombie feel where there are shadows, and the shadows want to eat me."

Kari stilled; that was the feeling she'd had before she had gotten dizzy. As if something watched her from the dark.

Kari watched as Ryuu moved quickly. One moment he was in the corner, the next kneeling beside his charge. "Why do you describe it like that?" He watched her face intently.

"I don't know," she admitted. "But the dark never bothered me before coming here."

He stood, looking first at Kuruk and then Sebastian, both men nodded. Ryuu looked down at Meryn. "If you would excuse me for a moment *denka*, I will be back momentarily." He quickly walked out of the dining room.

Meryn just stared at the door. "He left me," she muttered. She hopped down out of her chair and started to leave, but the door wouldn't budge. "He locked it!" She put her ear against the door and then spun to face the table, a look of disgust on her face. "And soundproofed it."

Aiden shrugged. "It's like he knows you or something," he said, his lips twitching.

Magnus, Adriel, and Declan all exchanged looks. Kari could understand exactly how they felt. What could possibly chase a squire as powerful as Ryuu out of the room?

After a couple minutes, Ryuu walked back into the room and took up his usual position behind Meryn without saying a word. Meryn got up on her knees and turned in her chair to face her squire. "Well?" she demanded.

"Well what?" he asked civilly.

"You know what I'm talking about. Why did you leave?"

"I just had to contact someone; it is nothing *denka*."

"Don't tell me it's nothing. You locked the door and soundproofed the room."

"And how would you know that?" he asked, raising an eyebrow.

"Fine!" Meryn sat back down in her chair. "But you have diaper duty for forever," she threatened.

He smiled softly. "Of course, *denka*." He bowed at the waist, his hand over his heart.

"Speaking of babies..." Aiden glared at Meryn. "Did you ever get Sascha out of jail?"

"Yeah, it was easy peezy. I updated their system; so he was released yesterday." She smirked. "But that wasn't before Colton got me a copy of his mug shot."

Aiden groaned. "Of course he did. I swear we won't have any units when we get back. They are going to kill each other."

"Consider it training." Meryn looked back at Ryuu. "Can I have some more pudding?"

Magnus put his fork down. "Meryn, normally, I would give you anything you wanted, but I am really concerned about your dietary habits. Eating pudding for a week cannot be healthy. Do you not need vitamins, vegetables, meat, anything else?"

Meryn shrugged. "Nothing else tastes good."

Ryuu placed a bowl of pudding in front of her with two pills. "At least take these. They are the vitamins that Broderick has created. They contain everything that a shifter or human could need." Meryn quickly swallowed down the pills and picked up her spoon.

Magnus sighed, watching Meryn, a concerned look on his face. Shaking his head, he turned to Declan. "To entice more of the women and some of the men to attend the interviews, I have arranged a chamber here on Level One. I know my people; most of them would accept doing the interview if only to say they had been to Level One."

"I am sure that will help enormously, thank you." Kari smiled at Magnus.

"I just hope that everyone you speak with today is mated of their own accord."

"Me too," she murmured.

Declan bumped her shoulder with his. "It will be fine."

I hope he didn't just jinx us.

CHAPTER TEN

KARI, FOR THE MOST PART, stayed in the background. She took a seat off to the left behind Declan and allowed him to do the talking. He knew most of the women, and he gently coaxed answers out of them. When he smiled, Kari could see the result in the women. They relaxed, took deep breaths, and answered his questions without hesitation. Kari was willing to say at least seventy percent of the interviewees were mated as true mates, but the remaining thirty percent had been arranged matings, and that bothered her.

One by one, the vampires admitted that they had mated to the men in their lives because of what their families and their mate's families had arranged. It had been a way to bring families together to form alliances and to keep their bloodlines pure. Kari made notes of all those that had admitted to arranged matings, and as she suspected, most of them had taken place on the levels that were obviously gearing up against Magnus.

They were on their last interview of the day when the hairs on the back of Kari's neck stood up. The woman who entered looked at Declan as if she already knew what his body was capable of.

"Hello, lover," the woman purred. "I would say you wanted an afternoon tryst, but we have an audience, or are you into that now?" she asked.

Kari simply began to tap her pen against the clipboard in front of her. She saw Declan wince at the sound.

"No Trish, that's not why you were called down here, you should know that. Magnus is interested in knowing who had matings arranged by their families."

Trish shrugged. "Mine was an arranged mating. I was not going to waste my time sitting around waiting for Prince Charming, and my family needed an alliance. The DuBois are doing fairly well, so I agreed. If I ever do meet my mate, I can always move on," she said flippantly.

Kari stared at this woman oozing apathy and immediately felt sorry for any future mate she would have.

Trish looked at Declan. "I have missed our nights together. Even if I am mated, you know I would not say no if you came knocking."

Declan fidgeted in his chair and cleared his throat. "Yes well, you are mated now and so am I. Even if I weren't, you know I don't mess around with mates."

"Too bad, my mate is not half as good as you are in bed."

Kari took a deep breath as the pen she had been writing with snapped when she clenched her hands. She watched as Declan's hand gripped his chair arm in response to the sound. "Well, that is all we needed to know. Thanks Trish."

Trish leaned forward as if to plant a kiss on Declan's lips. Before Kari realized what she was doing, she was standing beside her mate. She placed her clipboard in front of his face. Trish stood and met Kari's eyes. She smirked. "I do not mind having my leftovers being used by someone less fortunate."

Kari literally felt her blood pressure spike. Just as she was about to reach for Trish, Declan grabbed her around the waist to hold her back. Trish waved and shut the door behind her.

"That bitch!" she hissed.

Declan grimaced, releasing her. "Now Kari."

She spun to face her mate. "You knew who she was when she was scheduled for the interview. You saw her name on the list, and you did not prepare me?"

Declan scratched the side of his head. "I didn't think it would be that big a deal."

"You did not think it would be that big a deal?" she repeated.

Declan just stared at her. "I mean, I knew it was going to be a big deal," he backpedaled at her tone. "But I didn't know how to tell you," he rephrased his sentence.

Kari crossed her arms over her chest and tapped her foot. "How many women on this list have you slept with?"

Declan gulped. "I didn't sleep with any of them after they mated."

"How many of them have you slept with Declan?"

"Thirteen."

"Thirteen! Declan that is almost half of today's list!"

He winced. "I've been here a long time."

She took a deep breath. "You know it is not the fact that you slept with them. It was the fact that we would be doing interviews with them, and you never told me this could happen. She completely disrespected me. The entire city knows I am your mate, and because I was not prepared, she got away with treating me like a second-class citizen. I cannot afford for her to set this kind of precedent. What sort of message do you think that sends?"

"I'm sorry, Kari, I really am. I just didn't think of it that way," he admitted.

"No, you did not, and because of that, you are sleeping on the couch. No claiming sex for you."

His mouth dropped open, and he stared at her in shock. He looked so ridiculous she almost forgave him. When he started to say something, she bopped him on the head with her clipboard. "Couch, Declan." She sat down and made it look as though she was looking over her notes when, in fact, she was just trying to get her temper under control and not laugh at his desperate expression.

Declan dropped to his knees in front of her. "Kari, please! I never meant to hurt you. I guess I didn't think things all the way through. Please don't deny me as your mate." Declan begged.

She was trying to figure out what he was talking about when the door flew open. Nigel skidded to a halt in front of them. "Declan, why do you have your walkie-talkie off? We've been trying to reach you. You have got to get to Level Six. Warrick's family has gone bonkers. I think they're going after Avery!"

Kari was moving before she realized her legs were running. She raced toward the transport tunnel. She flew up the tunnel to Level Six, leaving Nigel to escort Declan behind her. She pushed her way through the crowd. Warrick was facing off against another man.

"Andre, you do not want to do this," Warrick said.

"No, I do not have to, but I am enjoying it. Father gave me a message. He said to tell you that you have been disowned. We do not want your kind in our family."

"Kind?" Warrick asked.

"Of course. Not only did you mate a shifter, but you mated a male one. You are not able to pass on the DuBois gift to another generation. You have polluted our pure bloodline."

Kari saw that Avery was shaking behind Warrick. He was clutching the back of his mate's shirt.

She stepped forward, growling low in her throat. "What is going on here," she demanded.

Andre turned, a smile on his face until he saw her expression. He looked at his cousin who stood almost seven feet tall and then to her, and he took a step back. "Nothing that concerns you, female. I hear you have whored yourself out to Prince Magnus for your quick promotion. No wonder my father is upset that my cousin mated the likes of your mongrel brother."

Kari inhaled at his words. But before she could reach out to choke the life out of him, Declan moved. He was a blur at her side before he raked his claws down Andre's chest. The vampire howled and clutched at the wound. Kari stepped around them to reach Avery. Warrick moved so that they were both behind him. Avery wrapped himself around her as they watched the scene before them.

"I will have you detained warrior! This is assault!" Andre cried.

Declan looked at him in disgust. "Quit whining, you useless sack of shit. The scratches are already healing. You're lucky I didn't return the favor your father paid me. You would be laid up in the infirmary."

Nigel walked over and took his place in front of her. Neil was next to him in front of Avery, creating another barrier between them and the threat. "Yeah! You're lucky!" Nigel yelled. "Yeah!" Neil echoed. Both men stood slightly behind Warrick glowering at the vampire.

Andre hissed up at Warrick. "You are forbidden to return to our level and may no longer interact with anyone in the family. You are completely cut off."

Warrick straightened his back. "I feel your father has done me a great service. I want nothing more to do with you."

Andre eyed Kari and Avery with an evil glint in his eye. "If the shifter has an accident and dies, you can come home." Andre licked his lips. "Or I am sure we could find a different use for him."

Kari blinked and almost missed it. Warrick stepped forward as he swung his right arm back. On the second step, he landed an uppercut that sent Andre flying. Kari realized that when one is almost seven feet tall an uppercut can go very, very high. Andre flew off of his feet and into the air. When he landed, everyone heard something snap. Nobody moved; they were shocked by Warrick's red eyes and his long black claws. "You go near my mate and I will rip you apart!" Warrick growled. When he received no response, Nigel edged around the crowd over to Andre and nudged him with the toe of his shoe. He looked up. "He may or may not be dead.

I'm not quite sure. I don't want to get close enough to look." Declan walked forward, reached down and grabbed Andre's shirt, and pulled him up. "He's still breathing." He dropped him back onto the floor.

Warrick sniffed. "Too bad."

Declan eyed his friend. "You do not want to kill your cousin, Warrick. You don't want to give Avery the grief of losing his mate. It wouldn't have been in self-defense."

"Who is to say it was not self-defense?" Old man Richter called out from the crowd. Mumblings of agreement sounded off all around them. Declan pinched the bridge of his nose. Kari felt tears gather. The people around her were supporting her and her brother. Kari ran a hand over his hair, trying to ease his shaking. "It is okay, baby boy, I am pretty sure that no one would be stupid enough to face your mate to get to you."

Warrick turned at her words, his eyes fading back to his normal color. He raced forward and dropped to his knees, and very gently, he pulled Avery away from Kari.

When Avery looked down at him, they were almost the same height. Warrick took both of his hands and kissed them. "I swear to you, I swear I will not let anyone hurt you." Avery just nodded. He lifted their hands up and began rubbing his cheek across Warrick's knuckles. Warrick looked at Kari as if asking permission. She rolled her eyes and nodded.

Warrick stood, scooping Avery up into his arms. Only then did Avery's trembles begin to dissipate.

"What in the hell have you guys done now?" Doc asked, hurrying over.

Declan looked around confused. Then, out of the corner of his eye, he saw a camera. He reached to his belt and grabbed his walkie-talkie. "Menace, did you send Doc?"

"Sure did, Simba," Meryn's voice came back.

"Thanks." He knelt beside Dr. St. John who began evaluating Andre's injuries. "I think he got his brain rattled a bit."

"What did you do hit him with, a steel bat?" The healer asked.

Declan jerked his thumb toward Warrick. "No, he punched him."

Dr. St. John looked all the way up, taking in Warrick's height. He turned to Declan. "Next time, you hit him with the bat; it might do less damage. Is this the DuBois boy?" he asked.

"Yep," Declan said grinning.

"Great. Just great." Dr. St. John looked around and stood. "You and you"—he pointed to Etain and Micah—"get this blockhead to the holding cells."

"Holding cell? Not the infirmary?" Declan asked also standing.

The healer shook his head. "I think he will be better off next to his father; he isn't dying or anything."

Declan grinned openly as Etain grabbed the back of Andre's collar, and Micah grabbed his pant legs. "Thank you for coming."

They nodded. "It's not like you needed us," Micah grinned. Together, they floated Andre from Level Six to Level One.

Doc waved. "You know the saying, 'When it rains, it pours.' They weren't kidding. I have gone years without returning to Noctem Falls, yet here I am on my third call this week." Shaking his head, he also walked over and jumped down the tunnel.

Declan headed over to Kari and took her hand. She appreciated the gesture. She felt like her emotions were racing out of control.

"Come on," he said, pulling her hand.

Kari hesitated, looking over at Avery. "You okay?" she asked.

He nodded blushing. "Warrick takes care of me."

"He better." She gave Warrick the evil eye. He nodded at her.

"You know"—Declan wrapped himself around her—"it's like I have my own personal tunnel escort."

"Do not get used to it. You know I will be busy with Magnus."

"How about you and I play hooky? The interviews are done, and we finished earlier than we thought. I could show you your new home."

"Really?"

"Of course, it is your home too."

They stepped into the tunnel and landed on the Unit Level. When they reached his house, he opened the panel on the back of the mailbox and punched in a code. "Give me your hand." He placed it on the biometric sensor and added her profile. "Now you can get in anytime you want."

They walked in. At first, she was a bit confused. The only thing she had seen of his house the night before was the foyer. She looked around, expecting something medieval given that it was a castle, but it wasn't like that at all. It looked warm and kind of rustic, almost like a cabin instead of the castle. Declan had decorated using log furniture, thick rugs, and dark colors.

"You could show me the bedroom," she suggested.

"Yeah?" he asked, his face brightening. "Does that mean I don't have to sleep on the couch and you won't deny our mating?"

She frowned. "You probably were not going to end up on the couch anyway; you were acting too adorable to stay mad at. But where on earth did you get the idea I would deny our mating?"

"You said 'no claiming'."

"Oh, Declan, I just meant that we would not be having sex because I was mad at you at the time. There is no way we can claim each other without sex."

"So bedroom?" asked his, eyes darkening to a dark honey color.

"Yes, but I am letting you know right now. I am not sleeping in that bed with you if you slept with any other woman there."

He shook his head quickly. "No, no one."

"I find that hard to believe, you did say you have been here a long time."

He shrugged. "It's the bro code."

"The what?"

"It's the pact all of us made. If a fellow unit warrior finds his mate, the first thing the unit does is to arrange for a new mattress. So I knew I didn't have to worry about it and could concentrate on you."

"Who did that for you?" she asked.

"Grant."

"So in the midst of everything happening, he arranged for a mattress to be delivered to the city estate and had set it up for you?"

"I'll do the same for him someday."

"He has access to your house?"

"All the guys from the Eta Unit do. Now, you and Avery."

"I seem to be getting access all over the place."

Declan looked at her. "What do you mean?"

"Magnus gave me access to Level One, including the infirmary, the gardens, the communications hub, the lab, his quarters, the guest quarters, and the Council quarters."

Declan whistled. "Look at my mate being all important."

"He is probably going to add you to all that as well considering that your brother will be staying here a little bit longer, and you have accepted an advisory role."

"He's only here for the trial," Declan countered.

"Whatever you say." Kari knew better than argue. Declan was too stubborn when it came to his older brother.

She looked over at the bed; it was huge. She walked closer and looked at the frame. "Did you do this?"

Declan nodded. "It took me about a decade."

"Declan, this is all hand carved."

He shrugged blushing. "It was something to do."

She walked over to the bed, taking in every detail. "How big was the tree that this came from?" she asked. She couldn't find any fittings. The pieces were not joined together; there were no screws, nails, or glue. The entire bed frame was one solid piece. "Declan, this is beautiful," she whispered. This kind of attention to detail and loving care spoke volumes about his character.

"Thanks, it's a hobby."

She shook her head and stood. "No, Declan, this is art. It is so beautiful, I am afraid to touch it."

"I wanted something special for my mate."

"And yet you brought other women here?"

He shrugged. "I never had sex with them in the bed," he stopped and looked up at the ceiling as if counting. "No not in the bed. Against the bed, one under the bed, one on the nightstand, in the closet, on the bathroom floor, in front of the fireplace..."

"Okay, I get the picture. If this is a custom made bed, where did Grant get the mattress?"

"After the bed was made I had a few extra made and put in storage. Every ten to fifteen years I replace them."

"How old is this one?"

His face became serious. "A couple months old."

"Good timing," she joked, but then stopped. The look on his face bordered on tragic. "What is it?"

"Did you dream before you came here?"

Kari looked at him. "What do you mean?"

"I had dreams before you got here. I could almost see a woman's face. She's screaming for me behind a locked door. I watch her burn to death through a small window."

"There is a fire?" She inhaled sharply, nodding. "I have had that dream. I thought it was just a night-mare. Are you the one I am calling out for?" He nodded. She went to him and wrapped her arms around his waist. "In my dreams, I knew that if whoever was on the other side of the door could just get to me, I would be okay. I just wanted to touch him one more time; that I would give anything to touch him one last time." Her voice broke, and he cupped her face with his large, warm hands.

He leaned down and kissed her gently. "You have me now."

When she opened her eyes and looked into his, they had shifted to a molten honey color. "Kari Delaney, would you allow me to mate with you?" he asked.

"Of course, you impossible man." And she meant it. There was no other path for her; there was no other man who could give her the sense of home and solace that she had been looking for most of her life. She knew she would crave Declan for the rest of eternity. Not even death could absolve her of this addiction. And she wasn't going to torture either of them by denying him a second longer.

She stepped back and pulled her sweater up over her head. She reached for her waist and unzipped her skirt's long zipper. Letting it pool at her feet, she stood in front of him in just her stockings, panties and bra.

He swallowed hard, looking at her. The emotion in his eyes made her feel bold and loved. It didn't take him two seconds to rip his clothes away.

"You might have wanted those pants later, now look at them," she teased.

He growled low in his throat, stalking forward. She thought he would pounce like his lion, but he didn't. He very gently picked her up and set her on the bed. He joined her there and looked down. Starting with her foot, he rubbed his cheek against her inner leg. He smiled. "Your stockings are silk," he stated.

"What?" she asked distracted by the feel of his warm hands on her legs.

"Silk. Your stockings are silk."

"Yes," she said closing her eyes.

Gently, he reached up to her upper thigh and

began to roll them down her leg. He left the garters in place but removed her panties. He ignored the juncture of her thighs and turned his attention back to her legs again. His stubbled cheek scratched and teased her. Now that the stockings were gone, she could feel his touch that much more. He made his way up one thigh, and just as she felt his breath on her mound, he switched legs and began rubbing his scent on her again.

He worshiped every inch of her legs. By the time he settled between her upper thighs and grasped her hips, she was a trembling mess.

"Please," she begged, wanting more.

"We haven't even gotten to the good part yet," he teased, gently reaching between her legs to spread her wide. He grinned and then bent his head. A second later, an orgasm took her by surprise as it ripped through her. His tongue felt like a thousand rough bristles. It bordered on painful but not enough to tell him to stop. Every time he caressed her, she jerked and moaned. He kept her on edge between one orgasm and the next. He flattened his tongue and licked her from her opening all the way to her clit. Over and over again, like a kitten with cream, he licked, nipped, and buried his tongue deep inside her.

When his coarse tongue stroked the inside of her channel, she came unglued. Never before had she experienced something like this. She buried her hands in his hair and tried to pull him closer. His hands came up under her ass and gripped each cheek. He went wild, alternating between gentle and primitive. When she finally didn't think she could handle anymore, he plunged two thick fingers deep inside her. The speed and the unexpectedness of the action drove her over the edge. She screamed again. He leaned up, licking his lips. "Are you ready, my love?" he asked.

"I think you have killed me," she replied, breathing heavily. He chuckled—the masculine sound of a lover who knew he had satisfied his partner beyond measure. "I do not know why you look so satisfied. I am the one who is perfectly sated." She reached out both arms. "Come to me," she said simply.

He reached down between them and guided the thick head of his cock deep inside her. After the wild abandon he'd shown her before, this was surprisingly gentle and tender. He took his time and seemed to be in no rush. His eyes never left hers, staying locked as he plunged deep and pulled out slowly. Gently, inch by inch, he penetrated her only to withdraw and slam back. He was taking his time and learning her body, what she liked, what she didn't.

He leaned forward, and she wrapped her arms around his neck. She wanted as much skin touching as possible as he slowly built the fire again. The longer they made love, the larger the head of his cock seemed to get. He stretched her, filled her, and rubbed over that one elusive spot that seemed to drive her crazy.

"Close," she whispered. She thought he would pick up the pace and send her out of control but he didn't. He continued a slow and steady grind, keeping her orgasm just out of reach. She pulled his body close, her fingers digging deep into his back. "Please," she begged. He stopped and gently kissed her on the lips. When he plunged deep inside her, he exposed his throat. She struck, sinking her fangs deep into his throat. Her feeding broke his control, and he snapped his hips repeatedly, driving her into the mattress. She was as deep inside him as she could get, and he was as deep inside her as he could get. He yelled out her name in a hoarse voice over her head, and she felt as if her body simply exploded.

No one could experience that much pleasure and live. Every drop of sweat merged them together, every drop of blood fused their hearts, and every wave of pleasure mixed and mingled their souls together. The core of their beings rose up out of their bodies like a mist. There was no Kari without a piece of Declan, and there was no Declan without a piece of Kari. There was now a new Kari and Declan. The new soul divided in half and returned to their bodies. When she licked the holes on his neck closed, he slumped to one side.

She never knew mating could be like this. She was no longer just Kari, she would never be just Kari again. She couldn't help it; she burst into tears.

Concerned, Declan immediately sat up in bed. "What did I do? Did I hurt you?"

She shook her head and covered her eyes with her hands. "No, it was perfect. I will never be alone again," she whispered.

"Of course not." He pulled her close. "Get some rest, we can lay here until dinner."

They dozed together for a couple hours before Kari woke and turned on her side. She ran a hand up and down his chest, from his collarbone to his abs, enjoying the freedom to touch him. "Can I bring up something without you getting angry?" She didn't want to spoil the afterglow of their mating.

He stirred and opened his eyes. "You can tell me anything. I doubt you could do anything to make me angry."

She snorted. "Do not make that bet."

He kissed the top of the head. "Go on," he urged.

"The thing is, growing up, I always wanted somewhere to call my own, with the furniture I had picked out, the kitchen set up the way I wanted, and the colors I liked. When my business was finally doing well and I had enough money, I bought my condo. It was this old brick building in the first town where I truly felt welcomed and where I met my adopted brother. It sort of became home for me. I visited and lived in other cities, but I always seemed to end up back there. So when it came time to settle my business, that's where I wanted to stay. It is just this small town, in the middle of nowhere, but it is home. I do not know how I can give that up."

"Do you want to move there?" he asked.

She sat up. "You would do that for me?"

"You're my mate; I would do anything for you. But you must have realized by now that you're needed here."

"So are you."

"Your happiness will always come first. Besides, Warrick just got disowned so I could see them living with us in your super condo."

She laughed then stopped. "Is he going to be okay?"

"Look who is now worried about Warrick?" he teased.

"He is just so...so..." she couldn't find the right word.

"Gentle?" he prompted.

"Yes. He is gentle. I feel like I have to take care of him." She gasped. "Oh gods, how can a man that size be my little brother?"

Declan laughed. "I know how you feel. Warrick is as old as most of us. But despite his size, a lot of guys find themselves watching out for him. It's not that he's naïve or innocent. It's his gentleness that makes us want to shield him so he doesn't lose it." His face darkened. "We have never seen him lose control like he did today with Andre. I know a lot of warriors who are going to be pissed that Warrick was pushed that far."

"What are we going to do about my condo? Do you think Warrick would move to be with Avery?"

"I'm pretty sure Warrick would walk through fire to be with Avery. As for your condo, let me see what I can do. There's not much I wouldn't do for you either." He sighed. "It must be nice to have a sibling that worries so much about you."

Kari turned her head. "You are kidding, right? Rex adores you."

Declan winced. "It's just hard trying to walk in those shoes. He casts such a large shadow."

"Then why try? You have Declan shoes, and he has Rex shoes. The only thing that man wants is for you to be happy, so cut him some slack."

"Since when are you team Rex?"

"Because he also loves the man I love." She heard his quick inhale at her declaration.

"I love you too, Kari; you are my heart now." His arms tightened.

She looked over to the nightstand at the alarm clock. "It is almost time for dinner."

"We do have a bathroom to break-in," he wagged

his eyebrows at her.

"No way, Declan. I heard shower sex sucks."

"There are many ways to do many things. If you're lucky, I'll show you a few of them." He hopped out of bed and strutted toward the bathroom. He turned and winked at her. With an exaggerated swagger, he marched into the bathroom.

I am mated to an absolute idiot, she said to herself.

And I would not change a single thing about him.

CHAPTER ELEVEN

BY THE TIME KARI AND Declan joined the others for dinner, the meal had already been served. Everyone was smiles as they sat down.

Meryn whistled. "Nice bite marks, Declan." He grinned and gave her two thumbs up.

"Congratulations on your mating," Magnus said.

"Thank you." Kari blushed.

She'd never admit it of course, but there was something a little bit embarrassing about everyone knowing you had just had sex and claimed your mate.

She looked around the table "Where is Avery?"

Sebastian cleared his throat. "Young master Avery went with young masters Nigel and Neil to their quarters on the Unit Level." He looked over at Magnus, who nodded. "Young master Avery has been offered a room here on Level One in the guest quarters for as long as he may need it. Consider it a mating present. So you have the privacy that each mated couple needs."

Kari fought back a wave of disappointment. For all intents and purposes, this was a celebratory meal for her mating. She wished her brother could have been there, but it warmed her heart to know that he had made friends. It was a bit sad watching him drift a little bit farther away.

"We can see him later," Declan said, bumping her shoulder.

She looked up, "You are right. Of course, you are right."

"Yeah, it's not like you'll disappear or anything." Meryn said, glaring at Eva in an accusatory manner.

Eva rolled her eyes, "I've been helping on Level Six. They know me. Things have been going much smoother with Adriel and me present among the refugees. Stefan has been coordinating with us to make sure that everyone's needs have been taken care of."

"Whatever. I guess I'm just nobody," Meryn complained loudly. Eva just shook her head.

Bethy looked at Kari, "Is it true what I've heard? Warrick has been disowned?"

Kari nodded as Declan turned to the prince. "Andre said he had met with his father and that his father gave him instructions to disown Warrick for mating a shifter and a man."

Magnus frowned. "Homosexuality has never been an issue in Noctem Falls before."

Declan thought about it a moment before he replied. "I think it was a combination of being gay and mating a shifter that pushed them over the edge.
"

"Not that I am not grateful, but why was Avery given a room here on Level One? Surely, that is a little too grand for him?" Kari asked.

Rex cleared his throat. "Since he is my little brother now, I'd like him on the same level as the Council estate so that I don't have to have a tunnel escort to visit him."

Kari blinked of course she was now related to the elder. "Have the twins been escorting Avery around?"

Meryn shook her head, "No, they made him a stone like I have."

"A stone? No way!" Declan protested. "I've been begging for one since I found out what they had done."

"What stone?" Kari repeated.

Meryn fished around in her pocket and held up a small stone. "It's a pumice stone they put a spell in. I can control it with a few words, and it allows me to float up and down the transport tunnel; Avery has one now."

Meryn looked at Declan who was still pouting. "I will see if I can ask them to move you up on the list."

He turned to her, looking incredulous. "There's a list?" Meryn began to giggle.

"Speaking of trouble," Aiden began, "Is Sascha talking to Noah?"

"Yes, the big baby. Honestly, you'd think spending the night in a county jail was the worst thing he'd ever experienced."

"I'm glad that's over." Aiden exhaled.

"I wouldn't say it's over," Meryn hedged.

"What?" Aiden responded apprehensively.

"Colton made copies of his mug shot and had Jaxon Photoshop them onto a *Babe* movie poster. They made it look like a dating app profile picture." Meryn smirked.

Bethy pulled out small legal pad and looked around the table. "So we'll add finding Aiden a new second in command to the list of things to do. How was everyone else's day?"

Magnus and Adriel, and Kari reached down in their satchels or under the table to pull out their own pads. They flipped the pages and looked around to see who would begin.

Magnus was about to speak when Meryn interrupted. "Why don't you guys have iPads?"

They looked at each other blankly. "An iPad?" Adriel asked.

"Yes, an iPad, you know, take notes, organize things, take pictures, video recordings, lists, calendar reminders, basically all the geeky stuff that you love. An iPad will make it much easier for you to keep track of everything."

"But I like to hand write my notes," Adriel confessed.

"You are able to write notes on the new iPad."

Adriel's eyes grew large. Meryn smiled. "I'll order y'all the new iPads and get them set up for you."

Magnus and Adriel looked at each other excitedly. Kari sighed. She'd used an iPad before, but there was just something about writing on paper. It seemed that she remembered it longer if she did.

Magnus tapped his pen on the table. "How were the interviews?" he asked.

Declan leaned back. "Most of them are true matings. They are meek, but willing. Those that are in the arranged matings aren't being forced. They understand that they could have mates out there, but they're not willing to rock the boat with their families. I'd like to make a suggestion though; have the warriors escort them to Level Six just to make sure we don't have any hidden mates anywhere. We don't want to repeat of what happened with DuBois."

"That is for sure," Kari muttered.

"It is a good idea." Magnus jotted down a note.

Kari looked at Bethy and Adriel. "How was the field trip?"

"Wonderful," Beth replied. "A lot of children were worried about you of course, but it was nice seeing them laugh and play despite your fall." Kari winced.

"Sorry!" Bethy apologized quickly. "Not that I'm one to talk, I trip over nothing," Bethy said smiling.

"What happened?" Adriel asked Kari.

Kari shrugged. "I have no idea, one second I was fine, the next I was dizzy, and then I woke up in the infirmary."

Declan turned to Magnus. "Did the parents say anything? Have they noticed a change in the children?"

Magnus nodded. "More than one parent came up later and said that their child seemed to be improved. That they were smiling more, though they all seemed tired at the end of the day, but I am sure that is because they have had more exercise in those few hours than they have had in the past week."

Magnus turned to Adriel. "How are you and Bethy coming along organizing the fair?

Bethy flip the pages back in her notebook. "I have contacted all of the paranormal vendors we'll need. They'll be here tomorrow to start setting up stalls and games."

Adriel nodded. "I have been working with the food vendors on Level Six; they are more than prepared to make extra. I think they are excited to be earning a little bit more money. All of them however want Declan's opinion of what they should offer." Adriel shot his second in command a wry expression.

Declan chuckled. "They love me as a taste tester,"

he admitted.

Kari looked at Adriel and winced. "I am so sorry. I did say I would help you with this."

Adriel gave her a look. "You have been pretty busy lately, Kari. Not only are you adapting to a new job, but you have also found your mate. Moving alone must be stressful."

Kari snapped her fingers. "Speaking of moving. Does anyone know a freight company that works between cities and is aware of paranormals?"

Bethy nodded and turned in her chair to face Sebastian.

Sebastian stepped forward. "I can contact the company that we used to send Bethy's things to Lycaonia. They are very reliable. If you have a contact in the city to let them in your home, they will be more than willing to pack your things for you and bring them here.

Kari nodded. "I would appreciate the name; I will call them myself later."

Magnus was looking at his list and turned to Rex. "I was busy with the children earlier. Were you and the other council members able to hammer out the details for the trial?"

Rex nodded "The trial is set for tomorrow at ten am. We're really not expecting a very long deliberation."

Magnus turned to Meryn. "Meryn, would you know anything about a very bright light that went off earlier in the detention cells?"

Meryn looked at him, her face taking on an innocent look. "Who me?" Magnus' eyes narrowed suspiciously. "Dinner looks good today," Meryn said, changing the subject. She started poking around her plate with a fork with gusto.

They had just started eating dinner when Meryn slammed her fork down and glared at Declan. "Declan, if you don't stop breathing, I'm going to throat punch you! I can hear you from here!"

Declan looked at her startled. "I...I can't stop breathing, Meryn." He looked around the table helplessly, looking for advice.

Kari patted his leg. "Do your best."

Meryn slumped back. "I am edgier than normal lately, everything irritates me. Then this damn misophonia popped up out of nowhere. Like I really fantasize about smothering Aiden in his sleep."

Aidan's fork stopped mid-shovel. "What?" he asked, looking spooked.

Eva nodded. "I get what you're saying."

Adriel froze. "Wait. What?"

Eva shrugged. "Sometimes you breathe so loudly I can't fall asleep. I'm so tired that well, sometimes I kind of would like for you to stop breathing so I could get some rest."

Aiden and Adriel exchanged terrified glances.

Aiden turned to his tiny mate. "Meryn, baby, please don't kill me in my sleep."

She held up her hand. "I make no promises."

Aiden just grumbled as he picked up another forkful of food and started eating his troubles.

Magnus was alternating between eating and looking at his notes. "I do have some good news. Thanks to Kari, we will be getting Leif Grassfield and Travis Hickory back." Magnus crossed something off his list. "Goddard was able to reach Leif and Travis while they were still in Vegas. They will be here in the next couple days. I am having them resume their duties. Nigel and Neil will remain assigned to their units as trainees with Travis and Leif as mentors."

Bethy clapped her hands "That's wonderful! You get the experienced witches back for the city, and we get to keep Meryn's twins."

Aiden grumbled at the phrase 'Meryn's twins'.

Magnus winked at her. "It was your idea."

As dinner began to wind down, Meryn patted her belly. "Well, that was good, but I gotta go; I have a date." She hopped from her chair.

Aiden grabbed the back of her shirt. "A date?" he asked.

"Well, yeah, if you're done, you can come too."

Aiden looked at his empty plate and shrugged. Sebastian and Ryuu stepped forward.

"If everyone would like to adjourn to the antechamber, we will be serving tea, coffee and dessert there, so that Ms. Meryn can have her date," Sebastian said winking at her.

Meryn popped out of Aiden's grasp and headed toward the antechamber. Kari walked with Declan into the room and sat down on one of the sofas. She didn't know how she'd missed it walking in, but Sebastian had transformed one wall of the antechamber into a media center. There were now three large TVs with game consoles, games controllers, and even a small lava light all geared for a true gaming experience.

Meryn plopped down in one of the gaming chairs in front of the television.

After a few minutes, there was a knock on the door. Sebastian opened it and Avery and Warrick walked in.

He looked around. "Hi everyone," he waved shyly.

He saw Kari and made a beeline to her. He was about to wrap his arms around her to give her a hug when he noticed the bite marks on Declan.

He grinned widely. "Congratulations."

She blushed. "Thanks. What is all this?" she asked him.

"Meryn, Nigel, and Neil have been teaching me how to play a game on their console, and now, Meryn wants to play with the group of us. We're going to be syncing up with Noah and Jaxon. Meryn says we have a kickass team even though I can't really walk in a straight line yet," he admitted.

Warrick walked over and placed a hand on the small of Avery's back. "You are getting better."

Kari began to crack her knuckles. "What game are you playing?"

"*Call of Duty*. Meryn's been into the zombie mode so we have been killing zombies,"Avery answered.

Kari looked over at the console wall. There were three: One for Nigel, one for Neil, and one for Meryn. Kari stood, grabbed a controller, and sat down in the gamer chair next to Meryn.

Meryn's mouth dropped open. "You're kidding right?"

Kari just winked. After the game was loaded, everyone logged in, and the game began. Kari had to admit she'd never met anyone as good as Meryn, except for her. After seeing how well the team was working together, Meryn asked them if they were willing to play against other teams and everyone agreed. Soon, they were playing with a team from Orlando.

"Fuck! Dammit!" Meryn growled, practically screeching at the television. "Camping bunch of fucktards!"

Kari nodded her agreement. "Amateurs."

Between Meryn and Kari, they were more than able to take on the other team single-handedly, the boys helping them when they could.

"All right, *denka,* it's time for you to settle down," Ryuu said, coming over to confiscate her controller.

"Kickass game! I haven't had this much fun in years," Meryn said excitedly

"Your blood pressure is too high." Ryuu handed her a cup of calming tea.

"Fine." She sulked for a moment before brightening. "I know! We can watch anime."

"What is anime?" Kari asked.

"A peep back home, Anne, introduced us to the stuff. The genre is called Boys Love, and I'm totally addicted," Meryn admitted. Using Kari's controller, she logged into one of the streaming apps and started an episode.

Kari got out of the gaming chair and walked over to the sofa to sit next to Declan. Meryn and Avery stayed in the chairs and began to watch the show. Avery's eyes were wide, and he kept peeking back at Warrick, who winked at him.

Adorable, Kari thought to herself.

"Look, look," Meryn said, pointing to television. "This is my favorite part."

Kari's attention went back to the television, and sure enough, the two boy characters had finally admitted their love for each other and were about to share a kiss. The tension built in the room, and then suddenly, in the show, the door swung open, and the two characters jumped apart. Avery gasped. The scene was over, and the end credits started.

"What?" he screeched to Meryn.

"What the fuck?" Meryn shook a fist at the television.

"I am so glad that you are relaxing while watching your anime," Ryuu said sarcastically.

"I didn't know they made the shows like that." Avery was blushing.

"They're totally hot, aren't they?" Meryn asked. Avery just nodded

"Oh my goodness, what is going on here?" Caspian asked as he walked in with Broderick.

"Papa, Daddy, where have you been? We had dinner ages ago," Bethy asked, looking concerned.

"We worked through dinner tonight, darling. I'm on the verge of figuring out one of the synthetic vitamins that I need. So we just ordered in from Level Six."

They both sat down as the next episode began. Caspian's attention was riveted on the show.

"What is this?" he asked.

Meryn gave him a sly look. "It gets better." Before they knew it, the two boys were now up in the older boy's bedroom. The older boy was trying to get the younger boy to sit on the bed.

Caspian's cheeks flushed. "Oh my, I think I know where this is going."

Broderick laughed. "This reminds me of our first date."

Meryn jumped and turned around in her gamers seat excitedly. "I just had the best idea!" she exclaimed. She looked at Caspian and Broderick. "I want to learn about the butt sex."

Aiden began to choke on his pie. Declan tried to help Aiden by hitting him on the back to clear his airway. Unfortunately, he was laughing so hard, most of the hits ended up pounding Aiden's arm.

Bethy and Gavriel just stared. Magnus shook his head, while Caspian and Broderick looked at her like she was crazy. Bethy finally gasped, inhaled, and began to choke on her tea.

Tarragon jumped up and quickly ran to her side. A faint yellow light appeared at her back, and slowly, Bethy was able to breathe again. Kari turned her attention back to Meryn. Meryn and Avery were now both on their knees on their gaming chairs and looking at Broderick and Caspian with big puppy dog eyes. Broderick looked at Caspian, who shook his head.

"I had the talk with Bethy; it's your turn."

"Meryn!" Aiden exclaimed, finally catching his breath. "You don't need to know about that."

Meryn scowled at him. "I'm not trying to get pregnant again."

Broderick rubbed his chin. "Technically, that could still happen."

Meryn shrugged. "I'll take my chances."

Broderick blushed as Bethy laughed at his discomfort. "I...I..." he stuttered. "I'm not quite sure where to start."

"Start with the butt," Meryn said, trying to help.

Broderick's mouth opened and closed and then opened and closed again. He looked at Caspian who was cracking up hysterically, his arms wrapped around his stomach.

Declan slipped his hand into hers. "Come on, I really don't need this lesson." He winked at her. "Let's go introduce you to the guys."

Kari ruffled Avery's hair and then winked at

Meryn. She knew that Meryn had broken the ice and had been asking these uncomfortable questions for Avery's sake. She couldn't love the little midget more.

Kari and Declan arrived at the Unit Level and Declan led the way. They stopped in front of a large building, and even from the outside, they could hear laughter behind the doors.

Declan turned to her. "We're having more fun now than we've had in decades. I'm not sure whether it's Adriel loosening up or having the twins here, but either way, it's becoming a common practice for the guys to meet up here. We call this the unit house. It has a large kitchen, eating room, and media center. Everything you need just to hang out." He opened the door, and Kari walked in behind him.

Somebody to their left shouted, "Congratulations!"

Another voice called, "Nice bite marks!"

Another male voice teased, "Lucky bastard!"

Declan laughed and wrapped a possessive arm around her waist. "Gentlemen, I would like you to meet my mate, Kari Delaney. Kari, these jokers are Noctem Falls' unit warriors."

"Is it true that your brother is mated to Warrick?" somebody asked.

"That's Viktor BelleRose," Declan said identifying the speaker.

Kari nodded. "Yes, though technically they will not be mated until next month when Avery turns one hundred."

"Any other cuties?" a handsome, sandy haired man asked.

"That is Beau Westerly," Declan said, offering

another name.

Kari turned to Beau. "Sorry no, just he and I."

Declan went around the room introducing the men, Kari was sure she'd never remember them all.

"Hey Kari, thanks for all your help here recently."

She looked over at the speaker, surprised. "What do you mean? You are?"

He shook his head "Sorry about that. All of us have been here for so long, we're just used to everyone knowing everyone's name. My name is Dimitri Romanov; I'm the unit leader for the Theta Unit."

"What do you mean, Dimitri? Thank you for what?"

"For helping Prince Magnus for one. Before you got here, there always seemed to be a tightness around his eyes like he was constantly frowning or worried about something. However, since you got here and took over for Cheryl, it is almost like he can relax. He is not afraid he is forgetting something."

Kari laughed. "I am glad that being here has made such a difference. He needs all the help he can get." The men around her nodded.

"So Declan, did you hear about Rachelle?" Beau asked.

Declan nodded. "Sure did. It makes getting cut up worthwhile. I can't imagine a baby being born here."

"Yeah, until it is your turn," Dimitri teased.

Declan turned pale, looked at him and then looked at Kari. She shrugged. To the right, uproarious laughter filled the air. She gave him a questioning look, and they both walked into the media room followed by the other warriors. In front of the television, Nigel and Neil were dancing around, bopping to the music. It looked as though they were playing some sort of dance game.

Goddard's eyes softened. "They can be a handful, but I would not trade them for anything. Their presence here has brought nothing but laughter and joy. You cannot pay for that kind of light. Most of us have forgotten what it is like to be young."

Declan, his arm still around her waist, steered her back toward the door. "Well guys, just wanted to make some introductions so she knows what your ugly faces look like."

The men laughed. "Get out of here. We can only imagine what it is like being newly mated," Goddard teased.

Declan chuckled and waved goodbye. They walked down the dark street that split the two rows of houses.

"You okay?" she asked.

He nodded. "It was just something they said."

Kari left it alone for the moment, but she could tell that whatever it was, bothered him. If he didn't speak up soon, she knew she would bug him about it later. They walked into the house, and he walked her to the kitchen, smiling. He pointed out a machine. It was all black and chrome.

"Now, I will show you how this works, but only on one condition."

She cocked an eyebrow. "What condition?"

"You must never tell Eva or Meryn that it's here. They would never leave."

"What is it?"

Smiling, he flipped a switch she heard a grinding sound and watched as a dark brown liquid began to stream into a small cup.

"It's an espresso machine. The one thing I can't

live without."

"You are right; Meryn would never leave. I have heard horror stories already about her and coffee. Magnus is evidently very entertained by them."

Declan took the two shots of espresso, walked over to the refrigerator, and opened the door. There was a small jar with a lid. He opened it and poured it in. He rinsed out the small cup and then set it on the counter.

"What will you do with that?" she asked.

"I'll use it later to make iced coffee."

They walked upstairs and got ready for bed. After the espresso demonstration, he hadn't said a word. She slipped on an old T-shirt and climbed into bed. When he still hadn't said anything by the time he climbed in behind her, she decided to say something.

"Penny for your thoughts," she started. He wrapped an arm around her waist and pulled her into the curve of his body. "Just a penny?"

"That is all I can afford right now."

He rested his chin on her shoulder. "Could you be pregnant?" he asked.

She stilled. She counted the days. During the move, she knew she had entered into her conception cycle. "It is possible."

Declan gave a happy sigh. "I think that's why I found you when I did. I think that was the reason why you came to me now."

"Declan, we have years, centuries even."

She felt his chin move across her shoulder as he shook his head. "I could've lost you. I can't even imagine..." his voice trailed off. "There's a killer on the loose and here you are, falling down the stairs."

She grabbed his forearm at her waist. "Can you

tell me more about the killer? I was with Magnus when Meryn showed him the security cameras, but no one filled in the details."

Declan began to rub her hand. "Just before you got here, we had three shifters murdered on Level Six. We think one of the wine vendors, a vampire, went feral when the refugees came in the first wave. There was so much blood, a lot of the vampires couldn't handle it. We think he snapped. Eva was able to track him down to the Pits, the lower levels underneath Level One. It's where city maintenance happens. She was attacked; we nearly lost her. Ever since Eva's attack, there haven't been any new murders. Poor Adriel is getting more frustrated as each day goes by without any new clues. We all hate to admit it, but unless he kills again, it may be impossible to find him."

"Maybe he left," she suggested.

"We sealed the maintenance shaft he used to get around the city, and he can't fly. He lost the ability when he became feral. No, he's still somewhere in the city, we just can't find him."

"What about Avery?" she exclaimed, "Avery is by himself, he..."

Declan nipped her shoulder "Do you really think Warrick is gonna let anything happen to him?"

She pulled her knees up closer to her chest. "Maybe we really would have been safer at home."

"No you wouldn't have. Three new families were discovered murdered just yesterday."

"What is going on? Why now?"

"I don't know, but it's like we're being hunted. My lion doesn't like it."

Kari fought back shivers. "That is how it felt in the

garden, just for a second before I got dizzy. There was this icy feeling of fear. I was dizzy, but I still looked around. I expected to see someone watching me."

"Why didn't you say anything?" He turned her in his arms.

"It was just a feeling."

"You and Meryn have said almost the same thing."

"It is difficult, I think," Kari started. "Being in a city you are not used to. There are so many tunnels and caverns. So many close spaces in darkness; in the shadows you almost expect something to be hiding there."

Declan shook his head. "I've been here for so long, it doesn't even bother me anymore. If you get that feeling again, you run, you find me, you find someone. I can't lose you." He pulled her against his chest and held her tight. "You see me. Not a mediator, not a Lionhart, just me. I can't lose that."

She rubbed her cheek against his chest. "I feel the same way. After my parents left, I was alone until my adopted brother found me. He helped me figure out what I could do and how to survive."

"Adopted?" he asked.

"Yes, I found him over one hundred and sixty years ago. It was right around the time the humans started heading west. I saw him doing some magic and stuck to him like a burr. He was the only paranormal I had seen since my parents left me. Eventually, I think he just took pity on me. He set me up with a piece of paper that changes depending on what I need it to be: A birth certificate, degree, or a marriage certificate. Anything that would help me get by in the human world and blend in."

"Where are your parents?"

"I have no idea. When I turned one hundred, they said I was old enough, and they left."

"Are they dead?"

"I do not know. That is why you and Avery are so important. You are my family now. I cannot lose the two of you."

He rubbed his chin over the top of her head. "You're never getting rid of me. If you ever wonder where I am, just look behind you. I'll be there to catch you or give you a push when you need it."

"I would rather you walk beside me." She smiled.

He snorted. "No way. I'd rather walk behind you so I can watch your ass."

She poked him in the ribs, and he laughed.

She got serious for a moment. "Do you really love me?"

He nodded. "So much it's frightening."

"Even though I am take-charge? Some guys I have dated said that I was too dominant and they did not feel they were needed."

"They just weren't strong enough to allow you to be who you are. For the most part, I go with the flow, it's just easier. But when it is just the two of us, when we are alone, my lion needs you to submit. Will that be a problem?"

She smiled and kissed his chest "If it results in a repeat of earlier, no."

He chuckled. "It's just the beginning of our mating heat, my little general."

She looked up; his eyes were laughing and sparkling.

"Why did you call me that?"

"Because you are like this little general who just

runs around telling people what to do and they do it."

"I do not." She swatted his arm.

He nodded. "Oh yes, you do. You even have the prince dancing to your tune; don't think we haven't noticed."

"I promise to use my powers for good."

He chuckled.

"So do you not want to?" she waggled her eyebrows at him.

He shook his head. "I'll always want you, but you got hurt today. The only reason I claimed you earlier, despite your injuries, is because my lion was frantic to do so after almost losing you. We can take the night off so your body can rest."

"So it is not that you did not enjoy..." He nipped her hard enough to almost draw blood and she squeaked.

"Don't even complete that sentence," he said in a deepened voice. "I'm being a gentleman."

Never before had a man put her needs— even the ones that she was ignoring— above his own.

"Thank you. Will you be a gentleman tomorrow?"

"I will be gentle, and I will be a man."

"Good." She turned back around and wiggled her butt.

Growling low in his throat, he gave her ass a gentle tap and stilled her hips with his hand.

"Careful, kitten." Laughing, she closed her eyes. She could get used to this growly lion.

CHAPTER TWELVE

WHEN SHE WOKE UP, SHE was alone. She stretched all four limbs, enjoying the feel of having the bed to herself. She looked around and saw a piece of paper on the nightstand. Declan had left. He had a workout meeting with the unit warriors, and he told her that he would meet her at the Council room for the trial. Kari stretched one last time and then hopped out of bed. She experienced a surreal moment seeing her suitcase against the wall. She lived here, but not really. She was still pulling clothes out of her suitcase to get dressed. She looked around; the man didn't even own a dresser.

She threw the suitcase up on the bed and dug out a change of clothes. She got ready and headed downstairs. When she got to the kitchen, she laughed. He had left a Post-it note on the espresso machine with a heart drawn on it with a little lion figure next to it. She opened the cabinets until she found what she was looking for, two reusable travel cups. She made two lattes, one for herself, and one for Avery.

With her portfolio bag slung over her shoulder and lattes in hand, she left the Unit Level and floated down to Level One. When she reached Magnus' office, she handed the latte to Avery. She noticed that Warrick was in the corner, his feet propped up on the desk, his eyes closed. When she walked up to the desk, Warrick opened his eyes. Even though he looked like he was relaxed, she knew he was on alert. Vin and Keegan were smirking at him, and Warrick winked at her. Avery grabbed the cup, inhaled, and his eyes practically rolled back in his head.

"Thank you!" he exclaimed.

He took a sip and then moaned. Warrick's gaze flew to his mate. She smiled at him, and he swallowed hard.

"One month," she announced.

"What?" he asked, never taking his eyes from Avery.

"His birthday is one month away. He was born late for shifter."

Avery sighed, blissfully happy, oblivious to his mate's discomfort. He was still dancing in his chair.

"Where did you find this?" he asked, opening his eyes.

"Declan has an espresso machine."

"I love your mate," Avery admitted, taking another sip. Warrick growled low at the declaration.

"On that note, bye darling, have fun."

"Oh, I will." Avery took another sip and then shuddered.

Chuckling to herself, Kari met up with Rex just past the transport tunnel on the way to the Council room. At the door, she saw Meryn standing with her hands on her hips, face turned up to the man at the door. Kari looked over at Rex who was now scowling. Rex and Kari walked up behind Meryn. Rex wrapped a protective arm around Meryn's shoulders.

"What seems to be a problem here?" he asked.

The man looked up, eyed Rex quickly. "No one is to be admitted, especially shifters."

"On whose authority?" Rex demanded.

"The Founding Families have determined these will be closed-door proceedings."

The guard never even looked up as he was speaking to Rex.

"Son, do you know who I am?" he asked.

The guard scoffed. "I am a vampire and probably older than you, shifter. Watch who you call son."

Kari heard a distinctive sound and then looked at Rex. He was grinding his teeth, his jaw muscles clenched. Declan shared the same habit when he was aggravated.

Meryn pointed at him. "Aiden does that a lot too."

Kari looked at her. "With you, I am not surprised."

"You have two seconds to move before I move you," Rex threatened.

The guard finally looked up and met his eyes. "I would like to see you try."

Without another word, Rex stepped away from Meryn, grabbed the guard by the collar with one arm, and threw him across the room. When the guard's body hit the stone wall, an echoing boom reverberated through the hall. The stone around his body cracked, leaving a huge crater. The guard fell to the floor, groaning.

"Holy shit, that was awesome!" Meryn exclaimed.

She turned to Rex. "Hey flex your arm," she asked.

Grinning, her mate's brother lifted his bicep and flexed. Meryn jumped up and began dangling from his arm. When the door opened, Aiden, Adriel,

Gavriel, and Declan stood there looking confused and shocked.

"What happened?" Adriel demanded.

Kari jerked her thumb to the wall. "The guard said that there were no shifters allowed and that these were closed-door proceedings."

"And evidently he doesn't recognize any of the elders here," Rex added, still holding his arm up for the giggling Meryn.

Aiden stepped forward. "Meryn, get off the Elder." He lifted her up and into his arms.

Declan was laughing. "Maybe if you visited more often, the locals would know what you looked like."

Kari smiled and walked past Rex. She wrapped her arms around Declan's neck and gave him a kiss. "I missed you this morning."

Declan smiled wide down at her. "I missed you too."

Magnus walked past them to stand beside Rex, looking at the wall. "For fuck's sake!" he exclaimed.

"Magnus cussed!" Meryn announced laughing.

Magnus turned to Rex. "My apologies. I had no idea that the guard was even here. He was not watching the door when we arrived."

Rex shrugged. "Shall we begin?"

They made their way inside the room, and the door closed behind them. DuBois and DeLaFontaine sat at one desk, Declan and Adriel at the other. Both desks faced a four-chair panel where the Elders sat. To the right were seats for any witnesses. Kari joined Aiden, Meryn, Beth, and Gavriel there. Rex glared at DuBois. Kari began to understand the term *if looks could kill.* Rex looked like he was two seconds away from ripping the man's head off.

"For the record, shifter Elder Rex Lionhart, vampire Elder Magnus Rioux, witch Elder Alastair Primrose, and fae Elder Dagda Vi'Ilsimir will be presiding over this case." Rex motioned with his hand to the men sitting beside him at the long desk. The witch Elder wore a deep green cloak over his clothes with the emblem of the triple moon embroidered on the chest in silver thread. The fae Elder wore a long gold and ivory formal robe, with a high collar that only seemed to accentuate his ethereal features. Both men stared at Ivan and Gerald with a flat look in their eyes.

"For the record, we need you to speak your name," Rex ordered Gerald.

Gerald DuBois stood. "My name is douchebag." Silence filled the room.

He frowned. "My name is douchebag!" he exclaimed.

Magnus and Rex along with the other elders' eyes went wide.

DuBois slammed his hands against the desktop. "I am douchebag." He looked around the room frantically.

Rex and Magnus could barely contain their chuckles. Elder Primrose flat out laughed, and Elder Vi'Ilsimir looked on, eyes wide and mouth twitching fiercely. When Gerald said, "I am douchebag," again, the fae Elder lost his sense of composure and began to pound on the elders' desk laughing uproariously.

After a few minutes the Elders regained their composure. Rex, wiping his eyes, spoke first. "We will skip your name for now."

Ivan DeLaFontaine stood. "I was told that the son

of the head of one of my Noble Houses was assaulted by Declan Lionhart yesterday," he began.

Elder Primrose waved a hand. "He was not assaulted. He received retribution for threatening a warrior's mate. He was taken to the detention cells for treatment and is fine. We are here today to address the charges against Gerald DuBois." Ivan sat down, looking thwarted.

Rex didn't even make a pretense of looking at any of the papers in front of him.

"Your sentence is..."

DeLaFontaine stood quickly, his chair hitting the floor.

"Sentence? I thought this was a trial."

Rex looked the man flatly. "It has been determined by the council that Gerald DuBois would not need a trial. Over two dozen witnesses have stepped forward to give statements. Regardless of the reason he assaulted a unit warrior, the fact remains that he resorted to violence." He turned to Gerald DuBois. "You are to pay a ten-million dollar fine for your assault on Declan Lionhart." Gerald's eyes bulged. Rex continued. "That money is to be set aside in a trust for any Noctem Falls citizen who may discover their mate among shifters and finds themselves needing assistance in starting over."

"This is biased panel! I demand that we replace Rex Lionhart with Elder Evreux for a more neutral and impartial deliberation. The defendant's own brother should not be part of the Council panel," Ivan DeLaFontaine protested.

Elder Primrose's eyes flashed. "Denied! If he does not want to be at the mercy of an elder whose family member he nearly killed, then he should not go around attacking people. He is lucky it wasn't my brother. He would have been gutted and the warriors would still be looking for his spleen."

Elder Vi'Ilsimir cleared his throat, smirking as he looked at Ivan DeLaFontaine. "Funds are to be transferred by close of business today. Do you have anything to add as the Founding Family head?"

Ivan turned to Magnus. "I will see you tonight for dinner, Prince Magnus."

Magnus inclined his head. "Of course."

Gerald stood and he and Ivan walked toward the door and left. Once the door closed behind them, Meryn broke down into a contagious fit of giggles. First Bethy and finally Kari got wrapped up in the infectious laughter. Elder Primrose chuckled along with them and turned to Magnus.

"I can see why you requested that Leif and Travis come back."

Magnus turned to him, an innocent look on his face. "Whatever do you mean?"

Elder Primrose winked. "I'm not saying Mr. DuBois was under a spell with Nigel and Neil Morninglory's magical signature all over it, but if he was, I would recommend that someone teach them a concealment spell."

"Good idea," Meryn murmured.

Elder Vi'Ilsimir bowed. "It was a pleasure to meet you, Meryn McKenzie. I received a report from Etain in regards to the standing invitation to Éire Danu by our Queen." He walked around the desk and up to the sections of seats where they had observed the sentencing. He handed her a small gold card. "If you need anything, anything at all, use that and it will contact me."

Magnus' eyes bugged out, and he practically raced around the desk to look at it.

"Cool beans. May I friend you on Facebook?" Meryn asked.

The Elder chuckled. "I think my mate has already friended you. She enjoys your hilarious updates."

Meryn winced. "I need to work on my phrasing."

"Oh, I do not know; I think your phrasing is just right," he said teasingly.

Meryn stuck the card in her pocket.

Aiden grimaced. "Meryn, that is a very, very important gift. It has been spelled so that it will allow you to contact Elder Vi'Ilsimir directly anytime you wish. If you stick it in your pocket, you may lose it."

"Dani wouldn't lose it. Besides changing into cool clothes, she is really good about keeping stuff in my pockets safe."

"Dani?" Elder Vi'Ilsimir asked, choking on the word. "Gods! Is that?"

Meryn nodded. "The Gown of Éire Danu," Meryn said, plucking at her T-shirt.

The fae Elder looked down at the small human and took in her scruffy shoes, her baggy jeans, Star Wars T-shirt, and large hoodie.

"That is the coveted Gown of Éire Danu?" he asked.

"Yeah, but that got to be a mouthful, now I call her Danu or Dani."

She reached into her pocket and pulled out a flash drive, two pieces of gum, five salt packets, a small stone, and what looked like to be a sonic screwdriver.

"See, she keeps things safe."

Aiden looked over her shoulder and down at her hands.

"Packets of salt?" he asked.

Meryn looked up, and with a very serious expression, said, "For demons."

The witch and the fae elders both turned deathly pale.

"There are demons here?" Elder Primrose whispered as if he were almost afraid to say the word.

Meryn paled and stuck the salt back in her pocket. "Wait, they're real, like, really real?"

They nodded. Elder Vi'Ilsimir turned to her. "Yes, but they have not been seen for many centuries, ever since their battle with the Dark Prince."

"I only started carrying them around since I started watching *Supernatural*."

The witch Elder shuddered. "The representation of witches in that show is ghastly."

Magnus nodded his agreement. "How do you think we feel about vampires? They made us look like piranhas."

Both the witch and fae Elders gave a half bow. "Well, if you'll excuse us, we've been asked to consult on different projects for the upcoming fair," Elder Primrose said, smiling.

Rex shook their hands. "Thank you for your help."

"I am sorry it happened at all," Magnus replied.

Elder Primrose clapped him on the back. "It is not your fault. On a different topic entirely, I wanted to thank you for hosting this fair; I haven't seen my mate this excited in decades."

Elder Vi'Ilsimir also smiled. "My mate is also very anxious to see what Noctem Falls' first fair will be like. You have given us something to look forward to." Together they left, and the door closed behind them.

"Speaking of the fair," Kari started. "What will everybody be contributing?"

Meryn waved her hand in the air. "I can use my drone to take pictures for people. That way we will have the entire thing documented."

Declan pointed to himself and Bethy. "We're talking to the vendors up on Level Six to make sure we have enough food. We've been having to place extra orders to the city estate. If the taste testing is a reflection of what will be available at the fair, I'm going to hurt myself eating."

Adriel looked at his clipboard. "Looks like Goddard is working with the units. They are going to be doing unit led activities for the children, including games. Eta has been acting as escorts for any vampire from the Noble and Founding Families to go to Level Six, but so far, there have been no new matches." He flipped a page. "Nigel and Neil are now with Emlyn Blackwood working on the net. It ripped when someone kicked Mr. DeLaFontaine into it."

Meryn lifted her foot and punched the air. "Ninja kick!"

Adriel laughed and ruffled her hair.

"You and my mate should not be allowed to be together."

"Don't hate on our badassery."

"Well, it sounds like we at least have starting points for the rest of the day," Magnus added. He looked at Kari. "I will see you in the office."

She nodded. "Of course."

They left as a group and everyone scattered to

go their different ways. Kari was surprised when Meryn hung back with Ryuu. She matched her pace to Meryn's. They walked slowly back towards Magnus' quarters.

Meryn looked up at her, stopping. "Doesn't your company also deal with security?"

Kari smiled. "Well knowing you, I am pretty sure you have already looked at that. You know we do."

"Can I hire them?" Meryn asked.

"You are mated to the Unit Commander. You are a guest of Prince Magnus, in his personal quarters. You have an amazing squire, and you are surrounded by unit warriors. Why on earth would you need additional security?"

Meryn shrugged and began scuffing her foot on the stone floor.

"It's just that eventually when the shit really hits the fan, and it will, I'm afraid that even Adriel will hesitate between protecting Magnus and Aiden. In his hesitation, we could lose them both."

Kari had a moment of clarity. "That was why you were really upset. It was not because *Doctor Who* was removed from Netflix. After Declan got hurt, it all started to come together for you. It got real."

Meryn looked up and met her eyes. "I was upset when I first heard about Declan's injuries. Then everybody was racing around helping, and I realized it could have just as easily been Aiden. He is just like Declan; he's the type to just jump right in, and he could have gotten really hurt. Then I thought if that could happen by accident, what could happen if someone was actually trying to hurt them. Adriel's loyalties would be torn between his Unit Commander and his prince. The vampires of the unit warriors would be torn. I think most of the shifters would help Aiden. I'm not sure about the fae or the witches. I think in those chaotic few seconds of confusion, we could lose a lot of people."

"Meryn, you are brilliant."

"Yeah, I know."

"If you do not mind, I can make some suggestions to Declan about hosting some drills or maybe just assigning the men people to protect, that way the men know instinctively where to go."

Meryn shrugged. "I think practicing will help, but how much practice can they possibly get to override centuries of association? It's the Prince of the Vampires we're talking about."

"Good point. Listen, I will call the head of security myself this afternoon. Since most of the security that works for me are paranormals, they should be able to get here right away. They just have to go to the closest portal."

"They will report to me right? Not Magnus or Adriel or Aiden. To me," she asked.

"Yes. That is the way it works. If you enter into the contract, they will belong to you. You can have them protect you, Bethy, Aiden, anyone. They will report to you and do as you ask."

"Good." Relief filled Meryn's eyes.

They had just walked past the transport tunnel when Kari began to feel dizzy again. She called out to Meryn, but then looked down. She watched the floor move under her feet, and suddenly, she was looking down the Transport Tunnel.

"Kari?" she heard a voice ask.

She blinked, and it seemed like the blink took forever. She blinked again; the dizziness overwhelmed her, and just before she lost consciousness, she heard a scream.

☾

WHEN SHE WOKE UP, SHE looked around and groaned; she was back in the infirmary.

"I am really beginning to hate this place," she muttered.

She opened her eyes and looked over to see Tarragon at her side.

"If I didn't know any better I would say you had Bethy's luck."

She looked to her left where Declan was clutching her hand with a sick look on his face.

"I am okay," she assured him.

He just shook his head, unable to speak.

She swallowed hard at the desperate look in his eyes. "Please tell me someone broke this to Avery gently?" she asked, noticing her brother's absence.

Tarragon winced. "I had to sedate him. I think he has had too much thrown at him in the past couple days. Warrick is watching over him. He promised that they would spend a relaxing day in Avery's room, followed up with a quiet dinner."

She looked down at Declan. "How bad?" she whispered.

"If it weren't for Meryn, we would have lost you," he replied, his voice cracking.

She frowned and looked past Declan to see Meryn looking pale sitting in Aiden's lap. She had her arm in a sling.

"Are you okay?"

Aiden shared Declan's sick look. "She jumped in after you."

"I used my stone," Meryn said, smiling weakly. "I think it reacted to my sense of urgency. I was able to fly down the tunnel after you, but I'm not that strong so my arm got pulled a little."

"*Denka* reacted very quickly to your fall," Ryuu said, his voice tight. Fear and anger was coming off of him in waves. Kari knew that the fear stemmed from almost losing Meryn. She was willing to bet that the anger was directed at himself for not stopping her.

"Oh Meryn, you should not have put yourself in danger like that." Kari felt terrible. She tried to sit up and groaned. Her head began to pound. "What exactly happened?"

Declan gently ran a hand over her hair. "Don't you remember?"

"I remember feeling dizzy, looking down the tunnel, and I think I fell." She looked over at Meryn. "I think you screamed."

Meryn nodded. "Your face got a funny look, and then you literally turned around and walked back toward the tunnel. I don't think you fell; it looked like you jumped in."

"How did you catch me?"

Meryn shrugged. "Kinda knew it was going to happen, so I was right behind you." She looked back at her squire, her eyes shining with unshed tears. "I'm sorry. I didn't mean to make you mad; I just moved before I knew it."

Ryuu was kneeling down beside her in an instant. "I would not change your courage for all the world. It just means I will have to work that much harder to be deserving of you as my charge."

"Just keep feeding me and we're cool," Meryn said, looking uncomfortable at her squire's compliment.

Ryuu simply brought her knuckles to his lips and raised them to his forehead in a sort of benediction. "Whatever you wish, *denka*." He stood and went back to his normal position of standing behind his charge.

Kari was touched at Ryuu's devotion. She couldn't imagine Meryn with any other squire. She looked around the room. "Is no one going to ask how she knew?"

Declan looked at Aiden who looked at Tarragon who shrugged.

Meryn sighed. "Don't ask, I have no idea; it might be this empathy thing."

Tarragon shook his head, bewildered, before he turned his attention back to Kari. "Is there any chance you could be pregnant?"

She shook her head and then blushed. "Wait...yes, it is a possibility."

"It only takes once," Meryn teased.

Tarragon just nodded before handing a small stone to Declan. "Would you like some privacy?" he asked. Declan nodded.

Tarragon turned to Aiden and Meryn. "Okay young lady, now that the major emergency is over, lets go work on that shoulder."

Aiden cradled his mate carefully to his chest, and he and Ryuu followed Tarragon out the door.

When the door closed, Declan just looked at her. "What do you want?"

"I do not know. What about you?"

"You know if you had asked me that this morning I would have been happy either way." He took a deep breath. "I heard the scream, and I knew it was you. So, I want it to be yes. I want a piece of you, a piece of us that we can raise and love. What about you? Yes? No?"

"Everything so crazy right now, but maybe that is why it should be yes. Maybe that is why it would be okay. It is important to hold onto the things that matter. Two days ago, I would have said no; I had too much changing. But now, maybe a little version of you would not be so bad. So, yes, I think I would be okay if I were."

Declan swallowed hard and held up the stone. She extended her hand palm up, and he placed the stone in the middle of her hand. Slowly, an amber light began to glow. Declan's eyes filled and sob escaped. He pulled her against him.

"Thank you," he murmured.

Kari knew she had said yes, but now that she knew it was yes, it was different. Things were so dangerous; it had her thinking that maybe they should've waited, but now it was too late. She was going to be a mother, and she didn't even know where she was going to be living. It wasn't until Declan began to shake her gently that she realized she'd been hyperventilating.

"Do I need to go get Tarragon? Are you okay?"

"I am fine. I am fine. Maybe you could get me a glass of water?"

She took another deep breath. Declan raced to the sink. When he dropped the cup for the third time, she had to smile. It was a good thing it was plastic. He filled the cup almost to the brim and carefully walked it over.

He handed it to her as if it were the Holy Grail. His reactions made her relax. He wasn't handling it any better than she was. Smiling, she drank enough that she wasn't worried about spilling any water. She set it down on the small stand beside her. Declan stood there, unsure what to do. Looking shell-shocked, he began to sway on his feet. She reached over and gently tugged on his hand until he sat down in the chair again.

"Kari, I could've lost you both." Growling, he reached for his walkie-talkie. "Grant, come in." Kari knew he was distracted if he didn't use a call sign.

"Yes, Simba. What's up?"

"Can you see if you find my brother and send him down to the infirmary?"

"Sure. Is Kari okay?"

"Yeah, she's fine, over."

Kari looked at him. "Your brother?"

"I'm not taking any more chances with the woman I love. I don't care if I have to become an elder. I'll do anything it takes to get you the protection you need and deserve."

Kari saw the stark terror in his eyes and wanted her goofy, smiling mate back. She didn't want the looming threat to ruin his moment. He had been so happy finding out he was going to be a father he had been shining, now he looked withdrawn. She reached out and rubbed the skin between his eyebrows where they were bunched together as he frowned.

"Do you have someone in mind for an *athair*?" she asked.

Slowly, a smile began to replace the blank look on his face. "Adriel," he said, nodding.

"Really?" she asked, surprised. "You seem closer to Grant or even Etain. Why Adriel?"

"Because Adriel would do anything in his power for our child. He has kept himself apart from the men because he didn't know he could be our leader and our friend. But over the past week, he has seen how Aiden is with Gavriel, and I think he has realized that he can be more than just a unit leader. I think what we have been seeing lately is his true self emerging. He's always been loyal and protective; he was great with Bethy when she was growing up. You couldn't ask for a better *athair*."

"Not even Warrick?" she asked.

He shook his head. "He's already going to be their uncle."

They both turned when there was a knock at the door. A second later, the door swung open in a concerned looking Rex walked in.

"No one told me what happened. Only that Kari was hurt. Is she okay?"

Declan nodded. "She's fine, but I have other concerns." He stood to face his brother. He placed both hands on his shoulders. "Brother, I have need of you," he said in a formal tone.

Kari could see the change in Rex immediately. It was as if Declan had hit a switch. Rex was suddenly surrounded by the power of his station.

"Declan, you know there is nothing I would deny you. You are flesh of my flesh and blood of my blood, and if there is anything you need, you have only to ask," Rex replied, placing his hands on top of Declan's shoulders.

Declan let his hands fall, and he practically collapsed into the chair. Concerned, Rex pulled one of the other chairs in the room over to sit beside his brother. "Tell me little brother, what is going on?"

Declan looked at Kari and then back to his brother. "I think someone is after my mate."

Kari gasped. "That cannot be right."

Declan raised an eyebrow. "Kari, have you ever had problems with dizzy spells, fainting, passing out before coming to Noctem Falls?" he asked.

She shook her head. "No, never."

"Don't you think it's highly suspicious that in the past two days you've fallen twice? At the very least, you have been gravely injured. Both falls could have been fatal, Kari."

Kari felt her stomach turn to ice. She didn't even realize she was shaking until Declan joined her on the bed, pulling her close.

Rex's eyes were flashing as he stood, growling. "Who would dare?"

Declan shrugged. "It could be anyone. Any one of the Founding Families or Noble Families that aren't happy with the progress that Magnus is making with Kari at his side. From what I heard, Kari clearly made her disdain of the ruling classes known when Cheryl got fired. It could be any of Cheryl's friends or family that felt like Kari had displaced her. It could be the feral..." Declan hesitated. "So far he's been going after blood. That requires up close and personal. Why would he suddenly switch to killing people from afar?"

Kari held up a hand. "How would this even happen?"

Rex and Declan exchanged surprised looks. "Kari,

you're a vampire."

"Yes, I know."

Declan looked at her carefully. "You do know that you have the ability to manipulate minds, right?" he asked.

She shook her head. "I had heard from others some of what we could do, but I have never seen it done. My parents did not teach me how." She frowned. "Wait, so you are saying that somebody could control my mind?"

Declan and Rex nodded. "It's not done normally. Besides being against our laws; it's very difficult to control another paranormal. We have an innate protection system built-in. Somebody might be able to manipulate your mind but they would have to be very, very strong, especially if they can do it without you being aware of it."

"So, what would they gain by making me take tumbles down stairs or down the transport tunnel?" she asked.

"If anything happened to you, Declan would be devastated. Adriel would lose his second in command," Rex answered pacing the room.

Kari disagreed. "It does not make sense to go after the mate of the second in command to distract the unit leader."

"It would upset Magnus," Rex added.

"He has only known me three days," Kari refuted.

"I don't care," Declan said quietly. "I really don't care why. I just don't want it to happen again." He looked up at Rex who nodded.

"I'll get on the phone with Mother and Father. We'll have some of our pride join us as soon as possible. She will be protected," Rex promised.

Declan looked at his brother, a smile forming on his face. "Yes, I think Mother and Father would be very agreeable to this, especially after they find out that Kari is having their first grandchild."

Rex's mouth dropped suddenly. His face broke out into a huge smile. He gave a loud whoop, and before she knew it, she had been plucked off the bed and swirled around the room.

Declan jumped up and batted his brother's hands. "Put her down, you idiot."

Rex looked instantly contrite and gently put her back on the bed. "Are you okay? I didn't break you?" he asked.

She rolled her eyes. "No, I am not broken. I am fine." She smiled up at him. "I take it you are excited about the idea of becoming an uncle."

Rex nodded, laughing. "Of course I am. My baby brother's having a baby." He clapped Declan on the back. "Good job, little brother."

Kari looked at them flatly. "Yes, because he will be doing all the work."

Both of them looked a little bit apprehensive. The expression on her face must've been formidable.

"Anything you want, baby, and I'll give it to you," Declan vowed, kissing her hand.

"I did hear that there was a really good chocolatier on Level Six." She winked at Rex.

He held up a hand. "Consider it done. With your permission I'll tell Avery the wonderful news. Then we can make plans for our future niece or nephew. I leave my sister in your care, Declan." Kari nodded her permission. In all honesty she wanted to be the one to tell Avery he was going to be an uncle, but she was already beginning to feel drained from the healing session. Rex would be able to share Avery's exuberant excitement and it would give them a chance to bond, further cementing the ties of their new family.

Declan rolled his eyes. "Yes, brother."

Rex left the room as Kari began to giggle. "He is a bit domineering, is he not?"

Declan sat down in the chair with an amused expression. "He really does care."

"You look surprised."

"We were never really very close. The age difference between us made things difficult."

"You are lucky; family like that is important." Kari looked over at her mate. "Are you sure you will not be in trouble for not calling your parents? I mean Rex is the one telling them everything."

Declan paled, reaching for a phone. "Thank the gods for Meryn. We now have cellular and Wi-Fi in the city." He put the phone on speaker and set it on the bed beside her. They heard it ring, and then a deep male voice came on the line.

"Jedrek Lionhart, Declan is this you?" the voice asked.

Declan swallowed. "Yes Father, it's me."

"Well it's about damn time you called, boy. Your brother gave us an update on what happened. You would think after finding your mate, you would've given us a call," his father said, sounding hurt.

Declan winced. "Father, she's right here."

Jedrek broke the momentary silence by clearing his throat. "I'm sorry, my dear, it's just I really am disappointed that Declan didn't call sooner."

Kari took Declan's hand. "Of course, I understand completely. You are his father and should have been one of the first people he called." She winked at Declan, who was rolling his eyes.

"You have no idea how happy I am to hear that, Kari. Sounds like you have a good head on your shoulders. You're a good match for my son."

"Father, the reason why I'm calling is..."

"Hold on, your brother's calling on the other line, it could be elder business."

"Don't answer it! It isn't." Declan called out.

"I'll call him back. Why should I not answer your brother's phone call?" his father asked.

"Because I bet you he's trying to beat me to the punch."

"What punch?" his father demanded.

"Is Mother there?"

"Hold on." They heard the sound of footsteps then a loud bellow. "Catherine!"

"Good gods, Jedrek! I believe the queen herself might have heard you. What is all the fuss about?" a soft feminine voice asked.

"Declan's on the phone with his mate, Kari."

"What?" They heard more footsteps before his mother's voice became louder. "Declan, darling, is that you?"

Declan's smile was soft. "Yes Mother, I'm here."

"Kari, oh, Kari, it's so good to finally be able to talk to you. When are you coming to visit?" his mother demanded.

Kari looked at Declan, who shrugged. "We are still trying to get settled here. Maybe after that," Kari suggested diplomatically.

"The sooner the better. I can't wait to meet my son's new mate. Finally, I have a daughter." They heard a chirp. "Why is Rex calling?" she asked.

"Hold on, dear, don't answer it quite yet. Declan has something he wants to tell us. Don't you, son?"

"Yes, Father. I just wanted to let you know that Kari and I just found out that we are expecting."

A loud screech practically broke the phone. Declan was shaking his head at the decibel level. Kari smiled.

"Now, you really have to come out, Declan. Bring her as soon as you can. I can't wait to see her. What joyous news." His mother's voice broke, and then she began to cry.

"There, there, sweetheart. Don't cry; this is happy news." Jedrek comforted his mate. "Declan, look what you did."

"I didn't mean make her cry," Declan protested.

"Of course, she's going to cry, it's our first grand-child," Jedrek said gruffly. "Is it permissible to answer your brother's phone call now?"

"Yes. I'll let him go explain what's going on. He's calling for reinforcements."

"Reinforcements?" Jedrek barked the question.

"Father, gotta go."

"Declan, I..."

Declan hung up the phone.

"That was rude, Declan," Kari admonished.

He shrugged. "Rex will be able to fill him in. Besides, you're looking tired. You're with child; you need to rest."

"I am not a—" A large yawn interrupted her. Then her stomach rumbled.

Declan frowned. He looked from her stomach to her face to her stomach. "Doc said you should rest, but you need to eat!" Declan looked confused and slightly panicked.

"Maybe a quick lunch and then a nap. Getting healed from a witch healer always makes me tired," Kari suggested.

"Okay, we go get lunch."

She went to get out of bed, he stood and began frantically waving his hands in front of her. "No, wait, stop, don't move."

She froze. "What am I supposed to do?"

Declan began pulling at his hair. "I don't know!" he exclaimed. "Should you move? Should you get out of bed? I mean you were hurt when you fell down the tunnel. Now you're having a baby."

Kari sat at the edge of the bed, her feet dangling. She watched as her mate slowly began to melt down before her very eyes. When he spun around aimlessly for the fourth time, she hopped off the bed, walked over to him, and placed both hands on his chest. He looked down at her with a wild look in his eyes.

"Darling, I am hungry."

"Right, hungry, food. You need food." He swept her up into his arms and began jogging out of the infirmary.

Kari sighed.

Wonderful. He has known for less than an hour, and this is how he is.

She laid her head down on his shoulder.

And I would not change a thing.

CHAPTER THIRTEEN

WHEN THEY WERE IN MAGNUS' quarters, Kari tapped Declan on the shoulders, and he set her down. She looked at him, "You go inside. I will be there in a moment."

He nodded his head up and down. "Of course. I'll make you a plate."

"That would be lovely," she said. As soon as he was in the dining room, Kari walked in and sat down on the sofa in the antechamber. She pulled out her cell phone and dialed a number she knew by heart.

"Hello," a familiar voice answered. "Kari, is that you?" he asked.

"Of course, it is me."

"Well, I'm not coming to get you. You need to stay there."

Kari rolled her eyes. "Actually Law, Avery and I have found our mates. We are staying here."

"What!" he exclaimed. "You were only supposed to stay there until it was safe to come back. You weren't supposed to move there."

"That is in part why I'm calling. I've met Meryn McKenzie, and she is requesting a security detail." She quickly went over what had been happening since she arrived: From Declan's assault to Meryn's concerns about the division of leadership. There was a brief silence on the phone.

"Come back home; it is not safe there."

"They are going to find the feral."

"What feral?" he demanded.

"Oh, you did not know about that."

"Safe haven, my magical ass." He quieted. "How soon do you need us?

"Well, I may or may not have a stalker trying to kill me too."

"Okay, we'll be there in an hour."

"And I am pregnant."

"We'll be there in fifteen minutes."

"There is no way that you could be here in fifteen minutes."

"Never mind that, I'm organizing my team and one other; we'll be there soon."

"Okay, but be safe."

"Me? I want you to go and stand beside Magnus until I get there."

"We are having lunch."

"Fine, go *sit* beside Magnus, it will be the safest place in the room." Sighing, he hung up the phone.

She thought about everything that had happened in the past couple days, and found herself smiling. No, Law wouldn't complicate things at all. She stood and walked into the dining room. She stopped and stared. Declan had piled her plate high with food. He stood and patted her chair. The other men stood smiling at her warmly.

"Food," he said, pointing to her chair.

She looked around the table to see amused expressions.

"Did he tell you?" she asked.

"We kind of put it together. All he was able to say was *food* and *baby*," Beth teased.

"Congratulations," Adriel said beaming.

"Come sit down and eat," Declan repeated.

"Look who's doing full sentences." Meryn laughed.

Kari sat down and the men resumed their seats. "Meryn, your security team should be here in about fifteen minutes." She turned to the Prince. "Magnus, you may want to alert the units so that our incoming teams do not get shot."

Adriel picked up his walkie-talkie. "Francis, we have incoming." He looked up at Kari. "How many?"

"Two teams of four that I know of."

"We have eight friendlies coming in; send them to Level One."

"Roger that. Uh, sir, can I can you a question?"

"Yes," Adriel replied.

"Why is my call sign Francis?"

Adriel looked over at Meryn who was snickering to herself. "Meryn?"

"His name is Ajax," she answered.

Kari looked around and saw that she wasn't the only one who didn't understand her explanation.

Meryn's mouth dropped. "Seriously?" She pinched the bridge of her nose much like her mate was wont to do when irritated. "We are going to have movie night soon."

"Francis, is an obscure movie reference," Adriel replied to Ajax.

"It is not obscure!" Meryn protested.

Adriel returned the walkie-talkie to his belt.

Kari eyed the spread of food her mate had picked

out for her. It looked as though he grabbed three of everything. "Though, knowing my brother, he might just pop up down here."

"How?" Gavriel asked.

"I have no idea. He is like that." She picked up one of the four sandwiches on her plate. "How is the fair coming along?"

Adriel nodded. "Quite nicely, actually. The vendors have really outdone themselves. Not only are we getting some of the city's favorites, but they have tried new recipes. They cannot wait to share them."

She looked over at Magnus. He was still beaming.

"Two babies plus my two nieces or nephews from Meryn and Bethy." He was practically vibrating in his chair.

Kari could tell he was truly excited about the prospect of new life. Any doubts she had about moving to Noctem Falls were eliminated. This man needed all the support he could get. Kari was halfway through her sandwich when the door chimed. A moment later, a familiar face appeared and a handsome smile greeted her.

"Law!" she exclaimed.

She jumped up out of her chair and raced over to him. He swung her up into his arms and twirled around. Behind her, she heard a few choking sounds.

He looked down at her. "Are you okay?" he asked, looking her over.

"Yes, I am fine. Meryn saved me." She pointed to Meryn who was sitting on Aiden's lap.

"So she's the smart one who identified the problem."

"Yes."

"What problem is this?" Adriel asked looking

confused.

"Meryn, go ahead; this was your idea," Kari prompted.

Meryn twisted her fingers, "Well it's just that I've noticed some things. Like Magnus gives an order and the warriors automatically look to Aiden to see if he agrees. If Aiden gives orders, some of the vampires look at Magnus to see if he agrees. And with Declan being hurt, I was afraid that if something happened to either of you, they would hesitate. We might end up losing you both."

Magnus, Adriel, and Aiden exchanged looks. From the rueful expressions, Kari could tell that none of them had noticed the problem.

Meryn scrunched up her nose. "Amelia's brother's name is Law. Is that you?" she asked.

"Yes, that's me." Law confirmed. "How do you know Amelia?" he asked.

"Amelia is my big sister cousin. Our mothers were sisters. That makes him my..." she paused. "My big sister cousin brother?" she asked the room. She turned her head. "Ryuu, how does family work again?"

Kari watched in amusement as Law's face froze. He blinked and then picked up his phone. He held it sideways, and it chirped like a walkie-talkie.

"Tom, send team seven down to Noctem Falls on the double; I need them here yesterday."

"Yes sir!"

Law clipped the walkie-talkie to his belt.

"Why add another team?" Adriel asked.

"I have two sisters here where the local populace is either attacking unit warriors or turning feral. One of them has a stalker. The other one is human.

And both are pregnant. We're surrounded by men who can't even identify a major chain of command issue. Of course, I'm bringing in another team," Law answered sarcastically.

Gavriel scowled. "You know, he reminds me of someone."

Law turned and looked at Gavriel. His eyes widened, and he inclined his head. "Looks as though I'm not the only one keeping secrets."

Gavriel gave him a flat look.

Law turned back to Meryn. "The word that you're looking for is brother. I am your brother. Amelia is my sister, and you're her little sister, so that makes you my sister." He smiled. "I can't wait until Thane and Justice find out."

"Why didn't you know about Meryn being related to Amelia?" Kari asked.

"I've been out on assignment."

Meryn's hands slammed the table.

"Say that again." she insisted, looking excited.

Law repeated. "I've been on assignment."

Meryn gasped, both hands rose to her mouth. "Deadpool?" she asked.

Law's mouth dropped open. "Red Queen?"

"Holy shit!" Meryn exclaimed.

"No way." Law stepped back and swung the dining room door open "Gimli, Gambit, Legolas get in here." Three large men filed in.

"Yes, sir?" The tall elegant blond asked.

Law pointed to Meryn. "That's Red Queen."

The large man with a shaggy beard and hair barked out his laughter. "Get the fuck outta here!" He ran over and scooped her right out of Aiden's lap. "Where have you been? We almost died in Afghanistan. They replaced you with an absolute idiot."

"We have missed you, little one." The tall, blond man lifted her out of his companion's arms and set her on her feet before kissing her hand.

"Let me at her." The dark-haired man stepped forward, kissed her on both cheeks, and then once on the lips. "You are absolutely adorable, little bit." Aiden began to growl low in his throat. The three men ignored him.

Aiden stood and pulled Meryn away from them, rubbing his cheek where they kissed her, and they laughed. He sat back down, holding Meryn close in his lap.

Aiden said, "Meryn, how on earth do you know them?"

"I worked with them to help them kill people."

Everyone froze, and there was silence. Aiden chuckled nervously. "You mean like on your zombie game?"

Meryn shook her head. "Nope, I hacked systems, opened doors, watched out for them on surveillance, made fake IDs. That sort of thing."

The one Law called Gambit brought a finger to his lips. "Hush shug, you givin' away all our secrets."

"Meryn?" Aiden looked down at his mate as if he had never seen her before.

"They were all bad," Meryn assured him.

"Security, huh?" Kari asked flatly.

Meryn gasped and began to laugh. "I thought you came because you're Kari's brother, I didn't know you were part of her security force." Meryn hooted as Law gave her a flat look. She continued to howl.

Bethy looked at her friend in confusion. "Meryn, what's going on?"

Meryn pointed a finger at Law. "He's a genius."

Law nodded. "Well..."

Gavriel looked around. "I do not understand."

Meryn wiped her eyes. "If you are paranoid and you think that someone is out to get you, what do you do?"

Kari frowned. "We would call in security." Her eyes widened and she looked over at her adopted brother. "Law!" she protested.

He held up both hands. "None of them were your contracts."

Gambit stepped forward. "Wait, sister?" he asked pointing at Kari.

Law nodded. "She's the ragamuffin I took in that I told you about." He turned to Kari. "Kari Delaney, I would like you to meet three of my oldest friends. Gambit or Emeric Foret, vampire." Emeric winked and blew her a kiss. "The rough looking redhead is Gimli or Gidan Campbell, a bear shifter. And our tall fae brother is Legolas or Idris Li'Mierlen." He turned to the table. "Meryn gave us call names the first day we worked together. She introduced herself as Red Queen, but we always called her Trouble."

Emeric looked Kari over. "Sir, this beautiful creature could never be a ragamuffin." Kari smiled at him and waved at the others.

Magnus turned to Adriel. "How do you think the team should be assigned?"

"Two on Kari..." Adriel started.

Law began to laugh and everyone turned to him. "I don't think you gentlemen understand. We only answer to the ones who call us in. That would be Kari and Meryn; they will decide where we go. We will do exactly as they order; no one can override their commands."

Magnus nodded, but didn't look very pleased. "I see."

Gidan put his hands on his hips. "You didn't say anything about taking care your sister."

Emeric shook his head. "We are gonna die. Law is gonna kill us if anything happens to these two angels."

"You want to head home?" Idris asked.

"No way!" Gidan replied. "We're not leaving our little queen here alone."

"I can look after my own mate," Aiden growled.

Grinning, Law turned to Kari. "So ladies, what are our orders?"

Kari looked at Meryn then turned and glanced at Declan, who was still stuffing his face. "Does having them here bother you?" she asked.

Declan looked up and shook his head. "The more people to protect you the better. Doesn't bother me at all."

Kari addressed Meryn. "All right, you're the one with the top score in battle combat or whatever. You decide."

Law looked impressed. "Really?"

"I tied with Byron," Meryn said, nodding.

"Byron McKenzie?" Idris asked.

"Yup, he's Aiden's dad."

"I always knew you were smart, Trouble," Law complimented.

"She is a little genius," Gidan elbowed Law.

"Of course," Law said, rubbing his ribs. "I let her direct us in the field, didn't I?"

They nodded. Meryn eyed him. "I was the only one good enough."

He just winked at her, and she laughed.

"Okay then," Meryn eyed Law. "We've got three four-man teams?"

Law nodded. "Yes, and my only request is that I personally guard either you or Kari."

Meryn bit her upper lip. "Okay Emeric and Gidan can go with Kari. Law and Idris with me. Split the other two teams up as follows: two assigned to Beth, two to Aiden, two to Adriel, and two to Magnus."

Law nodded. "Good choices."

"Even though you were not assigned to your sister?" Magnus asked.

Law grinned. "Tell them why you chose that way, Meryn."

"Two reasons. One: Personal feelings may impact his reaction time, and he might not follow proper protocol, which would endanger others." Meryn said, holding up one finger. Magnus blinked. "And two is because I need to ask Law magic stuff."

Law frowned at her a moment before he walked over to her. When he laid his hand on her shoulder, he jumped back as blue sparks flew. Cursing under his breath his sucked on his fingers. He looked around the room and then glared at Ryuu. "And you are?"

"My apologies. My name is Ryuu Sei. I am Meryn's squire. I've been helping her shield emotions. She was not reacting well. It should be safe now."

Meryn began to frown and shiver. She looked back at her squire. "You're the reason I was feeling better?"

Ryuu shrugged. "In part."

Law laid his hand on her shoulder. "You do have

magic. It's a small amount. Just enough to be bothersome."

"Empathy, that's what Kendrick said," Aiden added.

"You know Kendrick?" Law asked.

"Yeah, he moved to Lycaonia when Keelan's soul was ejected from his body," Meryn answered.

Law winced. "How much have I missed? Gods above, someone hurt Keelan! Is Lycaonia still standing?" he asked.

Meryn nodded. "Yeah, Kendrick's trying to stuff Keelan back into his body."

"What exactly happened to Keelan?" he asked.

Meryn glanced around the room. "That's classified."

Magnus and Adriel's eyebrows rose.

With his hand on her shoulder, Law leaned in. "If Kendrick OKs me, could you tell me then?"

"Sure, if he doesn't brief you himself."

Law closed his eyes. "Did Kendrick do the doors?"

"Yeah, but they're not working really well though."

Law shrugged one shoulder. "He's used to working with established witches. Your magic has been running wild all your life. You can't just shove this behind a door. You have to coax it there; otherwise, it will keep spilling out." Law removed his hand. "I'll work with you while I'm here. That should help."

"Thanks, crying and being all over the place sucks."

Law chuckled. "I can imagine."

Meryn turned to Magnus. "Where can the security peeps stay?"

Adriel turned to his Prince. "The teams for Kari

and I can stay on the Unit Level."

Magnus tapped the table. "We only have three guest rooms on this level. Aiden and Meryn are in one of them. Young Avery is in the other."

"Six," Sebastian volunteered, stepping forward.

Magnus turned his chair. "Since when?"

Sebastian put both hands on his hips and stared down at his charge. "Since we started running out of room. The boys expanded the guest quarters for us."

"Nigel and Neil?" Magnus asked. Sebastian nodded.

Magnus shook his head. "Those little devils."

Law nodded. "I'd like to get settled in and start assignments. We'll be doing twelve-hour shifts. Meryn, I'll be working with you a bit more. Idris, get the men assigned to their quarters. Adriel, if you could have someone help them to get acclimated."

Adriel reached for his walkie-talkie "Casanova, can you come down to Level One?"

"Yes sir."

"Casanova?" Kari asked out loud.

"Micah," numerous people responded. She laughed.

Bethy sat back smiling. "What else do we have for today?" she teased.

Magnus sighed. "The DeLaFontaine dinner."

"Douchebag," Meryn muttered. Law raised an eyebrow. She shook her head "Tell you later."

Magnus had a small smirk on his face, and he turned. "Law, will you be joining us for dinner?"

"Why would you join them, sir?" Gidan asked.

Law looked a bit uncomfortable. "My family is well known."

Gavriel, Aiden, Magnus, and Adriel began to

chuckle. Law eyed Meryn. "I think maybe I should join you."

Meryn grinned "Game on."

Kari sat back down and indicated for Law to join her at the table in the empty seat next to her. The men left with Micah to get assigned to their new quarters and be shown the city. She passed Law some of the sandwiches on her plate, and they began to wrap up their lunch. As people finished their lunches they left the room to get their assorted tasks completed before dinner.

She was walking out with Declan when she heard her name being called. She looked back to see Law jogging to catch up with her.

He looked down "So pregnant, huh? Emeric and Gidan will take good care of you."

Kari grinned. "Leaving you free to poke around."

He winked. "Meryn's squire has enough juice to take down an army. So she'll be okay with him while I snoop."

She laid a hand on his arm. "I am glad you are here."

"Me too, kiddo." Law ruffled her hair and then froze, looking at Declan. He dropped his hand. "Aren't lions supposed to be extremely possessive?"

Declan shrugged at the question. "I think my lion sees you as family. He knows that you will keep Kari safe so he approves."

"Lionhart? You're not at all like your brother."

"Who, Rex?" Kari asked. "He is very sweet."

Law snorted. "He's an arrogant ass."

Declan bristled. "It's just that he's that good."

Law smiled wide. "Just teasing. He'd swoon if he heard you sticking up for him like that. He dotes on you and Ari."

Declan grinned. "As if you now don't have six brothers and three sisters to take care of."

Law shrugged "Family's important. My future nieces and nephews come first though."

"Of course," Declan said.

"Speaking of family, where's Avery?" Law asked.

Kari sighed. "He didn't react well to the news of my 'second accident'." She held up her fingers in air quotes. "Tarragon had to sedate him. He and his mate will both be relaxing in Avery's room here on Level One."

Law's jaw tightened. "I'll check in on him and see what this new mate of his is like. I'm not sure I like the idea of my baby brother mated to a muscle-head."

"Hey!" Declan protested.

Law waved his hand. "Present company excluded of course." His eyes took on a devilish twinkle. "Maybe I should look in on Rex as well. I miss the time we spent together, one could almost describe those long weeks as magical," he sighed.

Declan's mouth opened, and he stared at Law.

Kari yawned, and Law steered her into Declan's arms, ignoring his shell-shocked expression. "She always tires after a healing, so go get her to bed before dinner."

"I can take care of my mate," Declan protested, still looking bewildered.

Law kissed her on the cheek then headed back to the dining room.

Yawning, Kari lifted them up to the Unit Level, and they made their way back to the house. Before she knew it, she was in their bedroom, and Declan had her undressed and in the bed.

"I think I like your brother. I wish you'd told me he was Law Ashleigh," Declan said.

"Why?"

"Because he's one of the most powerful witches in our world."

Kari snorted and buried her face in the pillow. "Surely not."

Declan poked her in the back. "Why do you think he was invited to dinner?"

She rolled over and looked at him. "He never said anything about being important."

"He wouldn't," Declan grunted. "I think that's why like him. I wonder if he was really involved with my brother?"

Kari hid a smile and ignored the question. She knew Law was having fun at her mate's expense, but she had to admit she was enjoying Declan's confused expressions too much to tell him otherwise. She crossed her fingers behind her head. "I wish I had known he was bringing me a security detail. We could have saved your father the trouble."

Declan pulled her into his arms. "You don't know my father; he won't be satisfied until you're surrounded by our pride members."

Declan buried his face in the back of her neck and placed a protective hand over her stomach. He began to purr. Ultimately, it was his purring that put her to sleep.

☾

WHEN KARI WOKE UP, DECLAN had already gone. On the nightstand, a single flower waited for her with a note.

Heading out to meet with the guys before dinner. Bethy dropped off a present. Miss you already. Love, Declan.

The flower was beautiful; it looked like mother-of-pearl and shimmered in the light. She had a sneaking suspicion that he had plucked it from the Royal Gardens. Smiling, she immediately jumped out of bed to look for a vase. She pulled one from the cabinet in the kitchen then ran back upstairs before adding some water from the bathroom and putting it on the nightstand.

After she got out of the shower and did her hair and makeup, she looked around and there, lying across the chair, was a gorgeous black silk dress. It was the gift from Bethy. She wouldn't have to worry about what to wear while she was here. At least, not until the rest of her things arrived. She sighed, thinking about leaving her condo, and then put that thought out of her head. Tonight, she would concentrate on the DeLaFontaine dinner. She slipped her feet into her own black heels, touched up her lip gloss and winked at herself in the mirror. As she exited the home Gidan stepped in behind her. She nodded at him and made her way to the transport tunnel. As she walked past the unit estate, she heard a few whistles. She turned and waved.

"Go get 'em," they yelled.

"You know I will," she said, waving.

She floated down to Level One and then rang the doorbell for the Magnus estate. Sebastian was there in a moment, opening it up and smiling at her.

"You look absolutely lovely," he commented.

"Thank you, Sebastian. Where is everyone?"

"Most of the men are in the antechamber having wine, and..."—he hesitated—"Bethy and Tarragon are fussing over Meryn."

Her eyes narrowed. "Is she being difficult?"

Sebastian smiled slyly. "When is she not being difficult? I think it is part of her charm."

Kari walked in, and Declan's head immediately turned to her. His eyes widened and low whistle escaped. "Baby, you look amazing."

He crossed the distance of the room and pulled her into his arms, before laying a hot kiss on her lips. When they broke apart, she looked up, and his eyes were shimmering gold.

She winked at him. "Did you miss me?" she asked

"Always," he took her hand.

Gidan nodded at Declan and took up his position in the corner.

Declan acknowledged the guard before his eyes darted to Adriel, and Kari nodded. They walked over to his unit leader where he was speaking with Magnus and Gavriel.

"Adriel, I've got something to ask you."

Adriel looked confused, and Declan smiled. "I have already discussed it with Kari, and we would like for you to be our child's *athair*."

Adriel's mouth dropped, and Eva began to smile "But I thought for sure it would be Grant or Etain," Adriel whispered. "Why me?"

Declan laid a hand on his shoulder. "Etain and Grant will make great uncles, but we all decided that you would make the best *athair*. The three of us watched how you were with Bethy. We know, no matter what, any child in your custody would receive the utmost care. Don't be surprised if they ask you to be *athair* for their children too. There's no one we trust more."

Kari was surprised to see Adriel had tears swimming in his eyes. His mate wrapped an arm around his waist as she laid her head on his shoulder. "See my love. I told you they knew you cared."

Adriel had to clear his throat twice before he could respond. "Declan Lionhart, it would be my honor to be your child's *athair.*"

Declan pulled him into a hug. "Of course, you may have to fight Rex to spoil her or him, but I think you're up to it."

Adriel gave them a rare open smile. "I am pretty sure I can hold my own."

A few moments later, the doorbell chimed again. This time it was Rex.

"There is my sister!" he exclaimed. Walking up to her, he pulled her into a gentle hug and kissed her on the forehead. "And how is my niece or nephew today?"

"The same as they were this morning," she commented.

Rex was beaming. "I took the liberty of picking out some of the bedroom furniture I think that my niece or nephew might like. Maybe we can go over my selections later."

Kari blinked. "We have not really gotten that far yet."

Rex waved a hand. "I can help."

"Evidently," she chuckled.

Rex looked around. "Where is Meryn?"

Gavriel, Adriel, Aiden, and Magnus exchanged

looks.

Aiden pointed to the far hallway. "Still in the bedroom."

Rex frowned "Isn't she supposed to be out here?"

Aiden spread his hands wide. "We're working on it."

Kari patted Declan's arm. "Give me a moment. I will see if I can go help Bethy."

He leaned down and nipped her ear. "Good luck."

Kari walked toward the guest quarters and stood at the open door. There, Tarragon was still fussing over Meryn's arm.

"It should be better by now, but I'm so hesitant, you're human after all."

"Get this freaking sling off me. I can't even wipe my butt," Meryn groused.

Tarragon rolled his eyes. "Thank the gods Bethy wasn't like you."

Meryn stuck her tongue out at him. He carefully removed the sling and gently made her extend and then flex her arm.

"Is there any pain?" he asked.

"Nope, I'm okay," Meryn insisted.

"Okay, I'm going to go to the antechamber for a glass of wine"—he looked at Bethy—"or three." Then he left the room.

Ryuu stood in the corner watching his charge, a smile on his face.

Bethy turned. "Meryn, you need to start getting ready."

"No," Meryn said. "I don't want to eat with that asshole."

"And I do?" Bethy asked. "Listen to your Yoda. Sometimes you have to make nice with jerks. It's part of being an adult."

"Fine," Meryn said.

"Fine?" Beth asked.

"Yeah, I quit being adult." Her clothes shimmered, and she stood before them in her Simba pajamas.

Kari laid a hand on Bethy's arm. "I guess this is just beyond her." She turned to Meryn. "Go eat your pudding, dear."

"What's beyond me?" Meryn asked, her eyes narrowing.

"This dinner." Kari clucked her tongue. "I keep forgetting how young you are."

"I'm not that young," she protested.

"It might be better if you do not attend. You are so very blunt."

"I totally nailed Daphne at that sewing circle."

"Oh yes, Bethy told me about that. Sweetheart, that is like bragging you stayed in your lane at the go kart track to an Formula One racer."

Meryn gasped. "I could totally do this."

Bethy looked unsure. "Maybe you should stay in tonight and get some sleep."

Kari nodded her agreement. "Meryn, there is nothing to be ashamed of. I think it is admirable you know your limitations."

"Whatever, heifer; I got this!" Her clothes shimmered again, and she was now wearing a red sequined dress.

Kari tilted her head. "Were you going for high class Vegas call girl?"

Meryn screeched in frustration. "Don't make me assume my ultimate form!"

"And what is that, dear? A homicidal hobbit?"

Meryn's mouth dropped, and then her lips began

to twitch. Soon, she was giggling. "Okay that was fun."

The red dress shimmered, and she was in a black dress with pearls. Kari winked at Bethy and then turned to Meryn "There is nothing more satisfying than winning the game."

Bethy's mouth dropped open. "You totally just handled Meryn."

"Game?" Meryn asked.

"Politics." Kari answered. "It is the ultimate strategy game."

"But how do you know if you're winning?"

Kari winked at her "You will know."

The doorbell rang, and she looked between Bethy and Meryn. "Game on," she said, echoing Meryn's earlier sentiment.

By the time the three of them arrived in the antechamber, tensions were already high and fake smiles were flashing all around. Holding a wine glass, Ivan DeLaFontaine stood between Magnus and Aiden.

"There have been too many changes lately, Prince Magnus, and much too quickly," Ivan observed.

"I disagree. If given a choice, the city would never change. Look how quickly they adapted to the wolves and Wi-Fi," Magnus pointed out.

"You are changing our way of life." Ivan protested.

"Ladies and gentlemen, sorry for the interruption, but dinner is now being served," Sebastian said bowing and indicating the dining room.

They filed in and sat down. Kari was relieved to be seated between Declan and Law. Across the table, she kept an eye on Meryn. Magnus lifted his spoon for the soup entrée. "You keep saying our way of life, but never have we had arranged matings before."

DeLaFontaine shrugged. "They are consenting adults; it is their choice."

Magnus turned to Kari. "Is this true?"

Kari knew that Magnus was asking for the results even though they had discussed it earlier to make a point with DeLaFontaine. She nodded. "In all of the interviews, everyone we spoke to was willing, however, most did point out that in the event that they found their true mate, they would dissolve their arranged mating immediately. If more citizens find their mates among the wolves, having the trust fund will go a long way to help those who may need to break away from their arranged matings if they are feeling trapped." Kari deliberately mentioned the trust fund. Ivan's eyes tightened at the word.

Kari's attention turned to Meryn when she began to rub her temples. Tarragon stepped from the corner where he stood next to Tarak and placed a hand on her shoulder. He frowned then looked around the table to Law.

Law stood, walked around the table, and laid a hand on her back; he whispered something, and Meryn's face began to clear.

"I say, is the human okay?" DeLaFontaine asked.

Meryn nodded. "Yes, I've been getting really bad sinus headaches lately. Tarragon and Law have been helping," she explained fibbing her butt off.

"That is kind of them," DeLaFontaine stared at Meryn, and then his eyes took on a different light. "Let us get an outside perspective. Meryn, what do you think of our way of life and the way we do things here in Noctem Falls?"

Kari could tell that she wasn't the only one holding their breath for Meryn's response. Bethy looked green around the gills.

Meryn shrugged. "It's a bit old-fashioned, but I think it's part of the city's charm."

Ivan nodded graciously. "Go on."

"But it could be better," Meryn continued. "In Lycaonia, there are people of all four races, so it's almost like we get the best of the four cities. Maybe a little bit of diversity would go a long way in helping people with changes."

Ivan took a sip of soup. "That is very forward thinking of you."

Meryn played with her spoon. "I just like my creature comforts."

"Like your Wi-Fi?" he asked. She nodded. "But not all races are the same," Ivan protested. "For example, take humans, they have very little to offer," he said, a smarmy look on his face. He was clearly baiting Meryn.

To everyone's astonishment, Meryn nodded her agreement. "Before I found Lycaonia, I pretty much stayed to myself. I didn't get along with those around me. I found them to be manipulative, greedy liars. I've found more friends amongst paranormals in the last six months than any humans in my entire life."

Kari could see the calculating look in Ivan's eyes. He looked too pleased. "I am pleasantly surprised to find that you are a very intelligent and objective young woman. We may have gotten off on the wrong foot earlier, when we had our little 'episode'. But I do believe you are a very fitting mate to one in power, like our Unit Commander."

Meryn smiled. Her acquiescent behavior had everyone wondering if a bomb was ticking in the corner. Kari found herself concerned about Meryn's statements. Did she really hate humans? Under the table, Declan gave her hand a squeeze. He met her eyes, and he gave a slight shake of his head. Kari began to relax. Of course, he was right, Meryn was not like DeLaFontaine at all.

Between Kari and Bethy, they managed to keep the topics neutral, and slowly and painfully, the dinner came to an end. In the antechamber, as they were saying goodbyes, DeLaFontaine shook hands with Magnus, who winced, and then Aiden.

Aiden frowned looking down. "You may want to get your cufflinks checked." He rubbed his hand.

Ivan shook his head "I told my squire to get that looked at, my apologies. My efforts to entice Sebastian to my home have failed, I have to make do with who I have." He looked over at Meryn. "This is been a most productive dinner."

Aiden stepped closer to his mate. With a final wave DeLaFontaine left and Sebastian closed the door firmly behind him.

Meryn yawned and then stretched. "Bedtime."

"Not so fast, pint size," Eva protested.

Kari wasn't the only one staring at Meryn. Ryuu walked up behind his charge. "She did not mean it the way it sounded."

Kari looked at Meryn. "So she did not mean to sound like a DeLaFontaine-human-hating sympathizer?"

Meryn's mouth dropped. "I'm not a douchebag."

"No, you're not, but you weren't lying; you weren't playing the game, and he knew that." Bethy chewed on her lower lip.

"No, but it was different before," Meryn said.

"Before I met you all, people sucked. I didn't like anyone..." she paused. "I didn't like humans..." Her eyes grew wide. "Oh my god," she whispered. "I'm a racist." Her voice sounded horrified.

Behind her, Ryuu snorted, Bethy slapped her forehead, and Kari began to laugh. Eva ruffled her hair, "Hey little bit, before you label yourself a racist, you might want to make sure you weren't just surrounded by assholes."

"Oh yeah, good point." Meryn looked a bit relieved.

Rex smiled down at Meryn. "I do not believe you hate someone for just being human. The fact that you grew up amongst humans and hated most of them is more a matter of statistics."

Meryn smirked up at him. "I was disappointed that you didn't beat him down with those muscular arms of yours."

Rex blushed a bit. "I wanted to, of course, but I was raised attending political dinners, as was Declan. We know when to act and when to keep quiet."

Meryn nodded. "Right. Bethy said something like that. Being an adult sucks."

Aiden turned to Law. "You were strangely quiet during dinner as well. Earlier, her headache, was that her magic?"

Law nodded. "Since it's so wild, I think we're gonna leave the door open for a bit."

Meryn looked up at him in confusion. "But isn't that a bad thing?"

Law shook his head. "No, I think it was fighting you so hard because it knew the door was closed, and it couldn't come out. If we leave it open just a bit and it knows it can come and go as it pleases that might actually make it easier for you."

Meryn nodded. "That makes sense."

"What I found interesting was that you were having such a reaction to DeLaFontaine. Do you want to know what I saw?" he asked, grinning.

Meryn closed her eyes. "Oil."

Law nodded. "All you could see was black oil. When did you start associating pictures with your feelings?"

"A couple of days ago; it was easier when certain feeling got a picture. That way I can understand what it was trying to tell me, and I could interpret it better. They would pop up, get identified and then go away. It didn't hurt as much."

"That's a really good idea." Law nodded his head approvingly.

Meryn flushed at his compliment.

"Oily?" Magnus asked. "He has always been a slippery one," he commented.

Meryn smiled up at Law. "Thanks for your help; those headaches kill me."

Behind her, Ryuu's eyes flashed. "You should have told me."

Meryn turned to her squire. "I didn't want to drain you."

Ryuu gave her an exasperated look. "Let me worry about that. I have more than enough power to help you, and your health comes first."

Kari watched as a group of men joined them in the antechamber. The twelve-hour shift was up, and there was about to be a change of guard.

Law kissed Meryn on one cheek then walked over and gave her a kiss. "Good night, ladies, I'll see you in the morning." He turned on his way out the door.

"Rex, you're welcome to visit anytime," he threw out.

Declan flinched, and his eyes widened as Rex's expression became confused. "Thank you for the invitation. I may take you up on that later to discuss some things."

My brother is going to hell. Kari decided to stay quiet and watch how this played out.

Meryn waved, and Kari gave her brother a salute. "Thanks again," she said.

"Anytime, ragamuffin," he said, shutting the door behind him.

The security detail went to their charges and everyone began saying good night.

Kari laughed when she heard Meryn. "Now that I have minions and mercenaries, I can take over the world."

Aiden looked down at his mate, a terrified look on his face.

"Okay, on that note, let's go check on Avery," Declan suggested. Kari eagerly headed toward the guest quarters with Declan. She couldn't wait to see Avery's reaction to her pregnancy news in person.

She knocked on the door. Avery answered almost immediately, looking happier than she'd ever seen him. He squealed loudly and wrapped his arms around her neck. "A baby! Our own baby! A real baby!" he rambled.

"I am happy to see you, too."

Avery danced from foot to foot. He was about to say something and then looked up and saw Declan. "Congratulations," he said, looking down at the floor. It was as if Avery had forgotten that Declan was there for a moment.

Kari looked at Avery. “Do you need sister time?”

He hesitated and nodded.

Declan smiled. “You’re not going to hurt my feelings, Avery. I’m sure there will be things you will need me for too.” He kissed the back of Kari’s neck. “I’ll be waiting for you by the tunnel.”

Kari shut the door, took Avery by the hand, and led him to the bed where they sat down. “Where’s Warrick?”

“He returned to his house, I could tell he wanted to stay but,” Avery pointed down to the double sized bed and giggled.

Kari shook her head at the image of Warrick trying to fit on the tiny bed. Then she looked at her brother. “Okay, what is going on?”

Avery shrugged. “There have been so many changes; everything is moving so fast.”

Kari wrapped her arm around his shoulder and pulled him close until his head rested on her shoulder.

“Warrick has not...” she started to ask.

Avery sat up straight and turned to her. “No, no, no! He’s been a perfect gentleman. He’s so sweet and kind and considerate,” he blushed furiously.

She smiled. “Good. You deserve all of those things.”

Avery’s smile faltered. “But I miss home. I miss my own room and my library.”

“I know; I miss home too. But I think we are needed here, and we have found our mates. I know they need us.”

“And I’m going to be an uncle,” his eyes widened. “When can we go shopping for the baby?”

She laughed. “No idea, we have only been here

three days. I think Rex has already picked out furniture."

Avery giggled. "He's really nice. He said I could call him brother now," Avery admitted.

The soft spot that Kari had for Rex grew larger.

"Hey, tomorrow is the fair. You're going to be there, right?" Avery asked.

"Of course."

Avery was quiet for another moment. "Do you think we are the way we are because fate needed us this way to help everyone? That we aren't broken? It's just that our pieces need to be put together differently to fit here?"

Kari blinked. She had always known that Avery considered himself different in a bad way. "I think so. I think Fate made us the way we are because she needed us this way. It helps knowing we are where we belong."

Avery nodded. "I could even give up my library for Warrick."

Kari laughed. "Remind me later to tell you about Magnus' library here in the city," she winked.

Avery's eyes grew wide. "Oh Kari, I would do anything to see his library."

"I will see what I can do, kiddo." She stood and kissed him on the forehead.

"Hey," he said. She turned. "Take care of my niece or nephew. I'm an uncle, after all."

She laughed. "Yes, you are."

She closed the door and walked down the hallway. She met Declan and Rex by the transport.

"So you let Mother and Father know what was happening?" Declan asked.

Rex nodded. "Father wasn't happy that you hung

up on him, but I think he understood that you needed more time with your mate. I can just as easily get him up to date. He'll be sending a lion security detail soon."

Kari shook her head. "Can we ask them to turn around? There are going to be so many people here."

Declan turned to her, not looking the least bit concerned. "They can stand all around you, for all I care. That said, the more people protecting you, the safer you will be."

Kari laid a hand on Rex's arm. "Will you be at the fair tomorrow?" she teased.

He rolled his eyes. "These things are not really my forte."

Declan elbowed him in the ribs. "Head to old man Richter's stand. He sells meat pies that are to die for. If you buy a couple dozen, they let you sit there at the stand and they serve beer."

Rex's face brightened. "That is not a bad idea." When Kari yawned, he pointed to the tunnel. "Go get your sleep. Your health is of the utmost importance, good night." Rex leaned at the waist until his face was near her belly. "Good night, baby Lionhart; your uncle loves you very much," he said in baby talk before walking away. Declan looked shocked.

"Why so surprised? He totally dotes on you."

"He drives me nuts."

"He is your brother."

"Yeah, I guess our child could do worse than Rex, Ari, Law, and Avery for uncles."

She giggled. "Avery kept saying 'uncle', 'niece' and 'nephew'. He is like Rex; he cannot wait to go shopping for the baby."

Declan took her hand. "Tomorrow, I'll make sure

Avery walks around and goes to the stalls. They have some handmade things that you can't buy anywhere else."

They returned to the Unit Level and were slowly walking down the main street toward their home when she turned to him. "You never doubted Meryn for a moment, did you?" she asked.

Declan shook his head. "She is the least judgmental person I've ever met in my entire existence. Her not liking somebody is almost like a knee-jerk reaction. The only person that gets that sort of reaction is an asshole."

Declan unlocked the door and they made their way upstairs to their bedroom. She sighed when she saw her suitcase. Declan simply stripped and got under the covers naked, his clothes in piles on the floor. She felt her eye twitch, but she was too tired to take him to task over it. She carefully laid the borrowed dress over a chair and dug out her favorite sleep shirt. She slipped under the covers then poked Declan until he moved over so she could take his warm spot. He grumbled, but moved over for her. She pulled his arm around her, holding it tight.

"What did Rex have to say about your parents?" she asked.

"That they're excited. My mother was still chattering away when Rex was on the phone with them. Father, of course, wasn't happy that I hung up on him, but he understood. He has a mate, after all. He'll be sending a lion detail to us. I'm pretty sure it might be a couple of cousins," he shrugged.

She yawned again. "Why am I so tired?" she asked.

"Oh, I don't know, probably because you've been

through a lot in the past couple of days."

"Avery misses home and his library. I do, too." She felt him tense under her hand. "This does not feel like home. It is like we are just visiting."

Declan tightened his hold. "Do whatever you need, change whatever you want at the house. As for Avery, you could tell him that Magnus has one of the largest libraries in the world."

Kari giggled. "I reminded Avery of that tonight."

"I'm serious, Kari; this is your home. We'll do whatever it takes to make you feel comfortable and wanted here."

"What about Avery? He cannot stay in Magnus' guest quarters forever."

"I was assuming he would be moving in with us."

"Really?" she asked. "You do not mind?"

Declan snorted. "Course not. That way I can keep an eye on little guy. In about a month or so, I'm pretty sure he will be moving in with Warrick."

She exhaled, sighing.

"We're right down the street, Kari; it's not like he's moving to a different level."

She brightened at that "You are right. Maybe I should just turn over both houses to him to decorate."

She felt Declan yawn. "Whatever the little guy needs."

"There is nothing that you would want for yourself? He and I show up and you are changing your entire life."

Declan shook his head. "Not life, existence. I existed before you. I may have smiled and laughed and spoke, but I didn't truly begin to live until I opened my eyes and saw you."

She clutched his arm to her tight. "Me too."

"Get some rest. We have a long day tomorrow and lots of food to eat."

She laughed. "You are just like one of the children. You are looking forward to the food and the games, are you not?"

She felt his lips on the back of her neck.

He smiled. "Of course. Like the children, I know what's important in life. And that's to have a good time and eat good food."

"Declan?"

"Yes?"

"I love you."

She felt one hot tear drop on her neck and then another. His voice was hoarse when he responded. "And I love you too, always."

Feeling more complete than she had in her entire life, she drifted off to sleep.

CHAPTER FOURTEEN

KARI AND DECLAN GOT READY. Each moving in different directions. It didn't take Declan long to get dressed, find his shoes, and make his way downstairs. After a minute, Kari smiled as the sound of the espresso machine grinding beans signified that Declan was still waking up.

She pulled on a pair of black slacks that were actually yoga pants made to look like business pants, a comfortable pair of black sneakers, a white shirt, and a black cardigan. She hoped to look professional but be comfortable during the fair. She grabbed her legal pad and walked downstairs. To her surprise, Declan stood in front of the espresso machine, a scowl on his face.

"You don't get any."

She opened her mouth to protest but then remembered why. Rolling her eyes she smiled at his misplaced concern, she'd just grab a coffee later from Sebastian. She went to the refrigerator and opened it. For someone who enjoyed food as much as Declan did, his refrigerator was surprisingly empty. She turned to glare at him. He held up both hands.

"We can stock it later. Besides it's a fair, I'm sure we'll be able to grab breakfast upstairs."

Grumbling about no caffeine, Kari walked with Declan out the door to the transport tunnel. She kept sneaking glances at his latte, which he carefully held in the other hand. Once they reached Level Six, he gave her a kiss on the cheek and they separated.

She immediately went to Magnus' side and helped to organize where the different stand locations were, who was running what event, and where to send the children. Every once in a while, she would hear Declan's laugh and would turn to see him surrounded by smiling people. Everywhere he went, he seemed to be a magnet. At first, he was helping the unit warriors with their activities for the children. Then, of course, he migrated over to the food stands. Every one of the vendors wanted him to be a taste tester. She watched her mate walk down the line, snagging treats from each stall.

She laughed as Adriel and Etain walked away with Prince Magnus. They somehow had managed to talk him into getting into a dunk tank. Magnus was a good sport, but being a vampire, of course he could levitate. So she knew he really wasn't worried about going in the water, unless one of the children succeeded in hitting the bullseye, then she knew he would be soaked.

Overhead, the witches had charged the crystals that brought a new bright daylight to Level Six. The children were able to experience a fairground as if they were topside.

Kari walked past the stand Meryn had proposed, bobbing for apples. The witches were murmuring spells to bring the apples close to them, while the wolves were trying to use their canines to secure their prize.

Avery had a booth set up and was doing face painting for the children, Warrick at his side. The children giggled as the large warrior insisted on adding his own touches to their new looks, often dotting them on the nose with a speck of black paint. Avery rolled his eyes at his mate's artistic abilities causing the children to laugh more.

She walked along the back wall and sure enough, as Declan had suggested, Rex was sitting at the stall that was selling meat pies. He had half a dozen empty tins in front of him, one in hand, and a beer at the table. She raised an eyebrow, and he just shrugged. She was astonished when he fit the entire meat pie in his mouth and then reached for another. Seeing that he was secure and happy in his choice of stalls, she kept walking. Behind her, Emeric trailed far enough away so as to not interfere with her day, but close enough that she knew he was close by.

Law was standing directly beside Meryn, pointing out different things, causing her to laugh. Ryuu was behind her off to one side, and Aiden was with Adriel directing the warriors.

After a few hours, the vendors came out and started to set up long tables at the stalls for their buffet lunch. Large bowls of pasta salad, potato salad, baked beans, stews, soups, chilis, breads, and sandwiches were piled high. Everyone began to dig in. Kari was reaching for her second sandwich when she heard the familiar sound of a fork on glass. Everyone quieted as Magnus stood in his chair to be seen by everyone.

"I want to thank everyone for coming today. It is

a first for Noctem Falls but not the last." Everyone laughed and clapped. "Today we are celebrating new friends, new family, and of course, new life."

Everyone clapped again, there was whistling and a few catcalls were heard around. Rachelle, Bethy, and Kari chuckled. Magnus was about to go on when, out of the corner of her eye, she saw that he turned his head. Her gaze followed his. At the back of the hall, at the transport tunnel, people were coming up, and a crowd began to appear. It was the Noble and Founding Families from the lower levels. Moving en masse, they marched through the fair-grounds, protesting the fair.

Loud shouts of 'Go home, you don't belong here!' were heard. The warriors formed a barrier between the fair attendees and the protesters. Kari began to move quickly to get through the crowd. The path behind her closed. She looked back to see Emeric cursing. She had to make her way toward Magnus to assist him in this.

She reached the opening where the families were walking. Gerald DuBois led the group as they marched directly up to the table where Magnus stood.

"We want them to leave. We were happy the way we were. Things were fine."

"We were not happy," one of the fair attending vampires called out.

Gerald hissed at the vendor. "You are lucky to have a place in the city," he said.

"Things are changing and for the better," another vampire yelled.

"Yeah, maybe you should be the ones to go," another vendor cried out.

Andre, Gerald's son, picked up an empty bottle and threw it into the crowd, hitting a wolf. Kari blinked, when she opened her eyes, chaos had broken out. The warriors were having a hard time maintaining their wall of bodies to protect the people because it wasn't just the Founding Families; the wolves wanted to fight as well, they had had enough.

She understood where they were coming from; this sort of active aggression could not go unanswered. She reached for Magnus. She was trying to break away when, all of a sudden, she was knocked to the floor, into the opening in front of the table. She gasped as the wind was knocked from her lungs and a loud roar echoed through the cavern. It was ear shattering. The hair on the back of her neck rose.

Everyone froze, looking at each other in confusion. In the back of the cavern, there was an answering roar. She looked up to see the sea of people part. Declan stalked toward her. For the rest of her life, she would never forget the sight. He seemed to have grown in size, bulked up his muscles, and expanded his shaggy blond hair. It had lengthened and seemed to billow about his head by an unseen wind, like a mane. His eyes were honey colored and his canines were extended. He snarled and growled. Everyone, friend or foe, quietly and carefully began to back away.

Declan reached for her and pulled her up and close to his body. He looked out at the crowd. "That is enough!" he bellowed. "Times are changing; if you don't like it, *leave!*" The word was roared and echoed through the chamber. "You're putting innocent people in danger, including my mate. If you have a valid complaint, step forward and use the appropriate channels. Your voices will be heard."

Kari laid a comforting hand on his chest as he breathed hard. She looked around at the faces. "Prince Magnus is not trying to take anything away from you. He is trying to give you so much."

"Liar!" a haughty voice cried out.

Kari looked to see Gerald hissing. She looked at the crowd of the Founding Family members behind him. "What has he told you?"

"That Prince Magnus gave away his mate to the wolves to keep them satisfied."

Kari blinked "That is not true. Rachelle is happy. She found her true mate amongst the wolves."

"It is true!" a female voice called.

The people stepped aside to allow Rachelle and Peter to step into the open circle.

"I am happy. I am truly happy. Prince Magnus has not forced me to do anything, in fact, he has supported me every step of the way."

Kari smiled. "The fair is part of a celebration for Rachelle as she is with child. The first for Noctem Falls in centuries."

The Founding Families looked shocked at the news.

"Truly?" one of the females asked, stepping forward. "Even though she is with a wolf shifter."

Kari nodded. "Yes, as am I." Everyone stared at her she placed a hand over her stomach. "I am a vampire." She looked up at Declan who was still scowling at the crowd. "My mate is a shifter. Rachelle is a vampire and her mate is a shifter. Our Prince's own niece is a shifter, and her mate is a vampire, and they are expecting. Your Prince is literally trying to breathe new life into the city. For the first time in ages, we will have children here, our own children."

Prince Magnus stepped off the table and stood behind her. "I could not have said it better myself. In the past week, we have had three pregnancies announced, and if that is not Fate telling us we are doing something right, I do not know what is. You do not have to like me, but you will respect me!"

Magnus never raised his voice, but the power emanating from him nearly drove Kari to her knees. If it weren't for Declan supporting her arm, she might've ended up on the floor like many of the Founding Family members. The energy pulsed and swirled around him like heat waves off of blacktop in summer. When she looked over, Rex and Emeric stood at the edge of the crowd looking pissed off.

Behind Magnus, in the silence, she heard a small voice.

"R.E.S.P.E.C.T find out what it means to me. Sock it to me, sock it to me, sock it to me, sock it to me."

Kari shook her head and rested her forehead on Declan's chest. Behind Magnus, Meryn was dancing, punching the air as if she was fake boxing and prancing back and forth. When Kari sneaked a glance, she saw that Magnus' lips were twitching violently. Though his eyes still remained a bit angry, he was having a hard time keeping up his scowl.

When she looked up, Declan now looked normal. He was watching Meryn, his eyes wide, and a smile on his face. Throughout the crowd, at first there were titters, then chuckles, and finally, open laughter.

Standing behind Meryn, watching her antics, Aiden shook his head, his cheeks flushed. Kari figured by now he was probably used to his little mate's crazy ways.

Trish, the aggravating woman that threw her past affair with Declan in her face stepped forward out of the throng of Founding Family members. She was fighting a smile as well.

"I do not know about the others, but I would be very interested in meeting some of these wolves. Especially if one of them could be my mate and give me a child." Trish winked up at one of the tall wolves whose eyes grew wide. He instinctively took a step back, unsure what to do. When her fangs extended and peeked out over her lips, he gulped. Finding his courage, he stepped forward and grinned at her.

Now that the violent tension was officially broken, Magnus walked toward Trish. "It would be my honor to introduce you."

Kari watched and identified the Founding Family members that turned on their heels and left. Not all of them were convinced, but she made note of which ones were walking away. Now that everyone was on more friendly terms, Tarragon and Dr. St. John were running around trying to treat some of the wounded. Declan kissed her on the top of the head.

"Are you hurt?" he asked.

"It was just a scuffle; I'm fine."

"And where in the hell was Emeric?" Declan demanded.

"Right behind her until those fools got in my way." Emeric's face was like a thundercloud. He jerked his thumb over and Kari saw where two wolves lay unconscious on the floor. "I moved them."

Declan nodded his approval. He kissed her forehead. "I need to help Adriel calm everyone down. Will you be okay?"

"Yes, I will be fine. I will be helping some of the shifter parents with the children."

"Meet me back here for dinner."

"It is a date." She stood up on tiptoe and kissed his full lips.

While Declan and Adriel worked with Magnus and Stefan to soothe the wolf shifters, Kari was assuring the skittish, scared children that everything was okay and that they would be resuming the games shortly. She was about to turn back to find Magnus when the scent of blood caught her attention. She walked over to see Tarragon frantically trying to save a wolf shifter.

"What on earth happened?" she demanded, kneeling down beside the healer.

Tarragon tore his eyes from his patient to look up at her furious. "I'm assuming one of the Founding Family members got a gouge or two in during the brawl. I need supplies." He blinked. "You have access to Level One, don't you?" She nodded. "Can you run down and get some bandages and supplies?"

"Of course."

Tarragon turned to Emeric. "I need you. Can you apply pressure?"

Emeric shook his head. "No, I'm sorry, I'm assigned to her."

Tarragon looked at him. "I will lose this patient if I don't get some help."

She laid a hand on Emeric's shoulder. "Apply pressure, that is an order. I will be right back."

Before he could answer, she dashed away. She flew down the transport tunnel and hurriedly walked through Level One to Broderick's laboratory. She was halfway down the hallway when she felt an overwhelming sense of dread.

She looked around and didn't see anything. She took a few uneasy steps and thought she heard steps behind her. She turned again and there was nothing.

Not taking any chances, she reached for her walkie-talkie. Just as she pressed the button, pain exploded at her back of her head. She saw stars and then darkness.

☾

WHEN HER EYES OPENED, SHE groaned; her head was killing her. She looked around, trying to identify where she was. The overwhelmingly strong astringent smell almost choked her. When she put her hands on the floor to stand up, they became soaked in liquid. She looked around, fear taking over.

Broderick's lab had been completely destroyed. In the back of the room, where the cabinets lined the wall, smoke billowed up from behind the long lab table.

She smelled her hands and knew she was covered in chemicals. It wouldn't be long before she too would end up like this room.

She went to the door, tried the doorknob, but it would not budge. She threw her shoulder against it and nothing. It was almost like it had been locked from the outside. She was looking out the window for help when a face appeared in the pane. She jumped back, startled.

The face was twisted in anger, eyes red. Was this the feral that they were looking for? Her eyes narrowed.

"Marcus?" she asked. He snarled, an evil smile on his lips.

"Marcus, what are you doing here?" she demanded.

"You are not my boss, not anymore. I came here to get even. I heard your little conversation with Law outside your office. I figured I would have ample opportunity to get even here. Then they found me and gave me a bigger purpose. They said they would make me a prince, and I believe them."

"Believe who? What in the hell you talking about? Get me out of here."

"No, you need to die. You need to be destroyed along with the lab. Enjoy your death," he sneered and then walked away.

She pounded on the steel door. "Marcus! Marcus!"

She reached for her belt but both her cell phone and her walkie-talkie were gone. She inhaled again and began to choke; the smoke was quickly filling the room. She leaned against the door and slumped down.

"Declan, where are you?"

☾

DECLAN WAS RACING AROUND WITH Adriel, making sure that those who were injured had received treatment and that the frightened families were settled. Everyone was concerned. Old wounds had been ripped open by the prejudices shown by the Founding Families. Surprisingly, his brother was at his side every step of the way. He took his cue from Declan and cajoled and joked with not only the wolves but also the other vampires.

He watched as the people around him slowly begin to relax and accept his brother. He had probably made more progress in the past thirty minutes with him than he had the past thirty years on his own. They made their way back over to where Magnus and Adriel stood comparing notes.

The fair began to kick off once again, mostly to keep the children calm and to lighten the atmosphere. The music resumed, and the games handlers were calling out about prizes once again.

"Well?" Magnus asked.

Adriel sighed, looking exhausted "Tarragon and Emeric are working on a wolf. It looks like he was gouged, just like Declan was. Might have been Andre. The wolf did not see who did it. I am not sure we have enough evidence to track the assailant down."

Declan nodded, then turned to Adriel.

"Emeric?" he asked.

"Yes," Adriel replied looking confused at Declan's urgent tone. Behind them, Law began cursing.

"Who's with Kari?" Declan asked.

Magnus paled.

"Where is Kari?" Declan demanded.

Everyone began to look around.

"Kari!" Declan yelled.

"Fire," Meryn said simply, her eyes slightly unfocused.

Everyone was still calling out for his mate and speaking at once, but Declan had locked in on Meryn. No one was paying her any attention except for him and Ryuu. Ryuu stood behind Meryn, his eyes concerned.

"*Denka*?" he asked.

"Fire," she repeated.

This time, Grant and Etain spun and looked at Declan. Adriel turned slowly, a look of horror on his face. His unit brothers knew what his nightmare had showed him.

"Kari," he whispered. "Where is she?" he asked

"Broderick's lab," Meryn answered, still looking dazed.

Law grabbed him by the arm, and they ran together. Using his magic, Law got them down to Level One, and they raced down the hallway.

At the end of the hall, they reached the door, only to see tendrils of smoke escaping tiny cracks. The lab had been made impenetrable and sealed. He tried the door, but the handle wouldn't even turn.

"I need somebody with access!" he screamed.

"Right behind you," Magnus put his hand on the biometric lock, and still it wouldn't turn.

"Hold on," Law ordered.

He closed his eyes and his hand began to glow. After a few seconds, Declan heard the tumblers turn and the door was unlocked. He tried the door again, but nothing happened.

Roaring, he felt his body completely expand. Bones began to crack as he grew taller and wider. His face began to form a muzzle. His teeth began to thicken and lengthen. His mane, which had been at his shoulders earlier, was now to his waist. A light gold fur covered his arms and his hands became black claws.

He dug the claws into the steel door and pulled, ripping it off the hinges. The people behind him cleared the way, and he threw the door down the hallway. Slumped to one side, Kari's small, pale body lay motionless on the floor.

Declan reached into the smoke, pulling her out. Around him, everyone began to cough. Law began to chant low, and soon, a bright light appeared, chasing away the smoke and putting out the flames.

"Kari!" Declan roared his frustration and fear.

Hands reached for her and he swiped his claws at them.

"Declan, you need to let us help her. She is not breathing," Magnus ordered.

He hissed and shook his head. They were trying to take his mate away. He snarled at everyone until he smelled something familiar. An arm was thrust under his nose. Pride. He looked up. His older brother stood over him, his eyes turned yellow and his hair billowing around him.

Though not in third form, Rex had also expanded with his own fear. He gently pulled Kari away from Declan, and Declan let him. This was family, this was his blood, and his blood would not hurt his mate.

Immediately, Rex began CPR. He breathed into her mouth and began chest compressions. Anytime, someone tried to get near, Declan swiped at them. After a few moments, Kari began to cough. Relief flooded his body. He pulled her into his arms, muttering her name over and over and over again.

She blinked up at him. "I am okay; I knew you would come."

She ran a hand over his muzzle, taking in every whisker. Her eyes were dancing with laughter. "I am not saying I could deal with this every day, but it is not so bad," she teased.

Relief and gratitude chased away the change. Declan felt his body shrinking back to normal again. He wrapped her in his arms and pulled her body between his legs and kept her caged there. "I'm never letting you out of my sight."

"What happened?" Magnus demanded

She gasped and turned to the Prince. "It was Marcus."

"Marcus!" Law exclaimed behind them.

She turned to her brother. "Yes, he is feral. He said something about serving a bigger purpose and that they would make him a prince. I am not sure what he was promised, but he came here after me. He is insane."

"I'll deal with him after I deal with Emeric," Law promised directly.

Kari shook her head. "You cannot get mad at him."

"Like hell, I can't!"

"You cannot, because even you said it yourself: They take orders from us, and I ordered him to help Tarragon to save the wolf shifter."

"His priority was you," Law argued.

"He was following chain of command as he was trained to do. Now, if you want to change the way teams are run, that is up to you, but this was my fault, not his."

Law took a deep breath and inclined his head. "I don't like it, but you're right. He only did as he was ordered. So after I find and destroy Marcus down to the cellular level, I will get together with our teams and establish a new set of rules." He glowered at her. "One where the safety of our charges are not compromised by orders from said charges."

She winced. Declan hissed at Law. Law growled right back. She could tell the two men were still fighting their own fear. She twisted her body to stand, but Declan growled, shaking his head. She took his face between her hands

"Are we going to live here in the hallway?" she asked.

He just gave her a helpless look. She put her hands on either side of his face and pulled him close, capturing his lips. He stiffened in surprise for a moment and then took over. She could feel his fear and desperation as he dominated her mouth, so she allowed him. When he pulled away and tucked her head under his chin, she let him. She knew his lion needed this, and frankly, so did she. With her still in his arms, he easily stood, carrying her weight. Rex was immediately at his side.

"Hey, little sister," he said. "Let us get you to Tarragon or to Dr. St. John to look you over."

"Oh, I am fine," she refuted. "As soon as I began to breathe in the smoke, I shut my body down. Vampires do not really need to breathe that much."

Declan blinked. "Thank the gods."

"How did you know where I was?" she asked.

"Meryn," Law, Rex, Magnus, and Declan replied at once.

"Miraculous little midget," Kari whispered.

"I'm not a midget," Meryn protested as she walked down the hallway with Aiden.

"I did say you were miraculous too," Kari pointed out.

Meryn eyed the blackened room, looking a bit shocked.

"There was a fire just as you predicted," Law said.

"So empathy and premonition. What a delightful little enigma you are, Meryn."

She shrugged. "That sounds like something Kendrick would say."

Law shrugged lazily. "Of course, he thinks like I do."

True to his word, Declan didn't let her out of his sight. In fact, he didn't even let her feet touch the floor for the rest of the afternoon. He walked around with her in his arms. Aiden or Adriel gave the order, and the unit warriors dispersed, searching for Marcus.

"How the hell is he getting around the city?" Declan growled.

Adriel winced. "We have been running lifts up and down the transport tunnel all afternoon for the families on the lower levels to come up to Level Six. Since it acts as a platform, anyone could have gotten on."

"Ferals smell, do they not?" Kari asked. "People would have known they were standing next to one, right?"

Aiden and Adriel exchanged uneasy glances. "Not necessarily," Aiden volunteered. "They have a new device that allows them to walk unnoticed in a crowd."

"What? That is impossible." Kari felt fear swirl around her heart.

Magnus shook his head. "I will get you up to speed later."

They stayed long enough for the fair to begin wrapping up. Making their excuses, everyone returned to Level One. Avery refused to leave her side and hadn't stopped shaking since she had told him what happened. Warrick sat on the other side of Avery gently rubbing his back.

Only when Kari was safely ensconced on Magnus' antechamber sofa with Avery and Warrick, did Declan allow himself to walk away. He and Law were in the corner discussing how they were going to find Marcus.

Emeric looked like his puppy had been killed in front of him. He kept shooting her guilty looks. She crooked her finger, and he walked over to sit in the chair beside her.

"*Cher*, I am so sorry," he stared down at his folded hands in his lap.

"Do not be," she said quickly. "It was not your fault." Law looked over, still scowling. She stuck her tongue out at him. "You did as I asked you to do. You are trained to follow my orders because I set priority, and in the moment, that man's life mattered more than me going down to get bandages. So it is not your fault Emeric. You did exactly as you were trained."

"More men will be arriving soon to assist," Rex volunteered. "There will be more than enough people here to protect the ladies."

"So now we have two ferals running around the city," Bethy whispered, her eyes fearful.

Gavriel held her close. "We will find him."

"I found the fucker!" Meryn crowed suddenly startling everyone.

Immediately, all eyes were on her. Standing behind Meryn, Nigel and Neil high-fived each other as Meryn continued to tap away on her laptop.

"That's impossible," Law protested. He stalked over to see what she was doing.

"No it's not; it's technology. You know, the thing you suck at?" A tiny finger pointed to a small white face on the screen. "Level Six, he's trying to blend in, but I'm using facial recognition software. I pulled his picture from the profile that Kari has on her company employee page. In fact, if you take a walkie-talkie, I can tell you if he moves."

Aiden threw Law a walkie-talkie, and he and Declan ran out the door. Kari and Avery stood and walked up behind Meryn. It wasn't a minute later that, using the camera surveillance, they saw Law and Declan running through Level Six. The people, seeing them coming, quickly got out of the way.

Marcus reached into his pocket to grab something, and Declan tackled him. Law was there a second later casting a spell. Marcus was now immobile.

"Geeks save the day!" Meryn celebrated.

"Every time I think that you have finished surprising me, you turn around and impress me further," Magnus said.

She looked up, blushing at the praise. Her attention turned back to the monitor. Kari's knees gave out with the relief. Instantly, Rex was at her side. She smiled her thanks up at him, and he winked. Avery wrapped his arm around her waist from her other side as Warrick placed both hands on her shoulders to steady her.

"That is gonna hurt tomorrow," Meryn said, giggling.

Kari's attention turned back to the monitor. Declan had Marcus by the ankles and was dragging him around the furniture, the stalls, and every sharp corner of Level Six, heading toward a transport tunnel. At one point, he stopped and pointed down at Marcus. Law shook his head, and Declan mouth opened and he hissed.

"Poor Simba is mad he can't kill him," Meryn said, laughing.

Before they continued their walk, Law waved a hand and Marcus' mouth opened in a silent scream. He then began thrashing around in agony causing Declan to lose his grip. Looking a bit mollified, Declan reached down to grab his ankle again. He bounced Marcus' body between two wooden stalls a few times, knocking his head about before they resumed their march back to the transport tunnel. Kari turned to Magnus and Adriel.

"I would get that detention cell ready if I were you."

Adriel was on the walkie-talkie in moments, calling down orders for the warriors to create a guard shift at the detention cells.

"One down, one to go," Meryn said.

"Seriously, from your lips to the gods' ears," Kari murmured.

LATER THAT EVENING, TWO LION shifters arrived from Éire Danu through the portal. They immediately checked in with Rex, and Declan introduced them to Kari. They were his first cousins Broden and Ramsey Lionhart. Ramsey smiled at her warmly as Broden winked at her cheekily, eliciting a snarl from her mate. She now had three shadows. Rex was not taking any chances with her. Though she felt like she was being a bit smothered, she never wanted to live through what she had again. Not just for herself, but also for Declan, she never wanted to see her mate that afraid again.

The guards handed something to Rex. Rex, in turn, presented it to Declan, who clapped his brother on the shoulder.

"What is that?" she asked him.

"I'm going to show you. Are you up to taking us to Unit Level? I can get a transport escort."

"Declan, I am fine." She took his hand. They floated up to the Unit Level.

"So what is it you are going to show me?"

"Not yet, we have to be in the house."

They walked in, and Kari kicked off her shoes.

"Okay, so..."

"Not yet"

They made their way up stairs to the long stretch of hallway. He stood in front of a blank wall.

"Okay?" she asked.

He winked at her. He reached into his pocket and pulled out a small stone. He set it on the wall and whispered a melodic phrase. The stone began to expand until it formed a beautiful archway, and within the archway stood a wooden door.

"What is that? she asked.

"You'll find out."

She nodded, more curious than scared. Declan opened the door, and it swung wide. Kari couldn't help the reaction she had next.

Tears began streaming down her face. She covered her mouth with both hands. On the other side of the door was her condo. Sobbing, she ran forward. She was home. Just exactly how she'd left it.

Declan followed her through and shut the door behind them. On her side of the portal there wasn't a stone archway with a wooden door; it was a standard door with white trim and satin nickel hardware. It fit perfectly with the decor in her house and, like in Declan's house, the portal had popped up in an empty space in the hallway. It simply looked like another bedroom door. "This is impossible!" She twirled, taking in every sight. How could she possibly be home? "Declan, what is this?" she asked.

"A favor." He walked over, took her hands into his, and kissed her fingers gently. "I was raised in Éire Danu, and I know Queen Aleksandra well. So when I told Rex of your concerns about your home and asked if anything could be done about it, Rex told Father, and he shared it with the Queen. This is our mating present."

"You got us a portal for a mating present?"

He grinned widely and nodded.

"But what about the city? The feral! Can anybody come through here?"

He shook his head "That's the beauty of it. It's keyed by blood. I activated it by nicking myself so I'm able to open the door. It only requires a few drops of blood when you say the spell. I'm thinking you, Avery, Warrick, and Rex. Just a handful of people."

"We have to bring Avery here; he has to see this."

"So will this work?" he asked, looking unsure.

She jumped up and threw her arms around him.

Laughing, he pulled her close "So I take it you're happy."

"Happy does not even begin to describe it. We could sleep here. Have breakfast, go through, and go to work. You can report to the units. I could work with Magnus. We could come back and go shopping. What? What is that look for?" she asked mid-ramble.

He shook his head, his eyes bright. "I just realized I've never seen you like this."

"Happy. Yes, you have," she said "I may not have been a rambling idiot, but I can guarantee you have seen me this happy. I have the proof right here." She placed his hand over her stomach.

Declan spread his fingers over her abdomen reverently. "I will always find a way to make you happy and to give you what you need, because you are everything I need."

"I love you, Declan."

"Even though I come to you with danger swirling around me? Even though by staying with me we have to worry about a crazy feral on the loose and a city on the brink of political disaster?"

"Did you ever stop to think that is why Fate sent me to you?" she asked.

He chuckled. "My little champion, your problem-solving skills will save us all."

Kari wrapped her arms around his waist. "I am no longer scared of the future. I do not fear the long empty days ahead." She rested her head on his chest and let the sound of his heartbeat soothe her.

"As long as we're together, we can do anything," he said rubbing his cheek on the top of her head.

In her heart, she knew he was right, and that they would both fight to stay together... always.

EPILOGUE

GRANT LEANED AGAINST THE WALL in Prince Magnus' antechamber. He watched as the leaders of the city sat around discussing what had happened at the fair that day. Out of the corner of his eye, he watched as Meryn sat down with a piece of paper and pencil. She placed the piece of paper on the coffee table and closed her eyes while holding the pencil. All around them the room was nothing but a cacophony of noise, but his attention was on the small human.

What on earth was she up to now?

After a few moments of her not moving, he became concerned. He walked over and sat beside her, tapping her on the shoulder. "You okay?" he asked.

She opened one green peeper and stared up at him for a moment, then opened both of her eyes. "I'm trying to predict the lottery numbers."

He blinked. "What?" he asked.

"Well, it seems like I can do this prediction thing. I want to hit the lottery at least once. Do you know how many Hot Pockets and how much Doctor Who stuff I could buy?" She closed her eyes and held the pencil on the paper again.

Shaking his head in amazement, he stood and

headed toward the door.

"Grant?" Adriel called out.

"Yes, sir" he replied, turning.

"I am assigning you Level Six tomorrow."

Grant nodded, wincing internally. There was no patrol he hated more than walking around Level Six. He wasn't the most social warrior and everyone, it seemed, wanted to talk to him. He had no idea what to do or what to say, especially to the wolves. All conversations with them seemed to circle back to his own pack.

"Yes, sir," he said.

Adriel nodded and then turned his attention back to Eva who was discussing some of the concerns that Stefan had brought to her concerning the Founding Families protest.

Grant shut the door behind him and headed toward the transport tunnel. He got to the edge and sighed. He really needed to get with Nigel and Neil to get one of those stones they'd given Meryn. Being in a city that required you to fly when you were a wolf just flat out sucked.

"Thought you'd be escaping soon," Micah teased.

He looked over at his warrior brother in relief. Etain and Micah were walking up behind him.

"Aren't you guys going to stick around to get orders?"

Micah shrugged. "I'm sure they'll let us know somehow. They're going to be busy for a while. There's a lot to discuss. We lowly warriors can go back to the Unit Level and get some grub."

Grant chuckled. It seemed as though after mating, Adriel and Declan had suddenly been pulled into the city's leadership circle. Adriel had been there almost from the beginning even if he refused to see it. Now Declan, with his political ties and multi-tasking mate, was getting pulled away from warrior duties more and more.

Before any of them knew it, Declan would probably get assigned as an elder somewhere. Micah and Etain floated them back up to the Unit Level and they headed toward the warrior estate.

"That's two for two," Etain said lowly.

Grant ground his teeth together but didn't say anything.

Etain met his eyes. "I know we discussed this earlier. I was apprehensive before, but now I'm downright terrified." Grant nodded.

"What? What am I missing?" Micah asked.

"Our mates are coming," Grant said

"You know that's not what I meant."

Etain stopped in the middle of the road, looking at Grant who shrugged.

"Seriously guys, unless you are going to break this down for me, I can go inside. No need to give each other secret glances or speak in code," Micah protested.

Etain shook his head. "You should be getting your dream soon."

"You mean about the mates?"

Etain nodded.

"That's great news. I would love to have a mate."

They both eyed him, sarcastic looks on their faces.

"What? Just because I love women doesn't mean I can't settle down with the right one." Micah laughed until he saw their somber expressions.

"What?" he asked. "What else is coming?"

There was a terror in Etain's eyes that Grant could

relate to. He looked at Micah. “Death,” he replied.
“Death is coming,” Etain echoed.

THANK YOU FOR READING! I hoped you enjoyed My Champion!

For a full listing of all my books please check out my Official Website: *www. alaneaalder.com*

I love to hear from readers so please feel free to follow me on Facebook, Twitter, Goodreads, AmazonCentral or Pinterest.

HUG me please!!

If you liked this book please let others know. Most people will trust a friend's opinion more than any ad. Also make sure to leave a review. I love to read what y'all have to say and find out what your favorite parts were. I always read your reviews.

IMPORTANT!!

As you know Facebook strictly controls what shows up on your newsfeed. To ensure that you are receiving all my latest news and teasers you can to sign up for my newsletters so you will receive regular updates concerning release information, promotions, random giveaways and future Live events.

I typically send only 1-2 updates per month and won't flood your inbox, promise! ;)

INCEPTION

Coming Soon!

WANDER THROUGH THE YEARS WHILE following one of Lycaonia's most dedicated unit warriors and discover how the Vanguard came to be.

OTHER BOOKS BY ALANEA ALDER

KINDRED OF ARKADIA SERIES

THIS SERIES IS ABOUT A shifter only town coming together as pack, pride, and sloth to defend the ones they love. Each book tells the story of a new couple or triad coming together and the hardships they face not only in their own Fated mating, but also in keeping their town safe against an unknown threat that looms just out of sight.

BOOK 1- FATE KNOWS BEST
BOOK 2- FATED TO BE FAMILY
BOOK 3- FATED FOR FOREVER
BOOK 4- FATED FORGIVENESS
BOOK 5- FATED HEALING
BOOK 6- FATED SURRENDER
BOOK 7- GIFTS OF FATE
BOOK 8- FATED REDEMPTION

BEWITCHED AND BEWILDERED SERIES

She's been Bewitched and he's Bewildered...

WHEN THE TOPIC OF GRANDCHILDREN comes up during a weekly sewing circle, the matriarchs of the founding families seek out the witch Elder to scry to see if their sons' have mates. They are shocked to discover that many of their sons' mates are out in the world and are human!

Fearing that their future daughters-in-law will end up dead before being claimed and providing them with grandchildren to spoil, they convince their own mates that something must be done. After gathering all of the warriors together in a fake award ceremony, the witch Elder casts a spell to pull the warrior's mates to them, whether they want it or not.

Each book will revolve around a unit warrior member finding his destined mate, and the challenges and dangers they face in trying to uncover the reason why ferals are working together for the first time in their history to kill off members of the paranormal community.

Book 1- My Commander
Book 2- My Protector

Book 3- My Healer
Book 4- My Savior
Book 5- My Brother's Keeper
Book 6- My Guardian
Book 7- My Champion
Book 8- My Defender

THE VANGUARD

We Hold the Line.

Book 1- Inception

40852329R00176

Printed in Poland
by Amazon Fulfillment
Poland Sp. z o.o., Wrocław